M G

Praise for *New York Times* bestselling author

ANNE
STUART

"A consummate mistress of her craft, Stuart crafts
a sophisticated romance that mirrors the rigors of the era
and adds her own punch of passion and adventure so
that her characters can have the time of their lives.
It is pure pleasure to indulge in this part lighthearted,
part deeply emotional and all-glorious story."
—*Romantic Times BOOKreviews* on *The Devil's Waltz*
[2007 RITA® Award nominee]

"Before I read...[a] Stuart book I make sure
my day is free.... Once I start, she has me hooked."
—*New York Times* bestselling author Debbie Macomber

"This taut romantic-suspense novel from RITA® Award
winner Stuart delivers deliciously evil baddies and
the type of disturbing male protagonist that only
she can transform into a convincing love interest....
Brilliant characterizations and a suitably moody
ambience drive this dark tale of unlikely love."
—*Publishers Weekly* on *Black Ice*

"[A] sexy, edgy, exceptionally well-plotted tale."
—*Library Journal* on *I*

"A master at creating
with a mod
—*Library*

D1020487

ICE STORM
ANNE STUART

MIRA

ISBN-13: 978-0-7783-2500-0
ISBN-10:   0-7783-2500-8

ICE STORM

www.MIRABooks.com

Printed in U.S.A.

With huge thanks to my fabulous wizard of an agent, Jane Dystel, and to my splendidly appreciative editor, Margaret O'Neill Marbury.

And a much-belated thank-you to Lynda Ward, who's helped me innumerable times.

Bless you all!

Prologue

Then

Mary Isobel Curwen had never shot a man before. She stood there, numb, unmoving. She'd never fired a gun before, and the feel of it in her grasp was disturbing. Her hand and arm tingled with the recoil, and she could smell the cordite, the blood. She wouldn't look at him— he was down, unmoving, and there was nothing on this earth that would make her walk over to him and see what she'd done.

Had she blown a hole through his head? His chest? Was he dead or just wounded? She knew she ought to check…. She'd had every reason to shoot him, but you couldn't very well let a man bleed to death, could you? she thought dazedly. Even if he'd been trying to kill you?

Or maybe you could. Maybe you could drop the gun, turn and run, as fast as possible, before he suddenly stood up and came after you, before one of his buddies came running to see where the noise had come from. Maybe you could take the gun with you, just in case.

She still had her backpack over her shoulder, which struck her as slightly crazy. She put the heavy handgun into it, noticing that her hands were shaking. Of course they were. She'd just killed a man.

He still wasn't moving, and she could see a pool of blood gathering beneath him. He was definitely dead.

How was she going to live without him?

It had begun to rain sometime during the last few hours. The streets were soaked, the lights glinting off the wet pavement as she ran out into the night, closing the heavy door of the abandoned building behind her without a sound. She was wearing loose sandals and wanted to kick them off, but you couldn't run barefoot when you were in the middle of a city. Even with a gun in your backpack and the man you loved lying dead in the dirt.

Running would attract too much attention. She shoved back her wild hair, trying to stuff the thick tangle into a knot. She straightened her shoulders and walked on in the rainy night, calm, composed, the scream buried so deep in her heart that it would never escape. By the time they found his body she'd be long gone, and there'd be nothing to connect Mary Isobel Curwen with a dead terrorist in a run-down part of Marseille. No one would ever know.

Except she would. And she'd live with it, as she'd learned to live with everything else life had handed her. Killian was dead. Long live Mary Isobel Curwen.

Without him.

1

Madame Isobel Lambert was exhausted. It had been a draining weekend in the Lake District—she'd played with her hosts' obstreperous children, gone on long hikes, eaten too much rich food, drank too much red wine, wrestled with her conscience and killed two men. All that without a cigarette. She was not in a good mood.

There was no question that the men had deserved to die. Manuel Kupersmith and Jorge Sullivan were the lowest of the low, and beyond the reach of traditional justice. Drug dealers with a taste for torture and a well-financed sympathy for terrorists, they'd covered their tracks too well. If she'd had to, she would have put a bullet in each of their dark, twisted brains.

As it was, she'd managed to sabotage their car, a nice, antiseptic kill. While she spent a social weekend with a member of parliament and his young family, it had been easy enough to wander past the inn where the two men had taken up residence, easy enough to sneak into the garage while the two were in bed. She knew a great deal about cars, and if her calculations were correct, the brakes would give out at the steep curve above the Lohan Cliffs and the car would end up on the rocks below. If the brakes failed too soon the car might hit a pedestrian; too late and they could run into the busy traffic of the neighboring town. Not something she'd be happy about, but a risk worth taking.

In the end, her timing had been perfect. As her hosts drove her to the train station in Lohan Downs they'd passed the police cars and the cordoned-off section of road, and her host had made important noises about road safety as Isobel breathed a silent sigh of relief. It was done.

She had the *Sunday Times* with her for the train ride back to London, and she finished the crossword puzzle in record time. Her flat in Bloomsbury was still and quiet as she let herself in, and she stripped off her clothes and headed straight for the shower, calm and impassive as always, ignoring her shaking hands.

She waited for the water to get hot, then stepped beneath it. And only then did she cry, silently, steadily. Not for the men. But for her own lost soul.

Peter Madsen looked up when Madame Lambert walked into the office the next morning, a cardboard cup of coffee in one hand, a newspaper under her arm. He had the same paper open in front of him.

"Shame about the car accident near the Lohan Cliffs," he said evenly, watching her out of the icy blue eyes that saw too much.

"Indeed," she said calmly. He would have been the one to do it, but he'd pulled back from that kind of work. Everyone reached their limit when it came to wet work—either they burned out or made one too many mistakes. Peter was deskbound, not because of his bad leg but because he'd seen and done too much. His focus had changed to his American wife and the semblance of a normal life, and Isobel wasn't going to do anything to change that, even though she could.

But she was running out of people she could trust to do what was necessary and nothing more. In the three years since she'd taken over Harry Thomason's role as head of the Committee, she'd lost three effective operatives. Bastien had disappeared into the mountains of North Carolina with his wife and family, Peter was no longer on active duty, and Takashi O'Brien was dividing his time between Tokyo and Los Angeles. He could still be counted on to do what was necessary, but Isobel was not the kind of woman who made other people do things she herself wouldn't. And Taka had a new life as well—he didn't need fresh blood on his hands.

Morrison in Germany, MacGowan in Central America were still working ops, and the Thai mission was almost complete. Takashi's young cousin,

Hiromasa Shinoda, was due to arrive any day now, and if he was half as good as Taka they'd be in decent shape. Though the learning curve was steep, and Isobel knew nothing about young Mr. Shinoda except that Taka recommended him, which was good enough. But he wouldn't be ready for solo assignments for quite a while, and she didn't know who she could assign to train him.

She hated not knowing things.

"You look rattled," Peter said, his voice cool and devoid of sympathy, as she needed it to be.

"I'm fine. It's just been awhile. Any sign of Taka's cousin?"

"Not yet. You had some calls."

There was something about the tone of his voice that twisted her stomach into a small knot of dread. She turned her impassive face back to him. "I imagine I did. Harry Thomason, I suppose?"

"Among others."

There were only the two of them in the Kensington offices of Spence-Pierce Financial Consultants, Ltd., their very effective cover. Anyone who managed to get through to them had every business doing so. More mundane matters were conducted at a distance.

Isobel took the leather club chair opposite Peter's desk, crossing her legs. Good legs for a woman in her sixties. Good legs for a woman in her forties. Not even bad for someone her real age.

"You may as well tell me." She pried the lid off the

coffee and took a drink. "I've never known you to spare my tender feelings."

Peter laughed, a sound she was slowly getting used to. In the first ten years she'd known him she didn't think she'd ever heard him laugh. "Sensitivity was never my forte," he said. "Thomason wants to know what you're going to do about the situation with Serafin."

"Thomason can blow himself," Isobel said sweetly. "Who have we got on him?"

"No one. Bastien did some of the preliminary work, as did I. But things stabilized and we had more important situations to deal with."

"Serafin," she said. "The Butcher." Her day had gone from bad to worse. "I thought he was just going to fade away like Qaddafi."

"No such luck. Only the good die young, and Josef Serafin doesn't fit that category."

She glanced longingly toward her office. She could go in there, close the door behind her and put her head down on the massive teak desk. Maybe bang it a few times for good measure. Peter was watching her, reading her mind. That was the problem with working with someone like Peter—he was smart enough and intuitive enough to know what she was thinking at all times.

She wasn't going anywhere. "Fill me in," she said. "Tell me we're finally going to get to kill him. Please."

"I'm afraid not. We're going to have to save the son of a bitch's life."

"I hate this job," Isobel said, leaning back and closing her eyes for a moment. She gripped the coffee tightly. If her hand revealed even the faintest tremor, Peter would see it. "Details. Everything we know about Serafin, and why in God's name we have to keep him alive. Maybe I'll figure a way around it."

"I doubt it. He's got nine lives. Even Bastien wasn't able to take him down when he was ordered to."

"I forgot about that. Details," she said again, wearily.

"Josef Serafin, somewhere in his early forties. It's anybody's guess where he was born—probably in a slum in Latin America. He first appeared on the scene in the late nineteen-eighties, part of an arms smuggling operation to the Congo. He branched out, became part of a drug cartel out of Colombia, just missing the big takedown in Cartagena, moved on and hired his services out as an assassin. He worked with the Shining Path in Peru, the Red Brigade in Italy, he'd worked in Croatia, Somalia, North Korea. Just about everywhere in the world where bad things happen. He's moved away from crime lords to politics, serving as second in command to three of the most ruthless dictators in recent history. He's managed to escape, unscathed, right before their governments came crashing down, and for the last five years he's been reported to be working in Africa, over-seeing ethnic cleansing and political purging."

"Lovely man," Isobel murmured. "And we're supposed to save his life?"

Peter didn't bother to answer her question. "He's

hiding out in Morocco for the time being, but we don't know how long that will last. He's got more enemies than bin Laden. Fouad Assawi was his most recent employer, but he was killed, part of the reason Serafin's on the run. Vladimir Busanovich is probably the biggest danger. He holds a grudge, and the last time Serafin worked for him he screwed up. Apparently something went wrong with the last round of executions, and at least three hundred of Busanovich's worst enemies escaped, right under Serafin's nose. Busanovich is not a tolerant man."

"And we're saving Serafin because…?"

"Because of the intel he brings with him. He knows just about all there is to know about the major players in the world of terrorism, and he's willing to trade that information for safe passage out of Morocco. That's where we come in."

She could always say no. She was the titular head of the Committee—in the end her word was law. Orders were handed down by a shadowy group of old men, the actual "committee," and her nemesis and former boss, the newly knighted Harry Thomason, had joined their ranks. She'd like to blame this mess on Thomason, but then, his major drawback had been his readiness to eliminate anyone on the slightest pretext, and Josef Serafin should have been dealt with long ago. Thomason himself had ordered hits on Serafin half a dozen times, but no one, not even Bastien or Peter, had ever been able to get close to him.

Until now. Mistakes happened—Serafin wouldn't be seeking asylum if he hadn't screwed up his deadly orders.

"So what's the plan?" she said, smoothing her perfect blond hair back from her face. "And don't tell me you don't have one—I know you too well. Who are we going to send? We're shorthanded right now, and Genevieve would cut my throat if I tried to send you."

He flashed another of those rare, unexpected smiles that still managed to surprise her. "And then she'd cut mine. I thought of Taka, but he's still cleaning up the cult mess in Japan. Besides, we haven't been given a choice in the matter."

She raised an eyebrow, waiting for it. "They want you to go," he said. "In fact, it's a direct order. You're to get to Morocco, make contact with Serafin, extract him and bring him to London, where we can debrief him."

"And then?"

Peter shrugged. "He's got to have millions salted away in some international account. He's spent the last twenty years or so selling his services to the highest bidder—he'd be well paid for it. Once we get the information from him he'll be able to disappear. With our help." He didn't look any happier about it than she felt.

"Maybe he could have a little accident once he's been debriefed," she said. "Accidents do happen, you know."

"Yes, they do," Peter said evenly. "I can see to it, if you'd like."

She didn't meet his eyes. *Never have someone do what you aren't willing to do yourself,* she thought. "Let's see if we can even bring him out alive. Do we know what the hell he looks like nowadays?"

"We've got some grainy surveillance photos from his time in Bosnia eight years ago, but they don't show much. Just a tall man with a beard and sunglasses. We've got a couple of recent descriptions from people who escaped ahead of the carnage. I'll put them together and see what we can come up with."

"You and your damn computers," Isobel said. Since Peter had come out of the field, he'd spent his time playing with technology—in all, a less emotionally damaging way to help the cause. Not that she would have thought Peter Madsen had emotions. Until she'd met his wife.

"See what you can come up with," Isobel said.

"How long have we known each other?"

Peter's question was unexpected, and Isobel almost dropped her guard. "Close to ten years by now. Why?"

"You look tired."

"Are you telling me I'm looking my age?" she said, her voice light.

"I don't know what the hell your age is," he grumbled. "You could be forty and you could be sixty."

"Or I could be twenty or eighty," she said. "I take very good care of myself. And I've had the very best of plastic surgeons. Why are you asking?"

"Because sooner or later this gets to be too much.

You and I both know it. And I'd like some warning if you're going to burn out."

"You think I'm getting too old for the game? I'll let you know when I'm contemplating retirement, if you're that eager for advancement. At this point I have a lot of good years left."

"Bastien retired in his thirties."

"So he did. And I expect if it weren't for me you'd be gone, as well. You don't really want my job at all, do you?"

"I've seen what it does to people. Turns them into monsters like Thomason, or comes close to breaking them, like..."

"Like me," she said.

"Like Bastien. Like me. Like you."

She rose with her usual perfect grace. "Tell you what, Peter," she said. "Find me a replacement with a conscience. Find yourself one as well. And then I'll quit."

"You can't do this job and have a conscience."

"It makes it hard," she said dryly. "But you need it as a fail-safe. Otherwise you become another Thomason, taking out your friends as well as your enemies." She moved toward her office. "Find me the best intel you've got on Serafin."

"I've already uploaded files to your computer," he said. He paused. "I could go."

"No," she said flatly.

"Taka's cousin whenever he shows up?"

"Taka would kill us. Getting someone as dangerous

as Serafin out of North Africa is hardly child's play. It would be like sending a lamb into a lion's den. Not that any relative of Taka could be a lamb, if his cousin Reno is anything to go by."

"Bastien…"

"Leave Bastien out of it. You think I can't handle it?" Her light mockery didn't bring one of Peter's infrequent smiles.

"You can handle anything, Isobel. I just don't know if you want to. You've changed."

She blinked. "I doubt it. I'm the same cold-blooded professional I've always been. You're just seeing things differently since you've been seduced by True Love."

He didn't bother to respond, just raised an eyebrow, and she wasn't going to argue. Why waste her breath lying to him, lying to herself? Sometime in the last five years, when she hadn't been looking, her nerve had begun to shred. Her emotionless practicality had turned into nothing more than an icy veneer, and beneath it ugly, painful emotions were beginning to roil. The Ice Queen was developing cracks in her facade.

And she wasn't going to argue. She was going to do what needed to be done. "How much time do we have?"

"Not much," he said. "Too many people want Serafin's head. The sooner we get him out the better."

She nodded, all business. "I'll leave tomorrow."

"It can wait a few days…."

"A few days won't make any difference," she said. A few years wouldn't make any difference. She had to keep going. If she stopped too long she'd start to think, start to feel, and then she might as well be dead. "Tomorrow."

Peter looked at her for a long hard moment, then nodded. "I'll make the arrangements."

She closed the door to her office, sinking down in the leather chair and closing her eyes. She needed a cigarette more than she needed air to breathe. The thought amused her. She certainly wasn't giving up cigarettes to prolong her life—she wasn't in the right profession to worry about longevity.

She didn't like the weakness. Didn't like the need. She reached forward and punched up the computer screen with the files that Peter had uploaded for her. A grainy photo of Josef Serafin popped up, and she glanced at it. Peter had used his computer tricks to clean it up, sharpen the focus, and suddenly her gaze narrowed. She leaned forward, her heart smashing against her ribs.

"Killian," she whispered. And the day went black.

2

Then

She'd been a wild child, with a tangled mane of curly red hair, a stubborn streak a mile wide, a passionate heart and an innocent soul. At the age of nineteen she'd shoved her belongings into a backpack, taken the first cheap flight to England and prepared to make her way to Paris and the Cordon Bleu at her own leisurely pace.

There was no longer anyone back home in Vermont to worry about her—her mother had died young and her father had a new family. Mary Isobel Curwen was simply a reminder of another lifetime. She didn't belong with them.

She wasn't stupidly reckless back then, just clueless. If she hadn't decided to hike around England before school started, if she'd waited to go with her friends, if she'd had enough sense not to go out into the slums of

Plymouth in the middle of the night... If, if, if. She was older and wiser now, and hindsight was a bitch.

She hadn't realized someone was following her that night. A group of someones, silent, predatory, moving through the darkness like a pack of starving wolves. When she finally realized she wasn't alone it was too late—she'd taken the wrong turn when leaving the pub, and was getting farther and farther away from the youth hostel where she'd left her backpack and sleeping bag.

She heard the scrape of a boot, a whispered laugh, and cold, icy fear had slid through her. She'd reached the end of the street and darted left, planning to disappear into the darkness of the alleyway. Only to find it was a dead end, lit by the fitful August moon.

And then they were there. A handful of them, some younger than she was, but she didn't make the mistake of thinking they were harmless. They were blocking her escape, and she froze, a thousand thoughts running through her mind. If she disappeared, no one would notice, no one would ask. Her father had already forgotten about her, and while her friends back in Vermont might worry, it would be too late when they realized something was wrong.

No one was going to save her, no one was going to miss her. She was on her own, and she was either going to die or be hurt very, very badly.

"I don't have much money," she said in a deceptively calm voice.

"Not interested in money," one of them said, as

they crowded together, advancing on her. "Who wants first go?"

"Me," said one of the younger ones, a skinny little rat with bad teeth and a feral look in his eyes. He was already reaching for his belt, and she opened her mouth to scream for help.

They were on her, slamming her onto the littered street, pawing at her, pressing her down, and no matter how she tried to kick or punch, someone always managed to stop her. She felt something sharp against her throat, and the young one grinned down at her. "I don't mind cutting your throat first. I ain't picky. I like a good fight, but if you want to lie there and bleed while I do you I'm not arguing."

"Please," she whispered, feeling the blade against her skin. She felt hands pulling at her jeans, trying to yank them down, and she kicked out, connecting with something painful, judging by the yelp of agony.

The boy straddling her turned and snarled, like a dog whose meal is threatened, and for a moment the pressure of the knife lessened. She slammed her head against his, feeling the blade knick her skin, knocking him off her and trying to roll away. But there were too many hands, too many bodies, and she knew there was nothing she could do but—

"Move away from her." The voice was cool, deadly and blessedly American. Enough of a shock to stop the pack of teenagers from ripping at her.

The ringleader rolled off her, peering into the night. "And who's going to stop us? There's one of you and seven of us, and I think you'd be smart to just keep on the way you were going. You can have a taste of what's left."

"Move away from her," he said again, stepping into the light. "Or I'll make you."

"You and what army?"

The scene was disjointed, crazy, dreamlike. There was a flash of light, and the boy was flung back, away from her, as if by unseen hands. A moment later the sound of a gun cracked the darkness, out of sync. And then they were scrambling away from her, disappearing into the shadows, and a moment later all was silent.

"Are you all right?" The man moved out of the darkness. In the bright moonlight he looked ordinary enough. Tall, in jeans and a T-shirt, maybe five years older than she was. Nothing to scare a gang intent on rape. But he had scared them. He saved her—he was one of the good guys.

He reached out a hand to her, and for a moment she wanted to shrink back, away from him. She was being stupid, and she took his hand, letting him pull her to her feet.

"Are you all right?" he asked again.

"Yes," she said. A lie. "How did you get them to run?"

He was taller than she was, lean and harmless looking. Not the type to frighten a bunch of creeps bent on rape.

"Car backfired," he said easily. "They must have thought I had a gun." He was still holding her hand, and she jerked away, suddenly nervous.

"I'm not going to hurt you," he said. He tilted his

head, looking down at her. He was wearing wire-rimmed glasses that gave him a slightly studious look. "Are you sure you're all right? I think I should take you to a hospital."

"I'm fine," she said, her voice stronger. "I just need to get back to the youth hostel."

"The one on Market Street? I'll take you there. I've got a car."

She just stared at him. "You really think I'm going to get into a car with a stranger, no matter how harmless he looks, a few moments after I was nearly raped and murdered? How stupid do you think I am?"

"I look harmless?" he replied, faintly amused. "I suppose I am. But I still managed to scare those boys away. And as for how stupid I think you are, pretty damn stupid to be walking alone in this part of town close to midnight. And whether you like it or not, I'm not leaving you until you're safe behind locked doors."

"They don't lock the doors at the hostel."

He just stared at her for a long moment. In the moonlit alleyway she couldn't see him that clearly. Just a tall figure, bordering on skinny, with long hair, and light glancing off his wire-rimmed glasses. Harmless. She was a good judge of character, or at least she always had been. He wasn't going to hurt her.

So she managed a tight smile. "Okay," she said. "You can drive me to the hostel on Market Street and chase away any wandering bad guys. Or you can walk me there—it's not far."

"If that's what you prefer. And you can tell me something about yourself, and why you aren't having hysterics over the fact that you just narrowly missed being raped and murdered."

"I'm practical, and having hysterics won't help me. I'll wait till I'm alone."

"There's not much privacy in a youth hostel."

She looked up at him. "You're far too nosy about me and my reactions."

"Hey, it's not every day I save a damsel in distress. I have a vested interest." His voice was light, careless, and the streetlights bounced off the thin glasses as they left the alley.

She shoved her tangle of red hair away from her face. "I'm not a damsel in distress. I'm a student on my way to the Cordon Bleu in Paris, and I can take care of myself."

"So I observed. Classes don't start for another three weeks. What are you doing wandering around England?"

The uneasiness that had almost ebbed away began to trickle back. "How do you know when the Cordon Bleu starts classes?"

"I've lived in France off and on for a number of years. I'm just about to head back there—I'm taking classes at a small art college in Paris and I planned to bum around the countryside for a bit. What's your excuse?"

The panic was fading, and she pushed her paranoia down. "I was going to do the same thing. I was told it was safe to hitchhike in Europe."

"Not when you look like you do."

It was a simple statement, not even a compliment, and there was no way she could respond. To her astonishment they were already at the door of her hostel, where a pool of yellow light surrounded the front door.

She held out her hand. "Thank you for helping me."

He looked at her hand for a moment, a smile quirking his mouth. She could see him better in the light—his hair was long, tied in the back with a leather loop, his face narrow and intelligent looking, his mouth the only anomaly. It was a rich, beautiful mouth in an otherwise austere face, particularly when he was smiling.

He took her hand and bowed low over it in an exaggerated gesture. "I live to serve. My name's Killian, by the way."

"Is that your first or last name?"

"Take your pick. I'm Thomas Henry Killian St. Claire, but I don't care much for the other ones. And you are…?"

"Mary."

He waited patiently, still holding her hand. "Mary Isobel Curwen," she said finally, snatching it away.

"Well, Mary Isobel Curwen, it's been an honor to have been of service. If you decide you want a ride to France just let me know."

"I don't think so. I'm fine on my own."

"Of course you are. I'll be at the ferry tomorrow morning—I've got a battered orange Citroën. If you want a ride, just show up. No strings attached. I've got a French girlfriend who'd cut my throat if I even looked at another woman. I'm just offering a ride to a fellow American."

"I'm fine," she said again.

"Suit yourself. I'm taking the ten o'clock ferry. In the meantime, stay out of dark alleyways, okay? France has even more of them."

"I will."

She half expected him to argue, but he simply walked away from her, down the deserted street, hands in his pockets, a man at ease with the world.

She watched him go. The whole evening had taken on a surreal feeling, and the sooner she got in the shower and into bed, the sooner she'd get past it. By ten tomorrow he'd be on his way to France and she would have forgotten entirely about him.

By ten o'clock she was sitting beside him in the disreputable orange Citroën, driving onto the ferry and wondering if she'd lost her mind.

She'd been a weakness, one Killian couldn't afford to have. He'd only been passing through Plymouth, trying to find a good cover to get into France to complete his mission, and the noise in the alleyway was none of his business. He'd accepted long ago that he couldn't save the world.

But something, probably simply the shitty luck that had currently plagued him, made him turn around and head back into the alleyway in time to stop some of the street rats from raping some stupid tourist.

He'd shot one, just because he'd wanted to. He could have gotten rid of them without the gun, but the sight of those pathetic, evil hoodlums annoyed him. They'd scattered, including the one he'd winged, and he was even more annoyed he hadn't killed him. And then he focused his attention on the woman.

He'd put on his best American student affability, reaching out a hand to pull her upright. She was slight, medium height, looking a bit shell-shocked. Just an idiot woman who'd wandered into the wrong place at the wrong time.

Pretty, too, if he'd been in the mood to consider such things. She had a mess of red hair, and he'd never particularly liked redheads. In the moonlight he could see she had unbelievably blue eyes—almost turquoise—and the kind of mouth that could distract most men.

It didn't distract him. Maybe playing Sir Galahad hadn't been such a stupid idea, after all. She'd provide the perfect cover—no one would be on the lookout for a couple of American students bumming around France.

He'd said all the right things, of course, and she'd taken him at face value. He couldn't fault her for that; most people looked at him and failed to see the wolf that lurked beneath his calm exterior.

He wasn't going to be able to take the easy route and sleep with her. The best way to get a woman to do what you wanted was to fuck her, but Mary Isobel Curwen had nearly been raped. She wasn't going to want any man putting moves on her for quite a while. If he needed to seal the deal later, before he'd finished his assignment, then he would, but it was always better if he kept things simple. Sex tended to make a woman possessive, or at the very least, curious. Curiosity was a liability in his line of work.

But a platonic, protective friend was another matter, and she fell for it. It was child's play—just the right amount of asexual charm and nonthreatening promise, and she was sitting next to him in the beater of a car that hid an engine that could outrun a Ferrari. She'd never know what hit her.

The wind was up and the ferry crossing was rough, but his newfound cover had a cast-iron stomach, and she stood up on deck, the wind whipping her wild red hair around her pale face, her eyes bright, lively. Another point in her favor—she wasn't easily frightened, either by storms or gangs of rapacious teenagers. As long as she stayed docile she'd be just fine.

She wasn't quite the perfect partner. If he'd been able to custom-order one he would have picked someone a little plainer, with dark hair, someone a little less complicated, who would enter into a sexual relationship without a lot of baggage. He liked sex, but he never let it get in the way of an assignment, and someone like Mary Curwen would definitely demand more than a vigorous workout. She'd get involved, making things a great deal more dangerous, so she was off-limits.

It would have been more convenient if she weren't so smart. That was mistake number one—thinking a cooking student would be less of a threat than someone attending the Sorbonne. Just because she'd been foolish enough to wander out alone didn't mean she couldn't put two and two together. He'd have to be careful.

Thinking it would be easy to keep his hands off her was the second mistake. And he wasn't sure which was worse.

But Killian was a man who took what was handed to him and worked with it. Mary Isobel Curwen, American student, had fallen into his lap quite nicely, and he had every intention of taking full advantage of her.

Two weeks until his rendezvous in Marseille. Two weeks to bum around France, setting up an innocent front for anyone who happened to be on the lookout for him, and there were doubtless any number of people who wanted to get to him before he could complete his assignment. He always worked alone—no one would ever expect him to have a woman in tow.

Two weeks to keep an unfortunately bright woman in the dark as to who and what he was, without even the benefit of sex to keep her distracted. It was going to be a long two weeks.

But worth it in the end. He'd make his meeting, complete his assignment and then disappear, and she'd never know her charming American buddy had just assassinated General Etienne Matanga, the best hope for peace in his small African nation.

She never could figure out why she'd woken up early that morning, shoved her clothes and books into her knapsack and made her way down to the ferry. The Citroën had been easy to find, and Killian had been leaning against the car, waiting for something. Waiting, it seemed, for her. He'd looked up when she approached, and simply opened the back door for her to throw her knapsack in.

"I've got a thermos of coffee," he'd said by way of greeting. "Black as the devil, hot as hell, pure as an angel, sweet as love."

She just looked at him. "I don't like sugar."

He shrugged. "Well, if we're going to be traveling together we'll have to compromise. There isn't really that much sugar in it."

"I thought you said 'sweet as love.'"

"I find love bittersweet, don't you?"

She opened the thermos and poured some into the cap, taking a tentative sip. "I'm not sure I find love at all," she replied. The coffee was good—hot and rich with just a trace of sweetness. "And who says we're traveling together?"

"That's up to you. I've got two weeks to kill before classes start. My girlfriend's stuck in Berlin on a photo shoot, and I'm just going to drive around the south of France. You've got a few weeks to kill as well, and you're welcome to join me, no strings attached. Maybe I'll even give up sugar in my coffee if you'll pitch in for gas."

"Your girlfriend's a photographer?"

He shook his head. "She's a fashion model."

That clinched it. No man with a fashion model girl-friend could have any ulterior motives in messing with red-haired Mary Curwen. He was absolutely right—she had three weeks until she could get into the cheap apartment waiting for her, and the fun of wandering on her own had permanently vanished last night in the alleyway.

"Lucky you," she murmured.

He laughed. "Hey, what about lucky her?"

He was right about that. Now that Mary Isobel could see him in the light of day she realized he was good-looking. Maybe beyond that. He was well over six feet tall, with long legs clad in faded jeans. He had a narrow, clever face and green eyes. And he was taken.

"Lucky her," she agreed with a smile. "You'll make very pretty children."

"If I can ever talk her into ruining her figure," he grumbled. "Got your passport? They'll be checking them."

"Of course."

"Hand it to me. It'll go faster if they know we're traveling together."

The nonchalant request bothered her. There was no reason for it, but it bothered her anyway, even as she put the dark navy passport in his outstretched hand. But he smiled at her, a warm, dazzling smile in the sunlit morning, and she knew she was being ridiculous. He was a fellow American, looking for company and someone to share the gas expenses, and she had nothing else to do for the next few weeks.

So she smiled back at him. "Very practical," she said,

as he pocketed her passport. And she took another sip of the hot, dark coffee and ignored her misgivings. The worst mistake of her life.

3

Now

The Moroccan sun was blazingly bright, a shock to the system after the dark rain of a London winter. Isobel Lambert drove very fast over the rutted roads. She was blessed with an unerring sense of direction, something that had saved her life on numerous occasions, and she knew she'd make her destination by nightfall. She ignored the fact that she didn't want to; she wasn't ready to face who and what was waiting for her in a tiny North African village at the edge of the desert.

At least he wouldn't have the faintest idea who Isobel Lambert was. She didn't know how he'd survived that night, but since he clearly had, he'd know that she, too, should have died. He would have forgotten all about the gullible young woman he'd used and tried to kill, even though she'd turned the tables and shot him. And he'd never connect cool, pale Isobel Lambert with the wild child he'd spent two short weeks with a lifetime ago.

And thank God that was who she was. An elegant, ageless automaton, with no desires, needs or emotions. Those had been scrubbed out of her over the long years, and after the initial shock of recognition, she could view her current mission with equanimity. Josef Serafin would be out of commission, and the world would be a marginally safer place.

The winter sun was blazing down on her open-topped vehicle. But the Jeep was the fastest, most rugged conveyance she could find, and if someone managed to track her, or Serafin, even an armored tank wouldn't keep them safe.

The tires were kicking up too much dust, but during the seven-hour drive from Agadir she'd seen only a handful of sheepherders and a few nomadic encampments. There was a good chance she was being tracked by satellite, but there wasn't much help for it. Killian... Serafin...was hidden in a deserted village near the Algerian border, and there was enough trouble in the neighboring areas that she had every confidence they'd manage to get away. But then, she never went into a mission without being convinced of its viability.

She could get Josef Serafin out of Morocco, back to London, without someone blowing his head off, no matter how many people wanted to do just that. Including his unwilling savior.

The sun was starting to set by the time she reached

the outskirts of the deserted village of Nazir, and a shiver danced across her skin. It was getting colder, as it did in the desert, the blistering daytime heat turning to a bone-numbing chill.

It looked as if no one had lived in the town of Nazir for years, perhaps decades. The doors with their faded blue paint were shut, the dusty streets empty, and for a moment she wondered if she'd come to the wrong place. Had her intel been faulty? Or was she walking into a trap?

No trap—her instincts, on high alert, told her nothing worse than Killian would be waiting for her in the abandoned rubble. Though she wasn't sure there *was* anything worse.

She pulled the Jeep behind the ruins of an old mosque, climbing out and stretching. She was a tourist who'd gotten lost—if she ran into anyone asking uncomfortable questions she could fend him off quite easily.

If she had any sense, she would have come in disguise. Someone younger, ditzier, so that her tale of getting lost on the road to Mauritania would seem plausible. But young and foolish was just a little too close to the woman Killian had known long ago. Even so, he would never recognize her. But she'd know. It would make her vulnerable.

Leaving the Jeep, she moved aimlessly down the deserted street. She had a knife at her ankle, a handgun at the small of her back, and the ability to kill swiftly and silently with her bare hands. No one would touch her, no one would get the upper hand....

"Hey, lady." The young voice came out of nowhere,

and she jumped like a startled kitten, too unnerved by the child's unheralded appearance to even draw her gun. Which was just as well—to any hidden observer she was simply a foolish tourist who happened to be in the wrong place at the wrong time.

"Lady," the child said. She looked down at the collection of rags and dirt in front of her. He was the size of a six-year-old, with the eyes of an ancient. "Lady, you come."

"Come where?" She hadn't missed the gun he was holding. An AK-47. An early model from Russian surplus, she guessed. She'd seen child soldiers before, but she'd never been able to get over the shock of heavy machinery held so easily in such small hands.

"You come, lady," he said again, seemingly the sum total of his English.

She touched the gun at the small of her back, to remind herself it was there, and followed the pitifully thin figure down the deserted streets. Killian ought to pay his stooges better, she thought, deliberately distancing herself. The child was skin and bones, held together by dirt. It was a wonder he could even lug that machine gun around with him.

They walked past crumbling buildings, some without roofs, the ubiquitous blue paint on the few remaining doors faded by the bright desert sun. She'd heard somewhere that blue deterred mosquitoes. Fortunately, there didn't seem to be any around. She hated bugs of any sort. Just one of the many reasons she lived in England.

The sun was a shrinking orange glow on the horizon, and already, in the east, a few stars were visible. She'd left her flashlight in the car—probably not a smart idea, but she'd wanted her hands free. She still wasn't quite sure for what.

The child came to a stop outside one of the larger houses. No windows looked onto the street, so there must be a courtyard within. The door was hanging on one hinge, and everything was silent.

The boy pointed with his gun, an unnerving gesture. "You go, lady."

Isobel looked at him for a long, contemplative moment, then did the only thing she could do. She went.

A man stood at the far end of the courtyard, a silhouette against the darkening sky. Isobel moved forward, keeping to the shadows, letting the cold settle within her. Since her first moment of shocked recognition she'd felt nothing, nothing at all. Now she was ice.

"Where's Bastien Toussaint?" His voice was that of a stranger—a mixture of ethnicities, a bit of Australian and South African, a touch of Spanish. Nothing like Killian's smooth, deep voice.

"He's retired," she said, skirting the open courtyard. "I'm here in his place."

"And who sent you?"

"I sent myself. I'm Isobel Lambert, head of the Committee."

"Madame Lambert herself? You must really want me." His tone was mocking, and her certainty was wavering. Had she been wrong? Even cleaned up, the grainy footage had been unreliable. Maybe it was a wild hallucination on her part; Peter had told her she was working too hard, burning out as everyone did, eventually. They burned out or were killed.

What she truly looking at a dead man? Or had the stress of her life finally caught up with her, making her see things that weren't real?

Her voice gave nothing away. "You have valuable information, Mr. Serafin, and you know it. You're bartering that information for your life. If it was worthless I wouldn't hesitate to get rid of you."

"How ruthless." The comment was light, mocking. Nothing like Killian. "I thought the days of Harry Thomason were long gone. No more random terminations."

"Most death sentences are the result of careful deliberation and examining all the options. You, Mr. Serafin, are a no-brainer. Blink, and I'll shoot you."

"I promise not to blink. Are you pointing a gun at me, Madame Lambert? You're skulking in the shadows. Maybe you've already made up your mind that what I have to offer isn't worth the price of letting me live."

"I'm keeping an open mind. Why don't you show yourself first?"

"Certainly." He stepped out, away from the wall, but it had grown too dark to see clearly. And suddenly the uncertainty was cracking the icy shell surrounding her.

"Do you have a light?" she asked.

"Why? Do you want a cigarette?"

She would have killed for a cigarette. Quite literally. "I'd like to take a good look at you before I come any closer."

"A wise precaution," he said. "After all, I'm considered to be the most dangerous man in the world. Didn't *Time* call me that?"

"You shouldn't believe your own press clippings."

"Mahmoud!" He raised his voice, and the small child appeared, carrying a lantern. The man took it, raising it with one hand and holding out his other. "Satisfied, Madame? I'm unarmed. Harmless."

She stared at his illuminated face, and the relief was so powerful she almost felt dizzy. How could she have made such a mistake? He was nothing at all like Killian. Killian was dead, and had been for eighteen years. The only thing this man had in common with him was his height. And the fact that he was a terrorist.

His eyes were dark, almost black, and Killian's eyes had been green. His thinning black hair was liberally streaked with gray. Half his face was covered with a salt-and-pepper beard, framing a mouthful of blackened teeth. He had a paunch, a generous ring of flesh around his belly that suggested years of good living.

"Do I look harmless enough?" he asked when she'd completed her long, shocked perusal.

"I'm not a fool, Mr. Serafin," she said. She couldn't afford to let her relief lower her guard. "Looks can be deceiving."

"Indeed," he said. "Are you going to show yourself?"

She stepped into the light, the 9 mm semiautomatic held tightly, trained at his chest. If she had to shoot she'd go lower or higher—the throat was efficient, the groin almost as painful. Both caused much more suffering than a bullet to the heart or the head, and if anyone deserved to suffer it was this man.

There was no expression in his flat black eyes as he looked at her and the gun. "Are you going to kill me?"

If this man had really been Killian, she would have been tempted. But she'd been wrong…plus tired and emotional and deluded. "Not until you give me reason to."

"You mean I haven't already? Given my activities during the last twenty years?" He was goading her, amused by her.

She hated killing, hated it with a sick, deep passion. But when they learned everything they needed to from this miserable excuse for a human being, she was going to enjoy putting a bullet in his head.

"Right now, you've got a free pass," she said, keeping her voice light. "Are you ready to go? My Jeep is waiting, and we'd do better to travel in the dark. We're heading down the coast highway to Mauritania and catching transport there."

"I don't think so. They'll be looking for me in Western Sahara, and I don't trust women drivers on these roads. We'll head east and go through Algeria."

"The border's closed."

"And that creates a problem?"

She controlled her temper. "You asked us to get you out of here and safely back to England. If you already made plans, then why did you bother with us?"

"I need cover. I need someone at my back, dubious as you now appear to be. And I need the resources of the Committee to get resettled in a new life. You've agreed to do that, much as it galls you, because of the intel I can bring to the table. We go through the mountains into Algeria. I drive. And I take Mahmoud with me."

"The arrangement was for you alone, not your plaything. You're not molesting children on my watch."

"What a cynic you are, Madame Lambert. I don't like young boys. I hate to deny you one more example of my infamy, but I'm not interested in raping children."

"What do you rape? Or is it only the soldiers you control who get to torture and murder?"

There was a long silence. "You knew who I was when you made the deal. It's a little late to change your mind."

"The most dangerous man in the world," she said, her tone mocking.

"But not, perhaps, the most evil man in the world. There's a difference."

"I don't really care. I don't have to like you, I just have to get you back to England. Alone."

She felt it—the sight of a weapon trained on the back of her head. She trusted her instincts implicitly. Someone was pointing a gun at her, someone who wouldn't hesitate to shoot.

Serafin must have read her expression even as she tried to keep it blank. "That would be Mahmoud aiming his AK-47 at you. And don't think for a moment he wouldn't use it. He has a vested interest in keeping me alive and within reach, and he won't hesitate to kill you if you get in his way."

"Wouldn't that interfere with your plans?" Her voice was level.

"It would," he said. "Unfortunately, Mahmoud is the one with the gun."

She held out both hands, her own gun visible. "The Jeep's big enough for three," she said. "As long as he doesn't get in *my* way."

Even without looking she knew the machine gun was no longer trained on her back, and she tucked her own weapon away, turning to look at the child behind her, an empty-eyed casualty of war and poverty. He was probably no more than ten and yet he was ageless, and already dead.

"You surprise me, Madame Lambert," Serafin said. "I thought a woman would be more tenderhearted. Surely you wouldn't want to leave a child alone and unprotected out here?"

"Considering that he's more than ready to kill me, I wouldn't hesitate. And don't assume anything because of my gender, Serafin. It's simply an accident of birth. I'm older and wiser and just as ruthless as you are."

"Are you really? Somehow I doubt that."

She said nothing. She could pass for a perfectly preserved woman in her fifties, and there was absolutely no way he could prove otherwise.

"So, we're agreed? We'll take the mountain route into Algeria, heading toward Bechar. I drive, Mahmoud comes along, and we're a happy little family."

"You don't give me much choice."

Somehow he must have seen behind her cultivated blankness. "You'd like to tell me to fuck off, wouldn't you? But you don't have that luxury. War makes strange bedfellows, Madame Lambert. You ought to have learned that by now, given your great age and experience."

There wasn't even a hint of mockery in his voice, but she still felt uneasy. "Hardly bedfellows, Mr. Serafin," she said. "Partners in crime, perhaps."

His smile exposed those darkened teeth behind the graying beard. "We'll have to agree to disagree." He looked past her. "Mahmoud?"

Her language training had included only the most basic Arabic, and she barely understood his orders, but the meaning was clear. Mahmoud darted past her, machine gun swung over his back, and picked up Serafin's battered duffel bag.

She could've reached out, snatched the gun from his shoulder as he went, neutralizing him long enough that they could get out of there without an albatross. The mission was going to be difficult enough with Serafin's meddling, and in the end a child soldier was still only a child.

But she didn't. The day she couldn't handle an over-the-hill mercenary and a young boy was the day she'd retire. And that day wasn't in sight, no matter how worried Peter seemed when he looked at her.

"I take it you're ready to leave?" she said.

"Whenever you are, princess."

It was too dark for him to see the fleeting reaction that managed to crack her perfect reserve. And the fact that she tripped was understandable—there was rubble underfoot. Unless he'd done it on purpose, he wouldn't know his casual word had been like a knife to the belly.

But it had been casual, automatic. She'd heard Killian call any number of women "princess"—from a toothless crone in Marseille to a White Russian countess in Nice, and they all preened just as she had, when he was inside her and whispered the word against her sweat-damp skin.

"After you," she said now, no catch in her voice, as she followed the first man she'd ever killed out into the twilight shadows of Morocco.

4

Peter Madsen looked at the man across from him, knowing that his own icy blue eyes gave away absolutely nothing. Sir Harry Thomason had never been able to read him, and he never would. It was part of what had led to Thomason's downfall—his inability to realize what his operatives, including Bastien Toussaint and Peter Madsen, were capable of. That, plus his ruthless destruction of anything that got in his way. Peter had been a star pupil, and even Isobel Lambert could issue termination orders without blinking.

There was one crucial difference between Thomason and the rest of the Committee. Thomason sacrificed everyone, operatives and enemies alike, with a total disregard for loyalty, and that could only carry him so far. It had carried him into forced early retirement and a seat on the Committee, the shadowy group of men who did their best to control the fate of the world.

Thomason wasn't nearly as good at hiding his resentment. He'd shown up at the Kensington offices the morning after Isobel had left, and Peter hadn't managed to budge him. And he needed to. Now.

"I was against this from the very beginning," Thomason was saying, and Peter dragged his attention back reluctantly. "You can't trust a woman in situations like this. We all know Isobel is more machine than human, thank God, but she's not completely devoid of hormones, at least not yet, and sending her after Serafin could be disastrous. I've been able to uncover some recent information that makes the situation untenable."

"Information I don't have?" Peter was frankly doubtful. As Thomason was kicked upstairs he'd also been stripped of his contacts. There was very little chance he had access to intel Peter had missed.

Thomason didn't blink. He was the epitome of an upper-class English civil servant—ruddy skin, spidery veins across his nose, colorless eyes and thinning white hair. "You forget—I've been in this business since before you were born. I have resources you wouldn't imagine."

"And you didn't consider it important to pass those resources along?"

"They won't talk to anyone but me. Are you in some kind of hurry? You keep looking at your watch. If I'm boring you, I can always leave. Isobel is an old hand at this sort of thing, and used to surprises. She'll probably survive."

In another lifetime Harry Thomason would be dead within minutes of walking in the door. Peter didn't like him, didn't trust him, which in the past would have been almost enough to find his death worth it. The fact that he wanted Isobel dead would have put him over the edge, and Thomason would be a corpse.

But Peter didn't do that anymore. For the sake of his wife, who was already waiting for him. For the sake of his old friends, who needed a stable presence in the Kensington office. Hell, for the sake of the new operative Peter was supposed to be picking up at Heathrow later that night, Sir Harry Thomason would live to cause trouble.

So Peter kept his hand away from the drawer that held his Glock, the drawer Thomason knew existed, and leaned back in the chair. His leg was bothering him—the cold damp was getting to it. His limp would be more pronounced by evening, and Genny would fuss. "I don't wish to be inhospitable, but I have a meeting."

"Don't let me keep you. I'll be fine here at the office, catching up on things. And don't think for a moment you can kick me out. I'm your boss, as I always was. Just one step higher up. I have access to all the information in this office anytime I want it."

"Then what are you doing here? Why don't you go back to your country house, have a brandy and ferret through our intel at your leisure?"

Thomason's smile was slow and annoying. "You don't like me, Madsen. You never did, and I expect my ordering you to terminate Bastien Toussaint was the final straw. I didn't realize you went both ways for pleasure as well as duty. I don't imagine your wife or Bastien's little hausfrau would be pleased to hear about that."

Peter merely looked at him. "Do you seriously believe you'll annoy me with something a puerile as that? You've lost your edge in your retirement."

The pale pink in Thomason's plump cheeks darkened. "Hardly retirement, dear boy. And your sexual activities are of no interest to me."

"I'm relieved to hear it. I've given up fucking for the Committee, so I'm afraid I'd have to turn you down."

That last was possibly a mistake. Thomason was a vindictive, petty man, and he wouldn't like having his virility questioned, particularly since he was so well closeted he was practically immured. But he was an old hand at this game, a worthy opponent, and he barely blinked, his pouchy eyes darting like a lizard's. "Let's keep this civilized, shall we? I know the veneer of breeding is particularly thin in your case, but I would hope it wouldn't crack so easily. You aren't so far removed from that bloody little brat who almost beat another child to death with his bare hands. Your talent for violence started early on, long before your pretensions to gentility. Just because your carelessness got you crippled and stuck in an office doesn't mean your killer instinct is gone."

"You should keep that in mind," Peter said, unmoved by Thomason's taunts. "In the meantime, whether or not you're my superior, I'm not leaving this office unlocked. If you're allowed access to our files, then you should be able to bring them up on your own computer." Thomason had always been a notorious technophobe, but it was also unlike him to trust anyone enough to help him. The life expectancy for his secretaries and personal assistants had been appallingly short.

Thomason made a sound halfway between a grunt and a snarl. "Then I take it you're not interested in the mess Isobel has gotten herself into?"

"In the years I've known Isobel I've never seen her unable to deal with what has to be done." Peter wasn't sure just how much Thomason knew about her current assignment, and he wasn't about to offer any information.

"Josef Serafin isn't only the most dangerous man in the world," Thomason said, watching him. "He's also someone from Isobel's past."

Peter didn't blink. "Indeed. And you think she didn't know that, going in?"

"Did she?"

"It's always a mistake to underestimate your enemy, sir," he said with exaggerated politeness.

"And you don't think Isobel made that mistake with Serafin?"

"I think you're making that mistake with her."

"She's hardly my enemy," he said loftily. "She's my employee."

"She's your replacement," Peter corrected him

bluntly. "And you're not the sort of man who takes forced retirement in stride."

"No, I'm not. But I don't expect I'll have to worry about it. Isobel is in over her head, and when she fails to complete her mission, there will be no one to turn to but me to fix the mess you've made."

"In the meantime I have work to do," Peter said, unmoved. "These are new offices since your tenure, but I'm sure you can find your way out."

He rose, ever the polite recruit. He was a long ways from the hybrid street rat Thomason had brought in, and he knew manners better than those who were born to it. Harry Thomason's jibes fell on deaf ears—if it were up to Peter he might have chosen his old life, not the bloody warfare thrust on him, along with the manners.

But then he wouldn't have run afoul of Genevieve Spenser, Esq., and despite everything he had done, she loved him. And sorry excuse that it was, it still made everything all right.

Peter waited until Thomason left, then sank back down in his chair again, rubbing his leg absently. Isobel was smarter and cooler than anyone in the business. If Josef Serafin was indeed someone from her past, she would most certainly have known, and she'd have her own good reasons for not telling him. There was no denying the fact that the job was getting to her. It got to everyone sooner or later, and no matter how adept she was at hiding things, he suspected she was paying a very high price for her cool efficiency.

But no, he didn't need to worry—he had enough on his own plate tonight, far more pleasant tasks. Picking up one of Takashi's cousins, Hiromasa Shinoda, at Heathrow, a new recruit for the Committee. And making a baby with Genevieve Spenser Madsen.

At least he could be certain of one incontrovertible fact. Isobel would be in control no matter what she faced. She was totally incapable of feeling weakness, or emotion.

She was made of ice, the way they all needed to be.

Isobel Lambert wasn't sure whether she wanted to throw up, burst into tears or laugh. Killian had been the epitome of her romantic dreams, tall and gorgeous. Despite her French husband's inventive talents, despite the intervening years, she still thought of Killian as the one man who'd ever been able to move her. Now he was simply a paunchy, balding mercenary with bad teeth. And the memory of that night in Marseille, the blood on her soul, had been washed clean.

He was driving through the cold dark night, much too fast for the mountain roads. His mascot was curled up in the rear of the Jeep, sound asleep, still cradling the gun that was almost bigger than he was. She could reach back and get the weapon away from his grubby little hands, but then, she probably could have done that at any point. She just didn't want to kill him.

"I wouldn't try it if I were you," the man beside her said. She noted again how his accent was different than Killian's—an amalgam of continents and cultures, since he'd sold his services all over the world, killed in every time zone. It was no wonder there was no tracing his background.

"I think I could manage to disarm a six-year-old with no problem," she said, turning to look at him. In the darkness, the differences weren't as noticeable—he still had that strong nose, the same wide mouth. His face was rounder, puffier than it had been, but in the dim light it was far too easy to remember another time, another car, another man and woman, both of whom were long gone. Killian and Mary were dead. Only their bloody ghosts remained.

"He's twelve," the man said in a flat tone. Roughened with age and probably cigarettes, his voice had the same timbre as Killian's. She'd be happier when she could see him more clearly, but his state of decay was at least a partial comfort. "And you shouldn't underestimate the power of a zealot. He has a task to accomplish before he meets Allah, and he's not going to let anyone or anything get in the way of it."

"And that task involves keeping you alive?"

"For the time being."

She was tired. She was usually impervious to such things—she'd learned to ignore the lack of food, sleep and shelter, and it had only been thirty-six hours since she'd slept. The night was cold, and the Jeep was open, providing no protection from the elements or snipers. She needed to be on high alert, and yet she could feel her thoughts drifting.

"And what is his divine task?" Isobel roused herself. She really needed to be pumping him for more important information, in case she didn't manage to get them out in one piece. With at least a partial debriefing the mission wouldn't be a total failure.

But the immediate safety of the mission was affected by the lethal bundle of rags in the backseat, a wild card she hadn't anticipated.

The man beside her shot her a glance. She could still only think of him as Serafin—it was better that way.

"To kill me."

The night had grown colder. "All right," she said. "That can hardly come as a surprise—anyone who's ever met you, even heard of you, probably wants to kill you. So why doesn't he? And why are you indulging him? I can't imagine you'd be squeamish about breaking the neck of a twelve-year-old who's as small as he is."

"Maybe I've gotten soft in my old age," he said.

She kept herself from glancing pointedly at the bulk around his middle. "The child wants to kill you and you're so sentimental you're going to let him?"

"Hardly. He has very clear plans, which he was kind enough to confide to me. He wants to wait until he's older, so that he can torture me slowly and I'll die in exquisite agony. He's too small to accomplish that as yet."

"Again, I understand and fully sympathize with his plans, and I'm sure most of the world would applaud him. The question is, why are you going along with this?"

"Otherwise he'll kill me now, and I prefer to chance waiting a few years."

"People have been trying to kill you for decades—my own organization tried twice. Even Bastien Toussaint failed, and he never missed. Why don't you just terminate the child and get it over with?"

"All right," Serafin said, putting his foot on the brake. "It shouldn't slow us down too much."

Isobel didn't play poker; real life was too full of bluffing, lies and high stakes. She silently drew a breath as he pulled over to the side of the deserted road, leaving the engine running. "This won't take long." He pulled out a knife from inside his shirt.

The moonlight glittered off the steel blade. German steel, the best in the world, and for a moment memories sliced into her brain, just as a knife like that one had slashed into her face and body. The face she'd once had.

"I don't think we have time for this," she said in a perfectly steady voice. "The sooner we're out of Morocco, the safer we'll be."

In the moonlight she could barely see his shadowed face, the ghost of his old smile. "Good point. We're meeting my contact at an appointed time, and it wouldn't serve to be late. Mahmoud can wait."

The sleeping child stirred at the sound of his name, or maybe he hadn't been sleeping at all. It didn't matter.

Serafin pulled back onto the narrow mountain road, and Isobel closed her eyes for a brief moment. It was going to be a long night. And there was no way she could keep from doing what she most wanted to avoid.

Remembering.

Then

It had been almost a week before Mary Isobel Curwen fell in love with a man who called himself Killian. She'd fought it, of course. After all, the man had a girlfriend, a French fashion model, no less, and even if Mary Isobel were the type to poach other women's boyfriends, she was hardly going to prove any competition. For one thing, she had a crazy mane of curly red hair, the bane of her existence. Plus she was curved rather than wraith-thin. Her last boyfriend had told her she looked better naked than with clothes on, but that was the kind of thing a single-minded boyfriend would say.

A French fashionista would have nothing but contempt for an American free spirit in gypsy layers.

And one thing Mary had known for certain: Killian was one of the good guys. He wouldn't simply take what was available. He wouldn't betray his girlfriend. He would provide the casual friendship and ride that he offered, and nothing more.

It wasn't his fault she'd fallen in love with him some-where between Brittany and the Loire. Maybe it was because he'd been so easy to talk to, his slow, deep voice sliding into her bones like liquid silk. Maybe it was because he was abso-fucking-lutely gorgeous. She wasn't used to beautiful men, and she hadn't realized until seeing him in the bright light of day, halfway across the water on their way to France, just how good-looking he was. Gorgeous men made her nervous, but somehow Killian managed to dispel that. Despite his green eyes and his beautiful mouth, despite his tall, rangy body that moved with an unconscious grace, he still seemed easier to be around than ordinary men, and she did her best not to stare at him when he wasn't looking. Why wouldn't a French fashion model have an equally gorgeous lover?

He treated Mary like a kid sister, and it made her feel safe, comfortable and deeply miserable. The one saving grace was that he had absolutely no idea how she felt. He was a good man, and he would never suspect that she was suffering the most ridiculously adolescent pangs of unrequited love she'd felt in her entire life. At least her dignity was safe.

He figured he'd fuck her when they got to Marseille. She was more than ready—he'd played her like the expert he was, and by the time he got her on her back she'd be begging, miserably guilty and totally vulnerable. The way he needed her to be, if she was going to provide the cover he required.

She was almost too easy. He'd only stepped into that alleyway in Plymouth on a whim—in general he didn't interfere with the local wildlife and their idea of sport, and whoever they'd set upon deserved what they got for being so fucking stupid.

It was a shame. If he'd been a different man, in a different world, he might have liked her. She was funny and smart, and had the most amazing freckles across her cheekbones and dusted above the rise of her very nice breasts. He was going to enjoy finding all the other places those freckles lurked when he got her on her back. Never let it be said he couldn't appreciate the more pleasant aspects of his line of work.

She was totally besotted already. He knew that beneath her colorful layers and free spirit she was imagining a safe little life with babies and a man who came home every night. A man who looked like him. She had no idea what she was dealing with.

In the end, he was probably doing her a favor. A bit of a walk on the wild side, though if he carried it off perfectly she'd have no idea she was only a few steps removed from a world of death and violence, danger most normal people couldn't even imagine. If he played his cards right she'd have a passionate fling with a man who would then, with a great show of reluctance, leave her to go back to his fictional French mistress. She'd go on to the Cordon Bleu in Paris, never realizing the assassination of General Matanga, head of the Coalition Armies trying to liberate a small country in West Africa, had been carried on right under her nose. And that Killian had washed his hands clean of the blood and then put them on her.

In a way it was a shame. Matanga was a decent enough man, the Coalition Armies were filled with citizens, not mercenaries, and ethnic cleansing was frowned upon. But Killian's employers had other plans for that war-torn area of Africa, and Matanga was counter to it, so he had to die. And it was Killian's job to do it. Plus tie it to a group of heroin smugglers in Marseille, destroying Matanga's reputation as well as his life.

Killian had everything planned, with a reasonable margin for error, because he was a man ready for the unexpected. Mary Isobel Curwen was unexpected, something he was using to excellent advantage. Word had gone out that he was coming into France, though no one knew what he looked like, what name he went by or what his current mission was. He was in so deep that he'd be hard to make, but with a hapless young woman beside him it would be almost impossible. They would have expected him to come from the south, but instead he'd crossed the Channel on a ferry, then driven his battered Citroën with the engine of a race car down the Loire Valley, the girl by his side, when everyone knew Killian only worked alone.

They'd make Marseille in a few days, their last stop before heading north to Paris. Maybe he wouldn't wait that long. He'd slept with his arms around her one night on the beach; the youth hostels with their cloistered dormitories, the ones that had provided such excellent cover, had been full so they'd camped. He'd been the perfect gentleman, the brotherly type, offering her warmth and a shoulder to rest on. And while he'd kept the greater part of his brain busy going over the details of his upcoming job, he'd allowed one small part to savor the smell of her skin at the nape of her neck. She used rose-scented soap, something delicate and sweetly, wildly erotic.

No, maybe he shouldn't wait for Marseille. The sooner he nailed her the blinder she'd be, and she'd never notice when he disappeared into the night. She'd believe his easy answers. All he had to do was make her come, and she wouldn't think at all. He was good at that.

He glanced over at her. They'd left the outskirts of Montpellier several hours ago, and they were heading for the Camargue, the ridiculously Texas-like section of France, full of horses and cowboys and dry landscape. There was a youth hostel in the tiny town Les Armes, and they could spend another cloistered night. Or he could make his move now, and they could end up at some cozy little inn, in a cozy little bed, with him inside her.

She was curled up in the seat beside him, her head against the window, staring out at the passing land-scape. In fact, she'd been a good traveling companion. She had an open mind, a willingness to try anything, a sensual delight in the wonders of France. If she brought all that to bed with her it might be better if he left her alone. It could prove a distraction.

No, that was bullshit. Nothing distracted him when he was on a job, not even the sweetest piece of tail in the world. And she wouldn't be that good—her sexual experience was limited. They'd talked a lot, about anything and everything, and right now he knew almost as much about Mary Isobel Curwen as she did herself. Out of place in her father's new family, at loose ends, she'd come to Europe to discover the world and discover herself, and during the two weeks they'd been together she hadn't called or written anyone. His kind of woman—isolated, vulnerable.

And she knew all about Killian, the graduate student from Indiana, with three sisters, a widowed mother, a small-town doctor for a father, a French girlfriend and a lifelong interest in botany. She knew nothing at all about the Killian who'd grown up on the streets of L.A., with a junkie for a mother and no father at all.

No, sweet, innocent Mary Isobel wouldn't know what a monster she was taking into her bed. With luck she'd never find out.

They'd reached a village about twenty miles inland, and he pulled over next to a pay phone. "Shit," he said.

She turned to look at him with those blue eyes. "What's wrong?"

"I forgot to call Marie-Claire." It had been a twist of black humor on his part; his contact was a mercenary with the unlikely name of Clarence. "She sounded strange last time I talked with her."

"Strange?"

He managed the perfect hint of a sigh. Too much would be out of character. "I think she might have found someone else," he said glumly. "She spent the last three weeks on a photo shoot in Germany, and she was going to meet up with me in Marseille. But when I talked to her last night she said she couldn't make it, and I got pissed off and hung up on her, which is not a smart thing to do with a Frenchwoman. They're far better at being pissed off than I am."

"I'm sorry. I'm sure it's nothing." Mary Isobel anxious, bless her heart. Worried about him, when the removal of the fictional Marie-Claire would clear the way for her.

"Maybe," he said, sliding out of the car and heading for the pay phone. Tonight. Two days before his rendezvous in Marseille. Two days to enjoy her and cement his cover. Before he turned her world upside down.

Now

Peter pulled the Saab into the underground parking garage at Heathrow, sliding it into the narrow space reserved for Spence-Pierce Financial Consultants, Ltd. He glanced over at his wife, Genevieve, who looked flushed, slightly rumpled and very happy. She smiled at him, and he found himself smiling back, against his will. It was good to see her happy again, at least for the time being. Maybe if he could keep her in bed twenty-four/seven she wouldn't cry. Maybe if he could keep her in bed twenty-four/seven they'd be able to make a baby, and she wouldn't greet each new month with silent tears. Trust him to fall in love with a woman with a wicked biological clock.

At least for now she was in a good mood, and he, simple creature that he was, was so well fucked that nothing could depress him. Not even the thought of training one of Takashi O'Brien's nerdy cousins.

Peter wouldn't have thought Taka could be related to nerds, given his Yakuza background and his admittedly dramatic presence. But Peter had read the dossier on Hiromasa Shinoda until his eyes began to glaze over. First in his class at Kansei University, experienced in software design and engineering, someone whose record was completely spotless. It didn't augur well for the life of a Committee operative.

But he trusted Taka as much as he trusted anyone, and if Taka thought one of his cousins would make a good recruit, then Peter would give him the benefit of the doubt. At least it wasn't his maniac punk cousin, Reno.

Genevieve threaded her hand through his as they headed for international arrivals. He could have arranged for a private meeting, but there was no reason to go to so much trouble. There was nothing to point suspicion at young Hiromasa Shinoda, just another studious Japanese salaryman arriving in London for a little international polish. Except that it would be in the world of death and danger, not banking and commerce.

"What are we supposed to do with Taka's cousin?" Genny said. "We don't have to bring him home with us, do we?"

"I have an apartment already set up at the office in Kensington. Taka says he's quite the student—I'll give him enough research to keep him out of our hair for at least two weeks."

She reached up and kissed the edge of Peter's jaw. "That would be very nice. Once I'm...once things are a little more settled, I wouldn't mind having him come out to stay for a bit. Just not right now."

"Not right now," Peter agreed, some of his sunny mood vanishing. By a little more settled she meant once she was pregnant. And while he would kill for her, change the world for her, no matter what he did he couldn't in fact guarantee she'd get pregnant. Though he certainly was putting a great amount of effort into the task.

The international arrivals lounge was jammed, the flights from the Far East arriving in droves. Hiromasa was apparently tall, like Taka—that was one way to identify him. Taka had said they'd know him when they saw him, but Peter stared at all the various Asian men and drew a total blank.

"What's he supposed to do, wear a rose in his teeth?" Genevieve whispered to him.

"I think I see him," Peter replied, zeroing in on a tall, slender man in an immaculate dark suit, looking around as if expecting someone. Isobel would approve; members of the Committee tended to be extremely well dressed. They didn't usually bother with the rank and file, but were more likely to interact with the movers and shakers of the dark world they lived in. The young man would fit in perfectly.

Peter headed for him, still holding Genny's hand. "Hiromasa Shinoda?" he said.

The young man blinked. "Sorry, my name is Weng Shui Lau."

Peter felt Genevieve's elbow in his ribs. "That's not him."

"I beg your pardon," he said politely, before turning to look at her. "I figured out that much, but why…" His voice trailed off. Someone was standing directly behind Genevieve, taller than her impressive height, and Peter's good mood vanished entirely.

"Oh, shit," he muttered.

Hiromasa Shinoda smirked, tossing his long red hair back from his tattooed face. "I'm glad to see you, too."

"Reno."

"In the flesh. That man wasn't even Japanese, he was Chinese. Believe me, we don't all look alike."

Peter ignored the jibe. "Taka sent you?"

A faintly disgruntled expression crossed Reno's face, and he dropped his sunglasses down onto his elegant nose, hiding the brilliant, fake green eyes and tattooed blood drops on his high cheekbones. "I was informed it would be a wise idea for me to leave Japan for a time, and Taka thought I should do some good for a change." He glanced around him with casual disdain.

"It would be a novelty," Peter said.

Genevieve smacked him in the arm. "Stop it, Peter. He helped save your life in Japan last year, and you know it. He just likes to pretend he's scary."

Reno growled, offended. "I am not interested in your idiot organization or your delusions of sainthood. I promised Taka I would come, and I will stay here and do what you want until it's safe for me to go home."

"And how long will that be?"

"It depends on how angry the police are, how unforgiving my grandfather is and how interested Taka is in letting me come home."

"What terrible thing did you do?" Genny asked, sounding fascinated.

"None of your business."

"Watch it," Peter warned him. "You don't want to mess with Genevieve—she can turn you into hamburger if you annoy her."

She laughed. "Nobody can keep secrets from me," she declared, and Peter remembered with depressing speed that his wife had always had a soft spot for Taka's punk cousin. She'd even tried a little bit of matchmaking between Reno and Taka's future seventeen-year-old sister-in-law, the Amazonian Jilly Lovitz, until Taka abruptly dragged him back to Japan.

And now he was here again, and likely to stay for a while, and it was up to Peter to ride herd on him. First Thomason, and now Reno. If it weren't for Genevieve he'd count the day a total disaster.

"You're coming home with us, aren't you?" she continued, ignoring Peter's horrified expression. "You know you're always welcome, and you can ride into London with Peter each morning. He's arranged for an apartment in Kensington, but I know you'd rather be with us."

Reno was looking just as aghast. "I like cities."

"But you really should—" Genevieve began to protest, until Peter interrupted her.

"You'll like the apartment. And besides, I don't think you'd enjoy it out in Wiltshire very much. Genny and I spend all our time in bed."

His wife kicked him, hard, avoiding his bad leg, and then realization obviously set in. They'd have a hard time making babies with a curious houseguest wandering around.

Reno lifted his sunglasses and gave Genevieve a cool, assessing look, one that Peter immediately wanted to wipe off his pretty face. "Taka promised me an apartment if I did this. Or do you think you need to babysit me?"

"I didn't know it was you," Peter grumbled. "I thought it was some nerd named Hiromasa Shinoda."

"I am some nerd named Hiromasa Shinoda. I just don't go by that name," he said loftily. "Are you going to take me somewhere to eat? I've been on a plane for thirteen hours."

Peter knew his wife very well. She was about to open her mouth to offer him a home-cooked meal, and the sooner he ditched Reno the better.

"We'll drive into London and take you to your apartment. There are several sushi places nearby."

"Fuck sushi," Reno said. "I want fish and chips. And beer."

"Great," Peter said. "At least you'll be a cheap date."

"Don't count on it," Reno said.

And Peter wondered how long it would take him to kill his old friend Taka. And how much he could make it hurt.

5

It seemed as if she'd been riding in a car with Killian for most of her life. After she'd shot him he'd haunted her dreams, and now, suddenly, she was back with him, almost twenty years later. The same, and yet everything was different. He didn't know who she was. And for the first time she knew exactly who and what *he* was.

They were climbing higher into the mountains; the air was thin and cold, and she hadn't brought warm clothing. She'd dealt with cold before. She didn't shiver—it would alert him, a sign of weakness. She simply concentrated, letting the cold sink into her bones and radiate outward. It would take longer to warm up, supposing she eventually got the chance, but it kept weakness at bay.

The sleeping child was impervious. The man beside her was wearing a heavy jacket, his concentration focused as he navigated the narrow, rutted roads. She glanced over at him, at the steering wheel, and for a brief moment wished she hadn't.

His hands were still the same. He'd always had the most beautiful hands—long-fingered, graceful. When she'd been young and stupid she'd thought he had the hands of an artist, a lover. They were the hands of a killer, stained with invisible blood.

She glanced down at her own hands, lying in her lap, then looked away.

"Do you have any particular reason for taking us across a closed border when I already made plans for our pickup in Mauritania?" she asked in an idle tone.

"I have my reasons."

"Then why did you bother insisting someone come and rescue you? It seems as if you're more than capable of getting yourself where you want to be."

"I don't need help getting out of here. I need help entering England, getting properly settled. My money's out of reach, and half the world wants me dead. You and your organization are going to see that I live a long, comfortable life somewhere far away from the people who want to kill me."

"I doubt that's possible," she muttered.

His mouth quirked in a smile. In the darkness it was the same mouth. She looked away. "You think people will always want to kill me?"

"I think it's likely. Even if your new cover is impenetrable, and you're some retired businessman in the Netherlands, you'll still manage to piss people off."

"Yes, but retired businessmen in the Netherlands don't get murdered because they're annoying. And I have no intention of living in the Netherlands. I thought England."

"Why not home to America?"

She could feel his eyes on her. "What makes you think I come from the United States?"

"Your past is very hard to pin down, but as far as we can tell you were born somewhere in the U.S. in the late sixties. Which makes you approaching middle-aged, ready for an early retirement. The perfect business-man."

"Perhaps. But we're not in the Netherlands. What about Ireland?"

"It's bloody enough."

"So which side of The Troubles are you on? Must be the English side, with that impeccable British accent of yours."

There was nothing beneath his noncommittal tone— no suggestion that the British accent wasn't quite real.

"Neither side. I don't like war."

"Then you picked the wrong line of work, Madame Lambert. Or is this just where your talents lie?"

It was meant to sting, but she'd made peace with all that a lifetime ago. "I'm very good at what I do, Mr. Serafin. It wouldn't be smart to underestimate me."

"Oh, I never would. I'm quite in awe of you, as a matter of fact. Not many women could immerse them-selves so totally in their role. And even a conservative guess at your number of terminations is quite impressive."

"You're responsible for the deaths of thousands,

probably tens of thousands. It will take me a long time to reach your level."

"If I were you I wouldn't even try. After all, there can only be one Butcher."

"True enough. I have no interest in being the most dangerous woman alive."

"My dear Isobel," he said in that voice she could almost remember, "you already are."

There was nothing she could say in response. She only hoped he was right. "I suggest you give me some warning when we're about to cross the border. I like to be prepared."

"It's actually a lot easier than you're expecting. Cigarette smugglers and poor families do it all the time. You just have to know the right route."

"And you do?"

"We crossed into Algeria over an hour ago, dear Isobel. There's nothing to worry about."

"Don't tempt fate. There's always something to worry about."

"Then that's the difference between you and me. Worry's a waste of time. You take what comes as it gets here."

"And how are we going to explain our entrance into Algeria? I have passports for the two of us, but not for Jack the Ripper, Junior in the backseat. And they show us entering Morocco, not Algeria."

"My contact has taken care of the necessary paperwork. I can get us out of the country. I presume you can get us into England, or I never would have contacted your people."

"I can. But you're taking a lot for granted. What if I came to kill you, not to rescue you?"

"Then one of us would already be dead," he replied. "I'm a valuable commodity and, despite your personal distaste, you're going to have to follow orders. I'm going to get away with murder and be handsomely rewarded for it."

He was wrong about one thing. Following orders had never been a high priority with her, and she was now in the unfortunate position of having to issue her own orders. To decide between life and death. The Committee might want this man alive, and there was no denying the wealth of information he could bring them.

But she had killed him once. She wouldn't hesitate to kill him again.

The sky was beginning to lighten, an eerily beautiful shade of blue across the mountainous landscape. They'd been descending for the last hour, and in the gathering dawn she could see signs of life in the distance. A small town, not much larger than the ruins of Nazir.

He didn't wait for her question. "We're meeting my contact outside the village. He's got the paperwork and a place to change clothes before we meet up with our flight."

"First of all, I don't have any clean clothes. This will just have to do. And—"

"Sorry, princess," he said, and her stomach automatically clenched. "You're wearing a burka. Best possible cover. Good thing you're not one of those lanky American women—you'd have a harder time passing. All you have to do is keep your eyes lowered and your mouth shut and follow my lead."

"And are you wearing a burka as well?" she inquired sweetly.

"I'll be a retired British Army officer and you're my Algerian wife. Not the best possible scenario—most cultures don't like it when you take their women."

"Something I expect you're more than familiar with," she muttered.

"I'm a man of strong appetites," he said lightly. "Anyway, Colonel Blimp and his wife won't attract that much attention in this little village—they're used to strangers. It's a center of the smuggling trade."

"And what are we supposed to be smuggling?"

"Mahmoud. The child sex trade is a very lucrative one, and beneath all that dirt he's quite pretty. We could get at least one hundred pounds for him."

She wasn't going to show how sick she was. "Only one hundred?" she said. "Hardly worth the effort. Though it is a good way to dispose of him."

"Don't bother. You aren't going to let me sell him, and I have no intention of unleashing him on an unsuspecting pedophile. Mahmoud would carve him into ribbons."

"You almost convince me. But no. I hope your contact has a plan for his safe disposal, because he's not coming to England."

"Samuel will do his best. I think he's got some Christian school lined up. But trust me, sooner or later Mahmoud will get his scrawny butt to England and to my door, no matter how well you hide me. One should never underestimate a zealot."

"And what happens then?"

"Then I'll kill him." His voice was light, sure.

It didn't make sense. He'd yet to give her a straight answer. A man like Serafin—like Killian—could kill a small boy quite easily, no matter how fanatical and well armed. Why didn't he put an end to this particular threat? Someone couldn't live the life Serafin had lived and have any qualms about killing a child.

It probably didn't matter. She wouldn't let him do it, but it was an anomaly. And anomalies made her nervous.

"When and where do we catch our plane?"

"You're not arguing?"

"About what? Killing Mahmoud or the burka?"

"Killing Mahmoud isn't on the table. I'm talking about the latter."

"Burkas are excellent for concealing weapons. I don't have any problem with it."

"A reasonable woman," he murmured in mock awe. "Mahmoud."

His response was instant. The child was awake, and clearly had been for quite a while.

Serafin's orders were brief and to the point, and Isobel once more cursed the fact that she couldn't understand more than a word or two of what he was saying. Not that further studies would have helped; it wasn't standard Arabic, but some sort of obscure dialect.

"Does he understand any English?" The ground had leveled out, and they were drawing closer to the edge of town. As the sun slowly rose the chill began to seep out of her bones. A stray shiver danced across her skin and then was gone.

"No. He has no idea that in twelve hours he'll be disarmed, scrubbed clean and praying to Jesus."

"If he didn't want to kill you already, then that would do it."

"I wouldn't blame him," Serafin said.

Mahmoud muttered something in a sharp voice, and he replied, then turned to her. "Actually, I lied. There is one word he understands—*kill*. He wants to know if he should kill you or if I should."

She glanced back at the empty eyes and blank face of the lost child. "And what did you tell him?"

"That you're my business. If you needed killing I'd see to it, but right now, you're more valuable alive."

"I'm thrilled to hear that."

"I'm sure you are." They'd reached an abandoned storage building, and he pulled the Jeep behind it, turning off the engine. "Darling, we're home."

Her body was cramped and stiff from the long ride, but she made no attempt to climb down. "And when is our plane?"

"Tonight, if we're lucky. Otherwise, tomorrow night at the latest. Trust me, I'm ready to get back to the world of hot running water and single malt whiskey."

"And where will we be until then?" The light of day was strong and clear, bringing blessed respite from the elusive cover of night. She could see him clearly—the puffy face, the balding head, the blackened teeth and middle-aged paunch.

"Samuel's house is quite well-equipped for this part of the world, and he has reasonable guest quarters. We'll be able to freshen up there, and if it becomes too dangerous we can always find a hotel and spend the night."

She bit back the impulse to say "lovely." She shouldn't care enough to be hostile. She'd made her reputation as the Ice Queen, a cool, emotionless creature that nothing touched. Every time she reacted to him she was betraying all her hard work.

Besides, it didn't matter. So she'd known him a lifetime ago. He'd been a bastard back then and was a triple bastard now. All that mattered was getting the job done, seeing it through to the end. And she had every intention of doing so.

A tall, thin Arab appeared out of the shadows. "My friend, I barely recognized you," he said in greeting.

"Samuel." Serafin climbed out of the Jeep and embraced the man. Isobel looked behind her, to see Mahmoud watching the two carefully, his hand on the weapon. They were going to have a hard time divesting him of the gun. Isobel was looking forward to watching the ensuing battle. She was keeping well out of it.

"This is the lady?" Samuel said, glancing toward her. "She looks like her passport photo. Unlike you, my friend. We're going to have to do something about that."

"How did you get a picture of me?" Isobel asked coolly. There were very few of her in existence—she was almost as hard to pin down as the Butcher himself.

"Samuel has the best resources," Serafin said. "Come along, princess. We have a bit of a walk before we get to his house."

"Please don't call me that." It was a weakness, admitting it bothered her, but if he called her that one more time she was going to scream.

"You don't like it? What shall I call you?"

"Madame Lambert. Or even 'hey, you.' I've never been a princess in my entire life."

He tilted his head, watching her. "Oh, I don't think that's true. I imagine you were quite the fragile little flower when you were young."

That stung, though it made no sense. She cultivated her agelessness, considering it a triumph when people assumed she was well past her youth. But for him to say it…

She wasn't as immune to him as she'd thought, damn it. If it kept up like this she was going to have to shoot him out of self-preservation.

"You have a vivid imagination," she said in a tight

voice. Mahmoud had already scrambled out of the Jeep, keeping close to Serafin, the gun cradled in his arms.

"We need to get under cover quickly," Samuel said, clearly impatient. "You can argue once we're safely inside."

"We're not arguing," Isobel said.

"Just a lovers' quarrel," Serafin said easily.

That settled it—she was going to kill him. As soon as humanly possible. Maybe she could push him out of the airplane as they flew over the Mediterranean. Or wait until they got back to England, found out everything they needed to know, and then let Peter finish him off.

Except she wouldn't do that to Peter.

Maybe Serafin would be the first mission for Taka's mysterious cousin. Or maybe they'd just let him live, fat and rich and untouchable.

In the meantime there wasn't a thing she could do but follow the two men, like a good Muslim wife, ten paces back, with the lethal child taking up the rear. Assuming Serafin had no more surprises to inflict on her, they'd arrive back in England by the next morning, and she could pass him on to Peter. Never have to see the man again.

Twenty-four hours, she promised herself. And then she could breathe.

6

It was almost full light by the time they managed to slip inside Samuel's house. The place was large and rambling, with an inner courtyard, a fountain and a burka'd wife to greet them without a word.

"Take the boy," Serafin said. "The sooner he's safely locked away the better."

Mahmoud had no idea what was coming. Samuel's wife sidled up behind him, putting her small hand on his shoulder. He whirled around, trying to aim the gun at her, but collapsed on the floor before he could even speak, and the woman dropped the hypodermic.

Serafin walked over to his unconscious little form and kicked the gun away. Then he glanced up at Isobel.

"He looks so innocent, doesn't he?" he said. "I can see your heart bleeding for him."

"Then you're having hallucinations," she said. "I've been telling you to ditch him for hours."

Serafin reached down and hauled the small figure into his arms. "Where do you want him, Samuel?"

"My wife can carry him. She's very strong."

The silent woman stepped closer, her arms out-stretched, but Serafin made no move to relinquish him. "That's all right," he said. "Just show me where you want him. You can take the first shower, princess."

Isobel gritted her teeth, then smiled sweetly. "How very thoughtful of you. But I imagine Samuel and his wife have more than one shower in this lovely house."

"We'll be in a back bedroom, out of sight," Serafin said, shifting the limp body in his arms. "Don't be squeamish, Madame Lambert. I promise your virtue is safe with me."

She bit back her instinctive snarl. "I'm relieved to hear it."

"Samuel, why don't you show her the room while I follow your wife?" Serafin said.

"Because, much as I trust you, old friend, an Arab never allows his wife to be alone with another man. Particularly one like you."

"I think your wife will be able to resist my charms," Serafin said. But he handed Mahmoud's limp body over to his friend. "I'll show Madame Lambert to our rooms."

Rooms? There was a plural there—a great relief to Isobel. She needed someplace alone, quiet, to sort things out in her head. Her meeting with the dead man hadn't gone the way she'd planned, and she needed time to put things in perspective.

He was looking down at her, large, bulky and unattractive—despite Samuel's concerns. And yet there was still some intangible something…. Maybe it was something inborn, something that had nothing to do with physical beauty. Because any beauty on Serafin's part had been shot to hell a long time ago. Thank God. It left her coolly, totally immune.

"What did she do to Mahmoud?" Isobel asked.

"A simple tranquilizer. He'll sleep for hours, wake up in his new life at the Christian school."

"Poor kid," she said reflexively.

"At least he'll be alive. None of his friends or family has survived, and if I'd left him in Lebanon he wouldn't have survived much longer himself."

"He came from Lebanon? What were you doing there? I thought your last job was working for Fouad Assawi."

"I get around," he said, telling her absolutely nothing. "We need to get back to the apartments. It wouldn't do for Samuel's servants to see us. He runs a pretty strict household, but people would pay a lot to find out where I am."

"And who could blame them?" she muttered, following him. She wasn't sure if she was relieved or not that they'd finally gotten rid of Mahmoud. Particularly since Serafin had yet to give her a straight answer as to why he'd kept the boy with him, why he was indulging someone determined to kill him.

The rooms at the back of the house were cool and dark, the windows shuttered, with fans turning lazily overhead. There was a sitting area with a cushioned bench and not much else, and a bedroom. One bed, and not a very big one at that. There were fresh clothes lying across it, including a dark blue burka that would disguise her completely. As long as she kept her mouth shut and her eyes demurely downcast. There were men's clothes, too, and she scooped hers up quickly, not wanting her clothing to be too close to his.

Serafin said nothing, but she could sense his amusement. "The bathroom's over there. Take your time. We've got all day."

She headed for the bathroom door. "You'd better see if Samuel's got other clothes for you," she said as a parting shot. "I don't think those are going to fit you."

And his laugh followed her into the bathroom.

She stripped off her clothes and stood under the shower, letting the hot water beat down over her weary, dusty body. She'd barely slept, and while she could manage for days without doing so, a few hours of rest would do wonders. Right now she didn't have to stop and make sense of the situation she found herself in; her actions would be the same no matter what. Her mission was to get Serafin into England without one of his legion of enemies putting a bullet in his head, and she had no intention of failing. One foot in front of the other. He had just as much of an interest in getting out of this country in one piece as she had, and she could presumably trust any escape route he'd come up with.

Sometimes the smartest thing was to let go and let someone else control the situation. It was the hardest lesson she'd ever had to learn, but she'd learned it well. Though she didn't have to like it.

There were clean underwear, jeans and a T-shirt to wear under the burka. Isobel had contact lenses to make her eyes a muddy hazel, but even so the color might trigger some kind of warning, and she yanked her silvery-blond hair into a tight ponytail. She was better off under the enveloping robe—no one looked twice at Arab women in purdah, and with luck she'd never have to use the considerable firepower tucked in her waistband. She'd just follow Serafin at a discreet distance, like a good Muslim wife.

She didn't want to leave the bathroom, face him again. She recognized the emotion, accepted it and pushed open the door to the bedroom. Serafin was sitting in a darkened corner, and there was coffee on the table.

"Bathroom's free," she said, trying not to stare at the coffee. She made it a practice never to take food or drink from an unknown source when she was on a mission, and she had absolutely no reason to trust Serafin's friends. Samuel's wife was far too familiar with knock-out drugs, as Mahmoud's unconscious body could attest, and Isobel had no intention of taking chances.

They had no reason to want to drug her. There was no reason to lure an agent of the Committee here just to incapacitate him or her, and they hadn't even been expecting her. Serafin had been expecting Bastien; her arrival had been a surprise.

And sweet Jesus, the coffee smelled divine. It was almost worth courting death and disaster for one small sip. Almost.

"Shiraz brought us coffee," Serafin said.

"No, thank you." There was another chair at the table. She could sit there, close to him and the smell of coffee, or she could sit on the bed. She chose to stand.

"It's not drugged or poisoned. I need you alert if we're going to get out of here in one piece." He took a sip of his own coffee, and Isobel wanted to weep.

"No, thank you," she said again, her voice perfectly expressionless.

"I'll tell you what. I'll take a drink of yours as well. If it's drugged then I'll be the one to show symptoms first. Samuel has no reason to drug either of us. He's here to help."

"But what about you? Maybe you think you're better off without me, that you can handle this on your own and that I'm just in the way. It's certainly how you're operating. I seem to be along for the ride."

"What can I say? I'm a man who likes to be in control of a situation. As soon as we leave Algerian airspace I'm putty in your hands. In the meantime these are my contacts, my people. You'd be wise to trust me."

How many people had trusted the man calling himself Serafin, and survived? If she thought about that she'd be sorely tempted to put a bullet in his brain right now. She wouldn't trust him, any more than she'd trust Killian. But then, she trusted very few people in this life, and wasn't about to start widening that exclusive circle now.

He reached for the second cup of coffee, took a deep swallow and set it back down as he rose. The passing years had changed almost everything but his height, and she took a step back, because she didn't like it. Didn't like the feeling of him looming over her. It reminded her of when she had liked it.

"Do I make you nervous, Madame Lambert?"

"No. I just prefer to keep my distance."

"Evil isn't contagious."

"I thought you said you weren't the most evil man in the world?"

"I'm not. But that doesn't mean I'm a good man."

"I don't think anyone would argue with that."

"Not even my mother," he said wryly. "It's a sad thing, don't you think?"

"That your mother didn't love you? Not particularly. Go take your shower."

"Yes, ma'am," he said with mock humility. "The pastries are good, too. Shiraz is an amazing cook."

Isobel hadn't even seen the honey-soaked pastries behind the coffee cups. "I'll pass."

She waited until he'd closed the bathroom door behind him, waited for the sound of the shower. There was always the chance that the coffee was drugged or poisoned and that he'd already taken an antidote, but right now her need for coffee was stronger than her reasonable paranoia. She reached for the second cup and sniffed it, then took a sip.

It was rich, strong and creamy. Just the way she'd always liked it. In the last few years she'd tried to wean herself to black coffee, but this was an unexpected treat. Double cream, with just a dash of sugar. It had been years since she'd had it that way, years since...

She wanted to throw up. She set the half-empty cup back down on the table. It was nothing but a coincidence. Coffee was very strong in the Arab world. There was nothing unlikely about the way this was served. And yet she still felt sick.

He was taking forever in the bathroom. The shower had stopped awhile ago, but the water in the sink had been running steadily, and she wondered what the hell he was doing in there. It didn't matter. It was only morning, and they weren't getting out of this place before nighttime. She was going to have to spend hours trapped in this room with her worst nightmare. The longer he spent in the bathroom, the better.

She was so weary, but the last place she was going was the bed. She sat on the floor, her back against the wall, and rested her arms on her drawn-up knees. How did the song go—"I'll sleep when I'm dead"? She felt half-dead already. But that meant half-alive, and it was going to take a hell of a lot to get past that other half. She closed her eyes, listening to the sound of the water, tasting the rich, creamy coffee on her tongue. Remembering things she wished she could have forgotten forever.

7

Then

"No room at the inn," Killian said. "The entire town is booked. Some kind of religious festival, I think. We've got two choices. Push on, drive until we find a town with some space, or spend the night on the beach. The problem is, it's supposed to rain, and apparently every town for miles around is booked solid for the weekend."

Mary Isobel was exhausted, bone weary. It seemed as if they'd been in the rickety old Citroën for centuries, and lunch had been nothing more than bread and cheese and fruit. She was grumpy, she was hungry and she was in love. Not the best possible circumstances.

"How far would we have to drive to find a hotel?" she asked. It was already after ten, and a light rain had begun to fall, fogging the windows of the small car.

Killian shrugged. He'd been quiet all day. She knew

it had to be Marie-Claire, and she felt that familiar-un-familiar knot of guilt and longing. He'd used a pay-phone just after lunch, and though he'd said nothing, she could guess there was trouble. "Probably two or three hours on these roads. And then only if we're lucky."

"Do you want to head straight to Paris?"

He turned his head, looking at her out of those mes-merizing green eyes, clearly surprised. "Why would we do that? Neither of us is starting classes for another week, and we wanted to see Marseille."

"I thought you might want to get back to Marie-Claire and patch things up. You've been quiet all day, and I know you're thinking about her. You could leave me here and I'll hitchhike to Paris. I'm sure I can find some cheap hotel to stay in until I get my student housing, and you've spent far too much time—"

"She's not in Paris." His voice was quiet, unemotional.

"Where is she?"

"In Austria, with someone named Wolfgang. Appar-ently she's fallen in love."

"Oh, Killian, I'm so sorry!" Mary Isobel said, her heart aching for him.

He looked out into the rainy night. They were parked on a side street of the small village, the motor running, and she watched his profile in the dim light. "I'm not sure I am," he said. "We'd been drifting apart for months now."

"But you loved her!"

"Maybe. Maybe it was just really good sex. It

doesn't matter—it's over now. And you can find really good sex anywhere."

She wasn't going to argue with that. Maybe it was easy for him. He was tall, strong and gorgeous, and not cursed with a crazy mane of red hair and a few too many pounds. She'd never had all that much luck with men and sex.

But talking about sex with Killian was something she intended to avoid. Particularly since every time he touched her, brushed against her, her nerve endings sang and her stomach clenched and she wanted to cry or fling herself at him.

"And I don't expect you're in any hurry," she said, trying to sound tranquil, and almost succeeding.

"No hurry," he said. "Since I've fallen in love with someone else, myself. This just makes it a little easier."

She'd been able to deal with Marie-Claire fairly well—after all, she'd been in place when Mary Isobel first met Killian, before she'd fallen deeply, hopelessly in love with him. But someone else, someone new, was a little harder to deal with.

She'd been around boys who were madly in love with other people, had listened to them pour out their hearts, oblivious to her. Killian was no boy, and he wasn't about to do that. But they were friends. They'd talked about everything over the last two weeks as they'd traveled around France. Of course he'd want to talk about the new woman in his life.

Funny that he hadn't mentioned her. He'd told Mary

Isobel enough about Marie-Claire to make her sicken-
ingly jealous. She didn't want to hear about the new one.
She knew he was out of her league—a good friend and
nothing more—but that didn't mean she wanted to listen
to him.

"Oh," she said, knowing she sounded idiotic. Not
caring. "So we don't bother with Paris. Where are we
going to spend the night?"

"Let's head for the Camargue. We both wanted to
see it—how many times do you get to see French cowboys? If we don't find a place to stay we can always
sleep in the car."

The rain grew harder, steadier, streaming across the
roads as he drove into the night. The Citroën was small
and boxy—she could always curl up on the backseat,
but he'd have a harder time folding his tall, lanky
frame into any kind of comfortable position in the
cramped quarters. At one point she fell asleep—easy
to do with the sound of the rain beating against the
canvas roof of the car, the even click of the windshield
wipers, the absolute peace and safety she felt beside
Killian. As long as she was with him nothing bad
could happen. He'd saved her once, and he looked out
for her. She'd put up with the ache of longing in return
for his friendship, which was as solid and real as
anything in her life.

When she woke up the car had stopped. The night
was black all around them, the rain still beating against
the windows and roof. The lights of the dashboard

provided only a small amount of illumination, and then none at all as he turned off the car.

"What's up?" she asked, sleepy, unalarmed.

"Believe it or not, I'm lost. I figure we can just spend the rest of the night here and wait until it gets light or the rain stops, whichever comes first." His voice was deep, soothing in the darkness.

"I'm sorry," she said.

"What for? It's not your fault I kept driving when I didn't know where the hell I was going. Go back to sleep."

She could always fake it. The night had grown colder, the rain icy and driving, and she was wearing only a T-shirt and one of her light gypsy skirts. Her bare toes were freezing, but it was too dark for him to see her shiver.

"You're cold," he said. His night vision was clearly better than hers. "Stay put and I'll get one of the sleeping bags to wrap around you." He started to open the door, and she put out her hand to stop him.

"You'll get soaked," she protested.

"I don't mind."

"You'll only make me colder."

She heard his laugh. "Point taken. I can reach in the back and find a blanket."

"Okay," she said. And then wished she hadn't. He turned in the seat, brushing against her, and she wasn't cold at all. A moment later he'd turned, no longer touching her, and she didn't know what was worse.

"Why don't you climb into the rear?" he said. "I don't think I'd fit, but you might be able to get comfortable."

"That's not fair...."

"Sure it is. That way I have the whole front seat to stretch out in."

The front seat of a Citroën 2 CV wasn't much bigger than a rabbit hutch, but there was no question he'd have more room without her. "Okay," she said, reaching for the door.

He put his hands on her, hauling her back. It was far from the first time he'd touched her, but in the dark, in the cavelike interior of the small car, it somehow felt more intimate. "If I'm not allowed out in the rain, neither are you," he said. "Climb over the seat."

"It would be a lot easier..."

His big hands were on her waist, and she was over the high-backed split bench seat a moment later, landing with a thud in the back. "There," he said, shifting his long body to the passenger side. There was an edge to his voice, one she wasn't used to hearing. "Now go to sleep."

"Is something wrong?"

"Nothing."

She'd been around grumpy men before; just because she hadn't seen Killian in this particular mood before didn't mean she couldn't handle it. After all, he'd lost his girlfriend, had spent the last few hours driving in heavy rain and was probably cold, hungry and uncomfortable. And no man she'd ever known was cheerful when admitting he was lost.

"All right," she said, hunching down on the small seat. She could just manage to curl up, and she tucked her hands under her head, closing her eyes and ignoring the cold.

Only to have something come sailing over the seat. The blanket he'd dragged into the front for her. "Wrap yourself up," he said, still sounding testy. "You're cold."

"You keep it. I've got more space back there, and you're cold, too."

"I'm wearing more than that skimpy little outfit you've got on."

"Skimpy little outfit?" she echoed, annoyed. "It was hot earlier today."

"It's cold now. And if you're going to try hitchhiking around France you might at least wear a bra. I'm not always going to be around to save you."

She sat up, pissed off and embarrassed at the same time. "I don't need a bra," she said. "It's just one more piece of laundry to deal with, and I'm not so well endowed that I need to bind myself—"

"It would make life easier on me if you did," he grumbled.

"What?"

"Never mind."

She leaned forward, putting her hands on the back of the seat. "What's going on with you? We're friends. As far as you're concerned I don't even have breasts."

"Princess, I'm a man. I always notice a woman's breasts."

"Okay, first stop tomorrow I'll buy a bra. Will that make you happy?"

"No."

"Killian…"

"Just go to sleep," he said. "I'm going for a walk." The blast of wind and rain swallowed her protest, and then the door slammed and she was alone in the car.

A moment later she was out in the night, chasing after him. He was barely visible, and the rain beat against her skin like tiny pellets. "Killian, get your ass over here!" she demanded.

"Get back in the car." His voice came from out of the darkness.

"Not until you do."

"Get back in the goddamn car, Mary." He was moving farther away, and the rain was icy, blinding.

She could be just as stubborn. "I'm not going anywhere until you come back." She started toward the sound of his voice, only to have him suddenly slam up against her out of the night, his arms around her, pulling her close.

"You idiot," he said. "You almost went over the cliff."

She tried to look up at him. "Why the hell did you park beside a cliff? Couldn't you find someplace safer?"

He pushed her up against the car, and she could feel him fumbling behind her for the door latch. "Please," he said, the word a growl, "get in the car and stay there. If you don't, I can't answer for the consequences."

"Consequences? What the hell are you talking about?"

"This," he said. And he kissed her.

Not the sweet lover's kiss she'd daydreamed about. Not the tender touch of his mouth on hers. This was rough, hard, deep—a kiss of such raw demand that it frightened her.

Her arms were trapped between their bodies, and she yanked them free, knowing she should shove him away. Knowing she was going to put them around his neck and pull him closer. Knowing she was going to kiss him back.

He got the door open and pushed her into the front seat, and if he'd had any thought of leaving her he was out of luck, because she held on, dragging him after her into the tiny space.

They were a tangle of arms and legs, mouths and tongues. She yanked at the denim shirt he was wearing, ripping off the buttons to expose the firm smooth flesh, as he pulled her T-shirt over her head and sent it sailing over the seat back. His hands covered her small breasts, and then his mouth, and the car was hot and dark, skin against skin. He pushed her into the driver's seat and reached under her skirt, finding the plain cotton underwear and yanking it down, putting his hand between her legs, where she was wet and aching.

He didn't say a word. He simply pulled her back to him, her legs straddling his thighs, and she heard the rasp of his zipper, his soft groan, and then he thrust up into her, pushing, thick and hard. Hard with wanting her, needing her. The thought was dizzying.

She wanted more, and he gave her more, until she was clawing at his shoulders, shaking with it, lost in a dark, wicked place with no words, no tenderness, just heat and need and his cock inside her. Pulsing, thrusting, and her own body shivering, trembling, taking him, all of him, until she burst, arching back, her hair rippling down her naked back, her breath caught in a silent scream.

He put his hands between them, touching her, prolonging it, not moving as wave after wave swept over her, stars and darkness and a thousand pinpricks against her skin. When she was finally able to draw breath into her lungs, he began to move again, thrusting up, hard, over and over and over and over until he was trembling. She was shaking, needing more, ready for him, when he suddenly pushed her off him, and she felt the dampness across her thighs as she fell back against the seat, against him, breathless, weak, and his climax spilled over their bodies.

She wanted to weep. Weep because she wanted everything. Weep because at the last moment he'd protected her. Weep because she loved him and it was never going to work.

She felt his lips behind her ear. "You're in love with me, princess. Fortunately, I'm in love with you. Now go to sleep, and as soon as it gets light we'll find a hotel and do this again."

"Again?" she whispered sleepily. *He loved her.* Astonishing, unbelievable, but true. He loved her.

"Again and again and again," he said.

And before she could come up with another word, she fell asleep in his arms in the cramped front seat of the Citroën.

* * *

He'd almost blown it, big time, Killian thought, shifting a little beneath his soft burden. He'd forgotten a condom, and the last thing in the world he needed was a pregnant mark. He had every intention of ditching her once he'd completed his assignment, but he was hoping to do it gently, without arousing any suspicions. Break her heart, maybe, but save her life.

If she got pregnant he'd have to kill her. He couldn't afford to let anything make him appear vulnerable.

But that wasn't going to happen. He had condoms in his backpack. Unfortunately, everything had happened too quickly for him to get to them.... He'd been meaning to wait until they reached a hotel, but whether he wanted to admit it or not, he'd been waiting for this moment since he'd seen another guy straddling her in the alley in Plymouth.

And it had only been a taste. Fast and hard and good, but it was going to be even better once he found a hotel. He had three days before he had to meet his man in Marseille, and he knew just how he planned to spend those days. Fucking his brains out with Mary Isobel Curwen.

She had perfect breasts. He'd known early on she was sensitive about them, even more than she was about her red hair and her curvy butt. Maybe if she'd worn a bra he could have waited until they got to a hotel room.

But in the end he'd gone with his instincts and his appetites. And she was now draped over him in a boneless little bundle of satisfaction, thinking she'd found her true love.

He still wasn't sure of the least painful way to get rid of her. Simply disappear? Tell her he was going back to the imaginary Marie-Claire? Pick a fight with her? That had worked this time, to get between her legs, but in general she wasn't easily riled. She loved him, which made her both tolerant and an idiot. He was a very dangerous man, though he went to great lengths to hide it. She was smart enough to have picked up on it if she'd used her brain.

But he'd done everything he could to keep her from doing just that. He'd kept her interested, aroused, frustrated for just long enough, and now he'd sealed the deal. She was his, body and soul, for as long as he needed her that way. When he was through, she'd be older and wiser. And he'd be long gone.

He wanted her again. Pulling out at the last minute had been the smart thing to do, and it had nearly killed him. When he got inside her again he was going to stay there a good long time. Until he'd had enough of her.

He just hoped three days would do it.

8

He'd left. Mary couldn't quite believe it. She'd crawled out of the rumpled bed a few hours ago, wrapping a sheet around her, and curled up next to the window, watching out over the rain-swept Marseille streets. It had been raining for three days now, and none of it had mattered. They'd spent those three days in bed, the first night at a small inn, the second two in this cheap hotel in one of the worst parts of the city.

She hadn't even looked at it when he brought her here. She'd simply followed him into the room, onto the bed, moving in the dark, her body caught up with his, and it wasn't until she woke up, late this afternoon, that she noticed just how run-down and dirty the place was.

She glanced over at the small, torn-up bed, at the remaining sheet. It was a badly laundered gray, and she shuddered, yanking the other sheet off her body and heading for the tiny bathroom, amazed that there was one en suite in this slum. The towels weren't any better than the grimy sheets. She used the rough soap on her body, her hair, and then dried herself with some of her clean clothes rather than touch the towels provided. And then she dressed and headed back to the window, to watch as the wet streets grew dark, watch and wait for a man who wasn't coming back.

She had no reason to believe that. He'd been the perfect lover, tender, sweet, so intent on pleasing her that he'd barely let her touch him. It had been strange, wonderful, dizzying, and she'd felt drugged with it, with him, with the sex and the darkness and the pleasure.

Drugged... She shook herself. Where was he? Strange, paranoid feelings were washing over her, ridiculous thoughts that she couldn't shake. She couldn't remember anything from the last few days, just flashes of sensation. Had she eaten? Had she used the bathroom? Had they talked?

She yanked up her sleeves, half expecting to see needle tracks on her arms. Her head was clearing, and she pushed open the window, letting some of the cold wet air in. Where was he? And what in God's name had happened?

Nothing of his remained in the room. There was no trace of him, though her things were intact. Including the small amount of money that needed to last, the credit cards and traveler's checks. Why had he disappeared?

He loved her. She'd believed him when he said it, but now a thousand doubts were beating at her brain. Why would he turn from friend to lover and then disappear?

They'd spent more than two weeks together, traveling the back roads of France. She knew everything about him, just as he knew everything about her. And then, suddenly, he was gone.

She couldn't just sit there. She shoved her clothes into her backpack, pulled on a sweater and headed out to the lobby of the hotel. Her French had improved exponentially during the time she'd been in the country, and she had no trouble making the old woman behind the desk understand her.

"He paid for two more nights," she said, "and told me to tell you he had to go back to Paris. He was sorry."

Mary just looked at her, uncomprehending. "Did he say why? Leave an address or a phone number?"

The concierge shook her head. "Monsieur Brown left nothing but cash for the room." She eyed Mary's backpack. "Are you leaving early? There are no refunds."

"Monsieur Brown?" He'd given a false name. Had he given *her* one, as well?

"We don't want any trouble here," the woman said. "Stay or go, it's up to you. But your boyfriend's left, and he went off with a group of men. Maybe you should just go back to America and forget about him."

That wasn't about to happen. At the very least, she needed some answers. "What kind of men? Do you have any idea where they went?"

The innkeeper, not much cleaner than her rooms, scratched the side of her face. "Bad men," she said finally. "Smugglers, terrorists. I've seen them around before, and you don't want to have anything to do with them. The police leave them alone, and you should, too. If your boyfriend is mixed up with the likes of them you don't want to be anywhere near him."

"Terrorists?"

"I don't want any trouble here. I think you should leave."

"Mr. Brown paid for two more nights and you don't give refunds."

The woman slapped some money on the desk. "You go."

Mary Isobel Curwen looked at the bills. She was still feeling drugged. The world had turned upside down, and she was lost. If nothing else, she needed some answers.

"Did you see where they took him?"

"They didn't take him, *mademoiselle*. He took *them*." She shoved the money toward her. "Go."

Blood money. For some strange reason the thought came to mind. What in God's name was Killian doing with smugglers and terrorists? He was a graduate student, a teacher, with a fashion model ex-girlfriend and a family back home in the Midwest. The woman had to be crazy.

"Did you see what direction they went? You can keep the money if you tell me." *Dumb,* Mary thought. The avaricious woman would probably just make up something.

"They were headed to the docks. I heard them say something about it. There are old warehouses down there, most of them boarded up. You'll never find him. Let him go, *chérie*." She'd already pulled the money back. "He's a bad one, and you were too blind to see."

Was she? Could she have been that wrong about him? For the first time in her life Mary Isobel had fallen in love. Had she been so stupid as to fall for a liar? And perhaps even worse?

"I don't know anything more. If you have any sense, you'll get the next train to Paris and go home. You seem like a nice young lady—these people aren't like anyone you've ever known, and the sooner you get away from them the better."

She'd go to Paris. But she wasn't going home—she was moving on with her life, her plans, her semester at the Cordon Bleu, where she'd learn to butcher meat, and think of a certain lying American while she did it. But before she left she needed more answers. "Which way are the docks?"

The old woman shook her head. "You're a foolish girl. You don't want to get mixed up in this business."

"Where are the docks?"

She jerked her head. "Turn right and follow your nose," she said, moving away. "And good luck to you."

Mary shouldered her backpack and stepped out into the rainy evening. She had no idea where she was—she couldn't remember when they'd arrived in Marseille, and she had no idea what part of town she was in. Some kind of slum, with narrow, hilly streets leading down toward what must be the docks. Killian had found her in a port city; it was only fitting that their friendship end in the same kind of place.

After the first half hour she stopped crying. Her red hair was a tangled mess from the rough soap she'd used, but the steady rain dampened it down, and she let it hang around her face, shielding her misery from the few people curious enough to look at her. There were clearly no tourists out and about, at least not in the section she was scouring, and the few people she came across weren't interested in a bedraggled young woman. She walked and she searched. Her sandaled feet were frozen, her fingers numb, but she kept trudging.

It was close to midnight when she finally found Killian's car hidden behind a warehouse in a relatively empty area of the docks. She'd been walking for hours, and her backpack weighed a ton. As far as she could tell she hadn't eaten in days, and at one point she'd had no choice but to stop in a corner café for a bowl of bouillabaisse and some crusty bread. At another time she would have savored it, tried to define the various fish and spices used. That night all she did was eat, trying to fuel her body enough to find Killian, slam him against a wall and get some answers.

The huge old warehouse looked deserted, with junk piled all around it, a rusted lock and chain on the doors that faced the narrow street. She wouldn't have seen the Citroën if she hadn't been searching—it was covered with a tarp, tucked back in a yard full of rusted machinery and the hulks of dead cars. But the wind caught a tail of the covering, flipping it back, and the familiar orange color caught her eye. She wound her way through debris that looked as if it had been piled there for decades, telling herself she was crazy, until she pushed the rest of the tarp back and saw the scratch on the side panel, a scratch he'd told her came from a rock. A scratch that looked more and more like it was from a ricocheting bullet.

"Crazy," she muttered under her breath, standing in the rain, staring at the abandoned car. She was imagining disasters, when the answer was probably much simpler. He'd tired of her and gone off with someone else. But why bother to hide his car? And what was he doing with people the innkeeper thought were smugglers?

When Mary Isobel first heard the voices, she thought she was imagining them. She was standing there in the pouring rain, stunned, for God knows how long, but the rough French made her suddenly dive down next to the car, purely on instinct, and yank the corner of the tarp over her as they drew nearer. Then the nightmare blossomed into full-out horror.

"I've sent Ahmad to take care of the girl," one man said. "I don't know why you didn't kill her when you had a chance. She served her purpose."

She heard Killian's voice, familiar and yet strange, cold-blooded and devoid of any emotion. "She provided excellent cover, and I pumped her so full of drugs she won't remember a thing. Another dead body will just bring more attention, particularly when it's a young American."

"I don't think that's all you pumped her with." The next speaker gave a snigger of a laugh. "Loose ends are a mistake."

"So is overkill," Killian said calmly.

"We'll live with the consequences. She's dead by now, and Ahmad will get rid of the body. Everyone minds their own business in that part of town, and no one's likely to question her disappearance. You're sure her family has no idea where she is?"

"She hasn't been in touch with them for the last two weeks. I made certain of it. I know my business. She was the perfect mark—no family or ties to speak of, entirely at loose ends. No one will miss her."

"So why didn't you finish her? You have a reputation for taking care of details."

"I've been more concerned with completing the job and killing General Matanga. The girl knew nothing— she wouldn't have caused us any trouble."

"And if she did?"

"Then I would have killed her," Killian said in a cool, dispassionate voice. "As it was, I didn't think she was worth the trouble...."

Their voices were trailing off. She didn't dare move, to see which direction they were heading, but the sound of a metal door opening and closing suggested they'd gone into the warehouse. She sank down slowly, the tarp still shielding her, so that she was sitting in the dirt and mud, her legs unable to hold her any longer.

She shut her eyes, forced herself to breathe deeply, steadily, when she wanted to scream. She didn't dare draw any attention to herself; if she was going to make it out of there alive she needed to run, fast, before anyone saw her.

But Etienne Matanga… She kept out of politics whenever she could, nonetheless even she had heard of him, head of the revolutionary forces in his small African nation. A decent man, a leader, despite the fact that most of the free world found him a threat. He was the best hope for stability in a diamond-rich nation torn by tribal warfare, genocide and lawlessness.

And Killian had murdered him.

She couldn't believe it. This freakish nightmare had to stop—she'd been a weak-minded idiot. She'd find gendarmes, bring them to the old warehouse, tell them everything. She had no idea what Matanga was doing in France, or what Killian had to do with him…. The smart thing would be to run, as far and as fast as she could, and forget all about it. Forget about Killian. She couldn't do it. During the long, cold hours she'd searched the docks, her anger had turned to a solid knot, mixed with an undeniable need for revenge. She wasn't going to let him get away with it. Get away with anything.

But maybe there was still time; maybe Killian hadn't killed Mantanga yet. She had no idea how long it was since he'd left her, drugged and helpless, at the hotel, but he might not have committed murder.

She shoved the tarp aside, struggling to her feet. If she moved fast, she could—

"There you are, *chérie,*" a rough voice said. "I've been looking for you."

She turned, slowly, to face a very large man with a very large gun.

Killian still had blood on his hands. They'd had to work quickly, arranging the bodies and scattering the broken packets of heroin. It was an expensive setup— the smack could have gone for half a million on the open market, but it was an important part of the show. The French police would confiscate it, and somewhere down the line someone who shouldn't would get his hands on it, but that wasn't Killian's business. His business was almost done.

Etienne Matanga, so-called savior of Western Leone, had died in a shoot-out with his fellow drug smugglers, leaving no one alive. That he'd been supporting his resistance movement with drug money would destroy any reputation the former priest had left. He had led his army of followers in attempting a peaceful coup, and he was so popular he'd almost made it. But his plans for the country were at odds with those of Killian's employers, and he had to die, disgraced and discounted. And Killian had seen to it, with his usual efficiency.

He was sorry about Mary Isobel. He'd tried to set it up so that she could get away unharmed. He'd found a great deal of pleasure in her semidrugged body the last few days, a good way to keep his mind off what he'd been ordered to do. And he'd found pleasure in the last few weeks, an odd kind of companionship he didn't remember feeling before.

Maybe if he'd lived a different life he really would have loved her. Instead of being the death of her.

He was sorry they'd sent Ahmad. The West African wouldn't have been able to linger over his work—time was of the essence. But he would have made it hurt, because he was a master at inflicting pain, and Mary Isobel Curwen hadn't deserved that. She hadn't deserved anything that she'd gotten, but then, life was a bitch and then you died.

She'd just died a little earlier than expected.

He glanced at his reflection in the bathroom mirror. As soon as he got to Southeast Asia, his next destination, he was going to dye his hair, maybe grow a beard. He popped out the green tinted contact lenses and stared back at his own grayish-blue eyes. He looked exactly like who he was—a cool, ruthless bastard who always finished what he started.

He heard noise in the warehouse—voices, when they shouldn't be talking. No doubt President Okawe's men were thinking he was dispensable. After all, they owed him a great deal of money for shepherding the current operation through to its successful conclusion, and dictators seldom liked to part with anything they didn't have to. Killian sighed. He wasn't in the mood for this. It had been a rough night.

Then again, he wouldn't mind putting a bullet between Ahmad's close-set eyes. Just because.

Someone rapped on the thin door of the toilet. *"Entrez,"* he grumbled.

"We've got a problem." It was Jules, the weasely half African, half French liaison.

"No, we don't," Killian said. "I did my part. I want my money, and then I'm out of here. The rest is up to you."

"Your girlfriend showed up."

He paused as he was shoving clothes into his duffel bag, just for a moment. "So?"

"So we don't know who she's talked to. You said you kept her drugged, but she seems to know far too much already. What the fuck is going on?"

"The drugs would have worn off by now," he said, weary. "And what's going on is that Ahmad blew it. When I left her she was out of it, and not likely to remember a thing."

"Then how did she get here? I don't think she's the innocent you think she is."

"Trust me, she's an innocent. Clueless to the point of recklessness. If she showed up here it's nothing more than dumb luck."

"Not lucky for her. Ahmad's got her out in the warehouse, and he's annoyed. He figures she owes him a little time for the aggravation she put him through searching for her."

Killian had seen Ahmad's handiwork in the past.

There wouldn't be much left of Mary Isobel Curwen when he was done. Which was probably the best thing that could happen.

"Then Ahmad's happy, you're happy, everyone's happy. Except for the girl, but she doesn't count. What's it got to do with me?"

Jules looked at him for a long, contemplative moment, searching for weakness, regret, any emotion whatsoever. He didn't find it. "All right," he said finally. "You can go out the back way if you don't want to see her. Just turn left."

It was a challenge, one that Killian had every intention of ignoring. He didn't need to see her again, didn't need to know what she was going to go through before she died. He already had a fairly good idea. The smartest thing to do was head out the back way, straight to the small cargo plane waiting to take him out of here. These things happened, and the wise decision was move on with his life.

"I couldn't care less," he said, shouldering his duffel. He headed toward the sound of voices. Ahmad's, low and menacing. And Mary's voice, the one that had whispered in his ear when he was inside her, the voice that had cried his name when she came. The voice that had kept him company the last two weeks, keeping him entertained, charmed, distracted.

He turned right, pushing open the metal door to the huge expanse of empty warehouse. She was standing there, silhouetted by the open door and the rainy night beyond, holding a gun in her hand.

He was momentarily astonished. Had he been that inept to not recognize an agent when he'd spent two weeks with her? But then he saw the way she was holding the gun, and it was clear she'd never touched one in her life.

There was no sign of Ahmad. Killian dropped his duffel. He had a handgun tucked in his belt—he didn't need to draw it. She could see it clearly enough, and he could move faster than she could. She'd be dead before she managed to pull the trigger, if that was the way he wanted it.

"Where's Ahmad?" he said.

She didn't blink. He wondered if all the drugs had left her system. She was staring at him as if seeing him for the first time, which, in fact, she was. "He left. He asked me if I wanted to kill you, and I said yes. So he gave me the gun and he left."

Killian couldn't help it—he laughed. If this was Jules's way of getting rid of him, it was a singularly ineffective way of doing so. If Mary Isobel had been a professional she'd still have been no match for him. As it was, she was doomed.

"You're not going to kill me, princess," he said. "You don't even know how to hold a gun. Just set it down, and maybe you can leave here without any more fuss."

The gun was shaking in her hands, and he couldn't see whether the safety was off. Ahmad was a thorough man; he'd probably set it for her before he disappeared.

"Did you murder Etienne Matanga?"

"Yes."

"Did you drug me?"

"Yes."

"Why did you save me in Plymouth, take me with you?"

"Because you provided a good cover. They were already looking for me—someone tipped off the authorities that a single male was planning a hit, but they didn't know who, and they didn't know where. I didn't want anyone looking too closely at me, and you were enough to distract them."

"Marie-Claire?"

"I made her up."

Mary Isobel didn't ask what else he'd made up. She knew. He'd made up everything. If he'd been a different man he would have felt sorry for her.

But he was who he was, and he felt nothing at all. Apart from a mild concern about the gun she was holding.

"If you shoot me, Ahmad and Jules will finish you off. You'd be smart to just put the gun down and walk away."

"And let a murderer go free?"

"It's not your business."

"You made it my business."

He sighed. He was going to have to kill her, after all. She was too hysterical for him to let her go, and her gun was wavering dangerously. He was seriously annoyed with Jules and Ahmad—this was the last thing he'd wanted to do.

"I'm afraid..." he began, reaching for the gun.

He flew backward, spun around and landed on the floor, momentarily stunned. The bitch had shot him. She had actually pulled the trigger. If he weren't so pissed off he would have laughed. She was more of a survivor than he would have guessed.

He was bleeding like a stuck pig, but he didn't move. As he'd fallen, he'd managed to get his hand on his gun, and if she approached him to finish the job, he'd roll over and shoot her before she could blink.

It's what he ought to do, anyway. She was just standing there, unmoving, and he could hear her choked breathing, as if she'd been running for a very long time. He waited for her, as he felt the blood pool beneath him.

A step. Two. She was coming to check on him. He should roll over now, shoot her between the eyes. It would be so fast she wouldn't have time to realize what was happening.

But he didn't move.

Then, a moment later, she was gone. She'd vanished into the rain-swept Marseille night. And he pushed himself up off the cement floor and started after her.

9

Now

The room was dark when Isobel opened her eyes. She'd somehow managed to fall asleep sitting on the floor in Samuel's back bedroom, and she scrambled to her feet, reaching behind her for her gun.

There was no sign of Serafin. The bathroom door was open, but he'd finished his shower long ago—there was no scent of water and soap in the air. His discarded clothes were piled on a chair, along with what looked like bandages and other trash. She checked the bathroom, but the surfaces were already dry. She checked the door to the main section of the house. Locked, of course.

If she wasn't so annoyed she would have laughed. Who did he think he was dealing with? Granted, she'd fallen asleep at an inappropriate time, and slept heavily. She could thank Shiraz's doctored coffee for that. She'd been a fool to drink it, but she'd needed the caffeine so badly she'd risked it, and now she was paying the price. Serafin must have been careful not to drink enough to affect him.

Unless his coffee had been drugged as well, and he'd been taken while she slept. Possible, but unlikely. If his enemies had found him they wouldn't have left her alive; they'd both be dead by now. She could only assume he'd watched her sleep and gone off on his own, for God knew what reason.

She wasn't happy. She'd come all this way to rescue a man who was, in every possible way, reprehensible. A mercenary, a warlord, a terrorist, a man responsible for thousands, if not hundreds of thousands, of deaths. A man who'd used her, betrayed her and planned to kill her. The first man she'd ever killed—or thought she'd killed. For all those years. She'd be entirely happy to have him be the last man she ever killed.

She had no choice. She never let emotions get in the way of her work, and she wasn't about to start. When she was finished she could let go. For now she had a job to do, a monster to find and protect.

It took her less than a minute to open the lock, only to find the door had been chained shut, as well, so she could only open it a few scant inches. She considered banging it until someone came, then rejected the thought. That would be childish, and, even if she felt like a thwarted child, she wasn't going to give in to it.

There was a large window looking onto the inner courtyard. She pushed the curtain aside, but the window was grilled and barred—probably to keep the women inside, she thought grimly. For now there was no way out. She had no choice but to wait until someone, presumably Serafin, returned.

She put her hands on the grille, yanking at it in frustration, only to find it moved. She looked up. The house was new, the grillwork fastened in with Phillips screws. And two of them were missing.

God bless MacGyver, she thought wistfully, and headed for the small duffel she'd brought with her. The Swiss Army knife was still there. In a matter of minutes she had the heavy ironwork unscrewed and out of its frame.

The courtyard was silent in the darkness. How long had she slept? She was still feeling slightly dazed from the drug, a fact that annoyed her enough to chase the last sleepiness out of her brain. She didn't like it when someone made a fool of her. Someone was going to be very sorry.

She climbed out the window, dropping to the ground below. The house was built Arab-style, with all the windows and doors opening onto a central, tiled courtyard. The only sound she could hear was the quiet splash of the fountain.

The rooms she and Serafin had been put in were at the bottom of the square courtyard, and from outside looked like storage space and nothing more. Maybe Samuel had a habit of hiding people. A safe haven would be a valuable commodity in any part of North Africa.

She ducked into the shadows, moving down the covered walkway that lined the courtyard and separated it from the house. She still had the gun tucked at the small of her back, and she was more than ready to use it. Preferably on Serafin.

There wasn't a sound in the entire place. It was getting close to dinnertime, and yet there were no lights, no murmur of voices. Just the steady splash of the fountain, strangely ominous. Something was very wrong.

She sensed someone there. The sound was so small another person might have missed it—just a faint breath of wind, a slight shuffle of clothing.

Then she heard voices, in a language she didn't recognize. Not Arabic—something European, maybe Slavic. Hadn't Serafin done some of his dirty work in Bosnia? Was there any trouble spot in the world that he hadn't contributed to?

And now they'd found him. Or at least they'd found where he was hiding—she could tell from the tone of the voices that they were frustrated, tense, still searching. So Samuel had managed to get him away, leaving her like a sitting duck. No matter. She could handle herself. Now she was going to have to incapacitate the men who were looking for Serafin, and there were at least three, from the sound of things. Once she got rid of them, she'd find the son of a bitch, her nemesis, and drag him back to England. She hadn't come this far to fail.

She'd started forward silently, heading toward the intruders, when she heard the sound again, the almost-not-there breath, and a moment later she was slammed against the wall by a large body.

He didn't bother slapping a hand over her mouth—

he knew she wouldn't scream and alert the Serbs. She let him push her back into a corner of the walkway, knowing who it was, hating him.

"Samuel sold us out," he whispered against her ear. In the darkness it was Killian, and eighteen years ago... and she wanted to weep.

"Who can blame him?" Her answering whisper was ice-cold. "I'd do the same."

"I'm sure you would. I happen to know a way out. Just be glad I decided to take you with me."

The lights in the courtyard came on suddenly, and the eerie sound of music filled the air. Either the stereo was wired with the light switches, or someone wanted some noise to cover his movements.

But it could work to *their* advantage, as well. She looked up at the man pinning her against the wall, and turned to ice.

It *was* Killian. Killian as she remembered him. The beard was gone, and so were the blackened teeth. He must have used wads of cotton to fill out his face. He still had his hair, and the bulk around his middle had been left in a pile with his discarded clothes. He was Killian, eighteen years older, and even more devastating than back then, when she'd been young and stupid.

She couldn't reach her gun, but the Swiss Army knife was close at hand, and even with a short blade she could do a lot of damage. She jerked against him, and the fool gave her enough room to get the knife open against his skin. He didn't react.

"I should gut you now and do the world a favor," she said, pressing the knife a little harder against the base of his throat.

"Maybe," he said. "But you aren't going to. You need me. And look at it this way—I came back for you."

"I didn't need your help. You don't know who you're dealing with."

"Of course I do," he said. "Hello, Mary Isobel. It's been a long time."

She had pale skin, her freckles long gone, and she didn't even blink. Her reactions were so well schooled that even he was impressed. If he'd rattled her she didn't show it.

She took a breath, and if it was just a trifle shakier than normal, most men wouldn't have noticed. But he wasn't most men. "I killed you once," she said calmly. "I wouldn't hesitate to kill you again."

"I imagine not. However, I'm your only chance of getting out of here. And you're not the sort of woman who'd let a mission fail because you were pissed off."

"You think you know me?" He could feel the knife nick his skin, the faint trickle of blood running down inside his collar.

"Better than you think. Are we going to stand here and rehash old times, or are we going to get the hell out of here?"

She appeared to consider it for a moment. She was more than capable of slicing his throat—he'd kept very close tabs on her activities for the last eighteen years for no reason he was willing to admit to. She was capable of it, but he was equally adept at stopping her. Because he did, in fact, know her better than she could ever guess. The truth would horrify her.

But he could save that news for later. In the meantime they had to get the hell away before the three Serbs caught up with them.

It must have taken a lot of money to turn Samuel. Each friend was only as good as the price paid for his loyalty, but Samuel knew Serafin was good for staggering amounts. It was hard to believe someone had a bigger pocketbook.

The knife pulled back from his throat, and he heard the almost silent click as she closed it. A fucking pocketknife—he'd been dangerously lax. "Lead on," she said. "But know that if you do anything funny I'll put a bullet in your back." She reached in her pocket and handed him a piece of white cloth.

"What's this?"

"A handkerchief. You're bleeding," she said. "I don't want you leaving a trail."

"Thoughtful," he murmured. "But you don't have to trail me like a Muslim wife. I prefer you where I can see you."

She said nothing. He could hear the voices in the courtyard now, the three men arguing. He'd already ascertained that they were heavily armed; if it was a question of firepower, he and Isobel were toast.

But the day he couldn't outthink and outrun even the best hired muscle would be the day he deserved to die. He looked down at Isobel—with her new face he couldn't think of her as anything but that. His body was on high alert, and he finally had some unfinished business by his side. This was what he loved.

"Then let's go, princess," he said. And he basked in the flash of hatred in her eyes.

He didn't bother trying to take her hand—she'd get that knife out in seconds flat, and this time she'd cut deeper. Not that he couldn't stop her, but he didn't want to waste a moment. He simply moved toward the back of the structure, keeping in the shadows, knowing she would follow his lead.

He paused before an open section of the walkway, half hoping she'd stumble into him, but she didn't. "I smell explosives," she whispered.

He shouldn't be surprised; he knew she was one of the best. "I set them. Samuel tends to keep things well-fortified, and it only took a moment."

"You're going to blow this place?"

"With the Serbs in it."

"But what about Samuel and Shiraz?"

"Who knows? Though I wouldn't give a rat's ass if they were caught in the blast. I don't like being sold out."

"Isn't the explosion going to draw too much attention?"

"A nice distraction. *We'll* be long gone by the time anyone realizes what happened."

She didn't argue, which surprised him. "Okay. But…" Her voice trailed off as they heard a muffled thump.

It was nearby, coming from behind a closed door. The three Serbs were still at the far end of the courtyard, and the noise of the fountain masked the bumping sound. For now.

"Shit," he said.

"What?"

"Go on ahead. Push the bed in our room out of the way and you'll find a broken screen that leads out into the desert at the back of the house. Climb through there and start running. There's a ridge about half a mile away—you'll see it if it's not too dark. I'll catch up with you."

"Don't you think Samuel knows about the screen?"

"Nope. I never go anywhere without a way out. Get going."

"And what are you doing?"

"Just checking out the noise. Don't tell me you're worried about me?"

It was the right thing to say. It annoyed her so much she pushed. "You're a job," she said.

"That's right. Keep remembering that, and I'll meet you behind the ridge."

He expected her to hesitate. He expected some sign—anger, regret. She just looked at him, her perfect face blank. "Be there," she said. "I don't like failure." And she was off.

* * *

Isobel figured she had no more than five minutes to cry. It was a simple release of stress, where no one could see her, and she did it silently. She did it silently as she moved, shoving the bed out of the way, scrambling through the broken screen and taking off across the rough ground. She was a good runner—she'd always made sure that when the cigarettes started to affect her wind she stopped smoking. But right now she wanted a cigarette even more than she wanted to make it over the ridge. By the time she slid over the top, onto the other side, the tears were gone and she was cool, collected and very very angry.

She shouldn't have left him behind. It had been a regrettable weakness on her part, but she was afraid if she'd stayed there she would have killed him.

He knew her.

It had been her one powerful weapon against the unwanted emotions that were roiling through her, that he had no idea who she was. She'd briefly entertained the fantasy of telling him just before she shoved a knife in his heart, and in her dreams it had always been a knife. She didn't want to shoot him. She wanted something up close and personal. She wanted to see the pain, wanted his blood on her hands, wanted...

To get over it. If he didn't make it out of the building she'd move on with her life. If he did, she'd protect him for as long as necessary. And in the best of all possible worlds she wouldn't even hate him anymore. She could let him go, to live out his murderous, evil existence in the luxury he'd earned in blood.

There was a Jeep waiting at the ridge, not hers but another one, and she could just imagine Thomason's reaction to her latest expense report. Sir Harry was a little man, and his loss of power had hit him hard. He made up for it by nickel-and-diming them as much as possible. The loss of her vehicle was not going to sit well. At least the thought of Thomason's displeasure gave her spirits a momentary lift. She shouldn't care, but she despised that man, and any way to make his life unpleasant cheered her.

She slid the rest of the way down the ridge and headed for the Jeep, giving it a quick once-over. No incendiary devices—it wasn't going to blow when she turned the key. Which she had every intention of doing if Killian didn't show up in the next few minutes. There was always the possibility that in this case a failed mission might be preferable to a successful one.

A moment later he appeared, moving fast, a bundle of rags in his arms. "Get in," he said. "I'm driving."

She didn't bother to argue. He dumped the bundle in the back, climbing into the front seat, and she had no doubt he would have taken off without her if she'd hesitated. Settling in the seat beside him, she glanced at the still form of the child in the back.

"Is he dead?"

"Just drugged to keep them out of trouble. I realized if Samuel was going to sell me out, then he probably

wasn't going to leave any traces. Too bad, too. The
Christian school would have done wonders." Killian
started the car, and at that very moment the sky erupted
in noise and smoke and flames. Samuel's expensive
house, gone in a moment, the flames shooting to the sky.

"Did you do that?" she asked.

"Of course."

"Let's hope your trusted friend was *really* well paid
for selling you out."

Killian headed into the night, driving fast, not even
looking at her. "Let's hope my trusted friend was still
inside and went up with the Serbs."

"Is that what they were? I didn't recognize the
language they were speaking."

"Serbs. I made a few enemies there."

She remembered the failed execution of thousands
of ethnic Bosnians. The notorious Serafin had been responsible for the screwup and the prisoners' subsequent
escape. Yes, he'd undoubtedly made enemies.

The Jeep went over a bump, and Mahmoud's unconscious form slid to the floor. "Don't worry about him,"
Killian said. "He's safer down there, anyway."

They were driving very fast over the rough terrain,
and all Isobel could do was hold on. "So you knew it
was Mahmoud when you stayed behind? Why?"

The night was mercifully dark, the headlights spearing straight out into the desert, so she couldn't see him
clearly. Sooner or later the moon would come out and
she'd have no choice but to look at him, search his face

for the ghost of the man she'd loved. But for now things were thankfully anonymous.

He didn't answer, and Isobel's senses went into high alert. "I thought you said he wasn't your sex slave."

"He's too young for me," Killian said, unruffled. "And stop being so obsessed about my sex life. I'm keeping Mahmoud alive because—" He stopped.

"Because?"

"I killed his sister," he said finally, his voice casual, belying his uncharacteristic hesitation.

"You probably killed a lot of people's sisters in your time. What makes this boy special?"

He didn't deny it. How could he, when she knew the facts? "Mahmoud was a street kid, recruited as a child soldier. He's probably killed more people than you have, princess. I'm guessing his mother's Arab, but no one knows for sure. The father's something else. Mahmoud's a mongrel, with no side to take him in."

"Except the people who put a gun in his hand. If he had no parents, how did he have a sister?"

"She wasn't really his sister. But she looked after him, and was the closest thing to family he had."

"How old was she?"

"Fifteen."

Isobel felt the cold settle in the pit of her stomach. "And you killed her?"

"Shot her in the head, point-blank," Killian said, with calm detachment. "She was seven months pregnant." There was no sound in the car, just the noise of the engine and the wind rushing past them. "So you see, he has a pretty good reason for wanting to torture me to death."

For a moment Isobel was speechless. "You could tell him you're sorry. Not that that would help much."

She could feel Killian's eyes on her as they sped through the night, but she wouldn't turn to face him. "I'm not sorry I killed her," he said. "And Mahmoud knows that. So in his mind I must pay, slowly and painfully."

"And you're encouraging him?"

"Let's just say I'm willing to accept him as the instrument of divine retribution if that's what's going to get me. He has as good a reason as anyone."

She glanced back at the small figure lying on the floor of the Jeep. He wasn't the first casualty of a crazy, violent world, and he wouldn't be the last. She'd learned long ago that she couldn't save anyone's soul, and she'd given up trying.

"Where are we heading?"

"Samuel said he'd arranged a plane over by the western cliffs. I figure he'd hedge his bets, have the plane there anyway and play innocent when he hears about the Serbs."

"Don't you think the plane could be a trap?"

"Anything's possible. But Samuel has no particular reason to want me dead, apart from material gain, and he'll have already been well paid. He wouldn't sell me out for less than twice what his house is worth, so he should be feeling benevolent. He gets the money, a new house and a good friend survives."

"You don't mind that he betrayed you?"

At that moment the moon came out over the desert landscape, and Killian looked as he had eighteen years before. Young and beautiful and honorable. "I'd have done the same thing, and he knows it. I'm not holding a grudge."

She stared at him. "I would."

He snorted. "I'm well aware of that. Which is why I'm going to watch my back. You killed me once—I'm guessing you'd be even better at it this time around."

"Count on it," she said in a cool, deadly voice.

He smiled at her. "I look forward to you trying," he said.

Isobel wondered if she could shove him out of the airplane somewhere over the Mediterranean. No, a knife would be best. Hand to hand, with blood. She leaned back in the bouncing car, still clinging tightly. For the first time in her life she was actually going to enjoy it.

10

The last thing Peter Madsen needed was Sir Harry Thomason sitting in his office, smoking a cigar and badgering him. Genevieve would smell the smoke on him and grumble, and he had more important things to concentrate on than keeping Thomason's nose out of their business. Business like the Japanese punk living upstairs, ostensibly perfecting his English but—from the credit card bills—spending far too much time playing video games, buying hip-hop and nailing every attractive female in the city. Peter once more cursed his old friend Takashi, who'd been remarkably unhelpful when he'd called him.

"We needed him out of the country," Taka had said in his slow, deep voice. "He got into a little trouble with the daughter of a rival *oyabun,* his grandfather's ready to chop off half his fingers, and the Tokyo police are on the lookout for him. To top that off, Summer's little sister is coming over for a few months, and I don't want Reno anywhere near her. He's smart, he's got skills and he's not nearly the punk he tries to be. You remember the night on White Crane Mountain—we might not have made it without his help. He's got potential."

"Like a slum apartment in Brighton," Peter said gloomily. "When can I send him home?"

"You can't. At least not until things quiet down around here and Jilly's gone back to the States. Besides, you're shorthanded, I'm tied up over here and Madame Lambert's on assignment. You need the help."

Peter had merely grunted. Taka was right—Reno was smart, ruthless, inventive and fresh blood. He could be useful, if Peter could just figure out how.

In the meantime, Sir Harry Thomason was a pimple on his ass when he was already beginning to worry about Isobel. She hadn't checked in. She hadn't met her transport in Morocco, she hadn't called in, and there'd been no word from Serafin. Peter had been monitoring trouble spots, looking for some clue, but the region was so fucked up that there was no way he could tell whether a car bombing or a kidnapping or a house exploding had anything to do with her.

Thomason was the last person with whom he was going to share his concerns. Their old boss had been sitting in Isobel's office when Peter came in, sitting in her chair as if he belonged there. It was no surprise that he wanted back in—Harry Thomason liked power. The only surprise was to see him being so blatant about it.

"Where is she?" he demanded now. "I gather she's

disappeared off the face of the earth, and you weren't going to tell me. Do you have even the faintest idea what kind of mess she's in?"

"Nothing she can't get out of," Peter said. Short of physically ejecting Thomason there was no way he could get him out of Isobel's chair, and, much as he'd love to do it, Thomason still held some power within the Committee.

Sir Harry frowned. "We're not running a rogue operation here, Madsen. You have to report to somebody."

"I do. I report to Isobel. If and when I deem it necessary to inform the Committee of any change in those circumstances, then I'll do so."

Thomason said nothing, puffing furiously on the cigar. It was an affectation; he wanted to be Winston Churchill and he'd ended up like Stalin. The thought would have amused Peter if he wasn't uneasy about Isobel.

"What's going on with the new recruit?" His old boss changed tactics. "How much goddamned money are you giving him?"

"He's new to the country. We set him up in an apartment, gave him spending money and a debit card. Relocating is expensive."

Thomason didn't look mollified. "I suppose he's going to get a Saville Row wardrobe to try to blend in. I'm not sure we ought to be hiring Taka's cousin. One Asian comes in handy. Two might stick out, no matter how well they dress."

Peter's expression didn't crack. "I already suggested a new wardrobe, but so far he's resistant. He's concentrating on English lessons and getting comfortable in his new environment. I have every expectation that he'll work out just fine." Actually, Peter felt nothing but gloom at the thought of the flamboyant Reno let loose on the world, but he wasn't about to share that information.

"I'm ready to meet him. If he can assimilate as well as the rest of you he might become the new Bastien. Things haven't been working that well since he left. He shouldn't have been allowed to retire."

"You put out a termination order on him. If that had been fulfilled he wouldn't have been around, anyway."

"I was precipitous. Operatives like Bastien Toussaint don't show up that often." Thomason glanced down at Peter's bad leg. "He never made mistakes."

Peter had wanted to kill Sir Harry for a long time, and the reasons just kept multiplying. But Isobel wouldn't like him bloodying her office, and he counted it a good test of his sangfroid to see how far Thomason could push him.

Besides, the old man was out of shape, smoked and drank—a walking heart attack. "I'll get Reno down here," Peter said in a dulcet tone.

"Reno? I thought he had a Japanese name…which we ought to change. Maybe some plastic surgery to fix his eyes."

Peter's mood had lightened considerably. At least this was something he was going to enjoy. He strolled back into his office, picked up the encoded cell phone and punched in a few letters. Reno was slavishly devoted to text messaging, and able to type faster than most court stenographers, even in a foreign language. He'd appear in a moment, and Thomason could enjoy him in all his glory.

In the meantime, Sir Harry could either sit alone in Isobel's office or come out here to badger him. Either way, Peter would win.

Thomason emerged just as Peter heard the clatter of Reno's high-heeled, pointy-toed boots on the staircase outside. His old boss looked distressed.

"Is that our new operative? Because he needs to learn to be a little quieter. You can't just announce your presence—you need to blend in, become a ghost, as you did, Peter."

"Not everyone needs to work that way. Bastien was never invisible."

"No, but he knew how to immerse himself in his character. Damned pretty boy should have been an actor," Harry grumbled. "He didn't have the stones for the job."

Peter just looked at Thomason. They both knew perfectly well just how efficiently cold-blooded Bastien Toussaint could be when called upon.

Reno punched in the security number in the keypad outside, pushing open the door without hesitating, and Peter leaned back in his chair, prepared to enjoy himself.

For once in his life Harry Thomason was struck dumb, and if for nothing else, Peter felt suddenly in charity with his new recruit. Reno was dressed in black leather, a lime-green T-shirt the only color besides his flame-red hair. He was wearing his omnipresent sunglasses, but when he saw Thomason he pushed them up, exposing his aquamarine-tinted eyes and the tattooed drops of blood on his high cheekbones.

"Who's the old dude?" he asked in a bored tone.

There was a reason Thomason had never been an operative. He had a singular inability to hide his reactions, and the sight of Reno was almost enough to send him into shock. As it was, he simply sank into a chair, staring at him in horror.

"Harry Thomason, this is our new recruit, known to all and sundry as Reno. And this is a member of the overseer board of the Committee, the man who used to be in charge of all this."

Reno looked him up and down with withering contempt. "I know who he is. Taka told me." He dismissed him, turning back to Peter. "What do you want?"

"How's the English coming? Better, I see."

"Fuck that," Reno said. "Where's Isobel?"

"Madame Lambert," Peter corrected.

"Fuck that," Reno said again. "This old fart know where she is?"

Thomason was looking apoplectic. "I haven't the faintest idea where she is, young man, and I'll have you know—"

"Later," Reno said. And he was gone, his boots clattering up the iron stairs once more.

Thomason had turned a satisfying red color, but it was already fading. No heart attack today, unfortunately, Peter thought. "That's Hiromasa Shinoda, Taka's cousin. He's quite smart, once you get past his appearance."

"Get rid of him," Sir Harry gasped. "Send him back to Japan or wherever the hell he came from. We can't use a freak like that."

"Oh, I think he might be very useful indeed, sir," Peter said, enjoying himself. "And that decision will be up to Isobel when she returns."

"And if she doesn't come back?"

What did the man know that he didn't? Peter's instincts were on full alert. Thomason's sudden haunting of the Kensington offices was more than suspicious, but how could he possibly have more intel than Peter had?

He was being paranoid, in general a sane and healthy thing to be in his line of work. And Thomason went out of his way to needle him; the last thing Peter was going to do was jump through his hoops.

"She'll be back," he said. "She's only a couple of days overdue. We sometimes have to go dark for weeks at a time. But then, you were never an operative, were you? More of a bean counter."

The cigar in Harry's hand snapped in half, the crunch audible in the soundproofed room.

"I'll let you know as soon as I hear from her," Peter continued. "But don't expect anything soon—these missions tend to be unpredictable. If something's happened to Serafin the entire world will know it, and we'll know that Isobel has been compromised. In the meantime, I wouldn't worry. She's the Ice Queen, the coolest, most capable human being I know. She can handle anything."

I can't handle this, Isobel thought numbly, clinging to the bouncing Jeep. Only the sliver of moon and the sand-covered headlights illuminated the desert landscape, and for the first time in more than a decade she felt out of control. Her world had turned upside down a few short days ago, with the sudden reappearance of Killian, and nothing had gone right since then. Now they were heading God knew where, a comatose child on the floor in the back, a ruthless killer at the wheel, and her only weapons were a small handgun, a Swiss Army knife and her wits. That would be more than enough in most circumstances, with most individuals. But this was Serafin the Butcher, the most dangerous man in the world, and he probably wanted her dead just as much as she wanted him gone.

When had he recognized her? She would have thought that was an impossibility. Her own father had known her for her first nineteen years, although admittedly he'd paid little attention. She'd run into him on purpose about eight years ago, just to see how well her new identity worked. He'd carried on a casual conversation with the elegant woman beside him on the plane, and not for one moment had he realized he was talking to his long-lost daughter.

Killian had known her little more than two weeks,

and he'd been lying the entire time. He was probably barely aware of her, using her as a shield while he completed his bloody job. During those long nights in the car, when they'd talked about anything and everything, his words had all been lies. And he probably hadn't heard a thing she'd said.

She wasn't naive enough to think the sex had mattered. Men could have sex anywhere, anytime, under any circumstances. Screwing her had been his way of keeping her compliant—it meant nothing. She remembered the earlier part of that final night with crystal clarity, even if what came after was a blur. He'd made no more than a token protest when he'd heard a killer had been sent to finish her.

"Don't you want to know what happened to me?" she said abruptly. "The last time you saw me I tried to kill you. That's not what you would have expected from the stupid girl you drove around France with."

He glanced at her. "All right, I'll bite. What happened to you?"

"I shot you, and I ran out of the warehouse."

"That much I remember." He didn't sound particularly interested, and she realized in his scheme of things it had been only a minor incident.

"You killed Etienne Matanga, didn't you?"

"That was my job."

"And you were going to kill me if I hadn't shot you."

"If you say so. But apparently you got away scot-free."

"Not exactly. Your friends caught up with me."

"Did they?" He sounded barely curious.

"Yes," she said. "They did. They were very good with knives, and they were very unhappy with me. I remember thinking I was going to die, and not caring."

"Such a very sad story. I expect you never made the mistake of falling in love with a mysterious stranger again."

"I didn't fall in love!" she snapped. "You used me."

"You enjoyed being used."

"You drugged me."

He shrugged. "Once we got to Marseille I wanted to hedge my bets. I couldn't afford to have you showing up in the middle of my job. Trust me, you would have done anything I told you to by that point. I just figured drugging you would make things a little easier."

She had a flash of memory; his hands holding her down, hot, wicked words in the darkness, as his mouth…

"Your friends left me for dead, lying in a pool of blood in a slum alleyway. If it hadn't been for a Good Samaritan, that would have been the end of me."

"How touching. I'm glad there are still good people in this world. So who was this Good Samaritan who saved your life?"

"I don't know. When I woke I was in a bed, covered with bandages. I was in such pain he kept me unconscious as much as he could."

"Your savior?"

"My doctor. My husband. He was a plastic surgeon

with a slightly shady clientele. He kept me hidden, rebuilt my face, rebuilt my life. And married me."

"Charming," Killian said, his voice cool. "Fairy tales do come true, after all. You should thank me for hooking you up with your true love."

"I should thank whoever knew the French underworld enough to dump me on his doorstep," she said. "Unfortunately, Stephan had no idea who had brought me there."

"Quel dommage," Killian murmured.

"I thought you were dead." It came out of the blue, and she would love to bite back the words.

"Unfortunately for you, you didn't know what you were doing. You winged me, and I decided I'd just stay down. I'm sure you're much better at it nowadays. Killing requires experience and expertise."

"I have both."

"Yes," he said.

"Your friends died that night. A few weeks later, when I was beginning to heal, Stephan brought me newspapers, with stories about General Matanga's assassination and the five people found dead with him in the warehouse."

"I was already blessed with experience and expertise."

"But how did the men who tried to kill me end up dead in the warehouse? And how did you escape?"

"Trade secrets, princess." He cut the wheel sharply as they skidded down a hill. "I figure I need every advantage I can get. You're a formidable enemy."

She didn't feel formidable. She felt crushed, aching.

She glanced at her reflection in the mirror. Dust-blown, shadowed, the elegant features that never showed emotion, contact lenses that muddied her blue eyes. How could he have known her?

That was a question she could, and should, ask. If she'd made a mistake, tipped him off somehow, she needed to be aware of it so it wouldn't happen again. Assuming she came out of this mess alive. Death was waiting for her, sooner or later, and she accepted that with equanimity. But she wasn't about to seek it out.

"How did you recognize me? And when?"

He didn't even glance at her. Once more she was driving into the night beside this man, looking at his slender, elegant hands on the steering wheel. Blood-stained hands, figuratively if not literally.

"I don't think you want the answer to that."

"I wouldn't have asked if I didn't. When did you know it was me? Was it my voice?"

"Your voice is very different. Deeper, and you have a British accent that's quite believable. Charming, as a matter of fact."

She gritted her teeth. "How did you know me?"

He said nothing. She could see the shadowed form of something in the distance, and as they drew closer she recognized the outlines of a plane. Maybe they were going to get out of this mess, after all.

"When did you realize who I was?" she pressed.

He pulled to a stop abruptly, and she put out a hand to brace herself. Mahmoud made a piteous sound from the floor of the backseat, and then Killian cut the motor. "Let's just say I'm very good at what I do. I'm not easily surprised."

He climbed out of the Jeep, reached in back and tossed something at her—the dark blue burka that she thought had gone up in flames. "Better put it on. This is going to be tricky enough—we don't need an anomaly like you getting people's attention." He picked up Mahmoud's slight frame, tossing it over his shoulder like a sack of potatoes. She hadn't moved, just sat there, holding the cloth. "Are you coming with us, or would you prefer to take your chances on the ground?"

Her small duffel was long gone, as well as anything he'd brought with him. She unfastened her seat belt and pulled the enveloping cloth over her head before climbing out. "I still have unfinished business," she said.

And she left it up to him to decide whether she was talking about the current mission or killing him. When in fact, it was both.

Hiromasa Shinoda was covered with sweat, dressed only in a traditional *fundoshi,* the strip of cloth that had served Japanese men as underwear for millennia. His was made of bright red fabric covered with tiny little Hello Kitty icons in combat gear, something that would have given his old-fashioned grandfather a heart attack. But his grandfather wasn't speaking to him. Reno was banished to this gray, gloomy place, and while there were as many women as he wanted, he was already getting tired of it all.

That son of a bitch Taka would approve, he thought, going through the prescribed moves.

Reno's English was becoming impressive, honed by language CDs and the assiduous study of American gangster movies. He'd started watching old Yakuza and Samurai movies dubbed in English, just to amuse himself, but he was tired of being cooped up in the city, tired of not being able to drive, tired of inaction. He had Dragon Ash on the stereo, turned up loud to annoy the man downstairs, but so far Peter Madsen had failed to rise to the bait.

Reno spun around, his long hair whipping his body, his reflexes perfectly honed. He was a weapon, waiting, and all he could do was work out in the sparsely furnished living room of the old apartment.

Not that it had come sparsely furnished; he'd shoved the chairs and sofa into the back bedroom, leaving only the wide-screen TV and stereo equipment, the coffee table and a few mats to sit on. He'd left the bed that filled up the main bedroom—he'd gotten to like the luxury of sleeping on softness rather than a thin futon. But he'd stomach even that if he could get back to Tokyo.

Not in the foreseeable future, his family had told him. The police were going to take awhile to forget his last escapade, and his grandfather's second-in-command had given him the choice of losing two fingers or getting out of the country.

Reno was very fond of his fingers. He could deliver—and subsequently receive—a great deal of pleasure via them, and he wasn't about to give them up lightly. He probably wouldn't have true Yakuza credibility until he lost at least part of one, but he didn't particularly care. When it came right down to it he could scare the shit out of most people, anyway.

Not the man downstairs. Not his cousin Taka, with his American wife and her gorgeous baby sister with the beautiful mouth who…

Not his grandfather. Reno was banished from Tokyo until they said he could come home. In the meantime he was going to raise all the hell London could handle, and more.

He stopped, breathing deeply, pulled his long hair out of the high ponytail and then stripped off the *fundoshi,* heading for the shower. Yes, he was sick of English women. But he might find an American, someone tall, and he could close his eyes and listen to her voice and pretend….

His eyes flew open. He didn't need to pretend anything. He needed to get laid, he needed to hit something, and he needed to get the hell out of London.

And he wondered how long this exile was going to last.

11

Isobel fastened the seat belt around the voluminous cloth of her burka as Killian tucked Mahmoud's unconscious body into the leather seat opposite her. The boy was so small he could almost curl up in it, and she watched as Killian adjusted the seat belt, then covered him with a blanket. Her nemesis knew she was studying him through the screened eyepiece of the blue garment, but he ignored her.

There had been two men waiting for them, strangers. One the pilot, one the money man. She'd caught enough of Killian's Arabic to figure out they were asking about his companions. Apparently they'd expected him to come alone, not with an Arab wife and child.

The very thought had been nauseating on many levels. That she was in any way connected to this man, even in disguise, was hateful. She was no man's wife. Her relationship with Stephan had been cool and efficient, and while pleasing her had been a matter of male pride to him, there'd been no emotion involved. He was thirty years older than she was, and when he'd died from cancer six years after they married, she'd felt a disconnected sort of relief. The Committee was her family. Her job was the only husband she needed.

"Stay put," Killian said. "I'm riding in the cockpit. I'm not sure I trust our pilot. If Mahmoud wakes up and starts causing trouble, just hit him with another shot of this." He tossed a syringe into her lap. "That should keep him out of commission long enough. We're landing in Spain—after that it's up to you to get us to London."

"I already had plans to get us out of Morocco. Why the hell did you drag us over an illegal border and into this mess?"

"Did I ever give you the impression that I wanted to confide in you, princess? We're doing this my way, and I don't have to give you reasons. I had an errand in Algeria. While you were sleeping I checked in with former employers of mine, one of the few who don't want me dead. I've taken care of it, we're on our way out, and now you can take over once more, as you've been itching to do. But Mahmoud comes with us, drugged or not."

She resisted the impulse to sweep the syringe off her lap. "How do you know this is even the right dosage? For that matter, why is he still asleep and I'm awake?"

"You were given enough that you should have been out for hours yet. Let's just say you're an exceptional woman."

"And if I were still unconscious? Would you have left me behind in the house?" She didn't know why she was asking. At least her voice sounded no more than casually curious, and he couldn't see the expression on her face.

"I'd already set the charges, and I only had time to bring one of you out. You or Mahmoud. What do you think?"

She tore the headpiece off, wanting to look at him without the screening between them. "I think you're a man who'd choose someone who wants to kill you over someone who wants to save you."

"You've learned a lot over the years, princess. Perhaps not as much as you think, but you're still quite observant. However, you're forgetting the fact that you want me dead with just as much passion as Mahmoud does. You're just not going to act on it."

She didn't bother denying that. "Not now."

"No, not now," he said thoughtfully. "Call me if you need anything." And a moment later he was gone, behind the door that separated the cockpit from the tiny, luxurious interior of the plane.

The takeoff into the desert night was smooth and effortless; at least the pilot knew what he was doing. Once they were at a decent altitude she unfastened her seat belt and pulled the burka over her head, shoving it under the seat. She would have preferred to throw it out the window, set it on fire, anything to get rid of it, but she wasn't that stupid. Spain had a large Muslim population, and a woman observing purdah would hardly be remarkable. It would require life-or-death circumstances to make her put that thing on again, but unfortunately, such circumstances were the norm right now.

She looked over at the sleeping Mahmoud. She'd seen child soldiers before, of course. Seen them kill, seen them die, and Mahmoud was just one of a long line of faceless bodies. She didn't believe in the power of redemption, or second chances—she'd been in the business too long. But she also knew that anything was possible. If Killian were dead, Mahmoud would have nothing driving him. Maybe then he might have a future.

She leaned back, looking out into the dark night, then reached inside her bra for the small device that contained her world. It was a cross between a Blackberry, a PDA and a cell phone, so advanced no one could hack into it, at least not as of the day she'd left England. Fortunately, no one had touched her, searched her. She opened the keyboard and began to text, hoping to God Peter was on call.

But of course he was. The only thing that could distract him was Genevieve, and at this hour she was probably lying in bed next to him, sound asleep.

A few minutes later Isobel snapped the phone shut, tucking it back inside her bra. Mr. and Mrs. Smith were bringing their adopted child back to the U.K. via the Bilbao to Portsmouth ferry, a nice, leisurely ride where no one would think of looking for them. Someone would meet them at the ferry terminal with the proper IDs.

How Peter would get an updated photo of Killian was beyond Isobel's comprehension, but she didn't doubt he could do it. He could do anything. In the meantime, she needed to get them to the northern port from wherever they were going to land. She pushed herself out of the chair and headed for the cockpit door.

It was locked. "Bastard," she muttered under her breath, rattling the latch. "Open the goddamn door," she snapped.

There was a low murmur of Arabic, and then Killian's voice, clear and cool. "What do you want?"

"I want you to open the door."

"Don't be tiresome." Did his tone sound odd? She couldn't be certain. "Go and sit down. We should be landing before long."

"Landing where? I need to make arrangements." She rattled the door again.

"We can make arrangements when we land, Sarah. In the meantime take care of little Benjamin."

She froze. As a code it was far from sophisticated, but the message was clear. Something was wrong, and it didn't sound as if Killian was going to be able to fix it.

Which left things up to her. She still had the Swiss Army knife, and the engine noise was loud enough to cover her work. In less than a minute the lock clicked open, and she pulled the gun from her waist and pushed at the door.

Killian was sitting in the copilot's seat, handcuffed, and the pilot was holding a pistol to his head. "Go back in the plane," the man ordered. "Or I'll shoot your friend."

"Looks like you're going to shoot him anyway," Isobel said, not moving. Killian appeared singularly unalarmed, a fact that annoyed her.

"He's worth more alive than dead, and I like money. You, however, don't matter." The plane must have been on autopilot, for he turned away from the controls and aimed the gun at her.

A mistake. Killian slammed his head against the pilot's, so hard the man jerked in his seat, and a moment later the two of them were down on the floor, sprawling into the plane, Killian's hands still bound. Isobel stepped back, out of the way. If she came too close she could be pulled into it, and if she tried to shoot the pilot they could end up with a depressurized cabin. Besides, she might miss and get Killian, which would be a great tragedy to someone in this world, if not to her. She watched, unmoving, as the pilot slammed his elbow into Killian's unprotected stomach.

She'd witnessed violence before, participated in it. The strange silence of this life-and-death struggle gave it an eerie sense of unreality, as the unpiloted plane flew through the desert night. She ought to do something, ought to stop them, but some small part of her was taking a savage delight in watching Killian get the shit beat out of him.

Except that he was winning. He had the man under him, his knee on his neck. The cracking sound was unmistakable, and then the pilot lay still in the narrow walkway.

Killian rose, falling back into the seat, slightly out of breath. "Get the keys to the handcuffs, would you, princess?"

She didn't move. "I think I like you better when you're tied up."

He didn't even blink. "It didn't stop me from killing him, and it wouldn't stop me from killing you. Can you fly a plane?"

"No. Can you?"

"Of course. I was going to wait until we were closer to landing before I killed him, but you did have to blunder in and precipitate things, didn't you?" He sounded vaguely annoyed. "Next time, remember I don't need rescuing."

"Next time, I'll let you die," she said, kneeling down and going through the dead man's pockets with efficient distaste. She found the keys and threw them to Killian. Found a crumpled back of cigarettes and palmed them, sliding them into her pants pocket.

"You can try," he said, unfastening the cuffs and tossing them on the body. "Cover him with a blanket or something, will you? I don't want Mahmoud to wake up and see him. Another dead Arab won't increase his trust in me."

"You expect him to trust you?"

"Not exactly. But I'd prefer not to push him over the edge right now. He's happy to wait to kill me, but he could always change his mind, and I'm not in the mood to break his scrawny little neck." Killian slid over into the pilot's seat, checking the gauges with reassuring confidence. But then, when had he ever seemed less than confident? "Close the door and go back to your seat. I'll let you know when we're getting close to landing."

"Landing where? I've made arrangements to get us from Spain to England, but I need to know our starting point."

"Our pilot was heading toward Málaga, where I expect we had a welcoming committee. I'm heading farther up the coast—there's an airport in Almeria and one in Murcia. I don't think this plane holds enough gas to get farther."

"All right. We'll rent a car to take us up to Bilbao."

"We're leaving from Bilbao? That's a pretty busy airport."

"We're not flying," she said, and closed the door before he could ask any more questions.

At least she could be enigmatic, too. It wasn't much of a weapon against someone like Killian, but it was better than vulnerability. She looked down at the dead man on the floor. Someone had betrayed them again, maybe Samuel, maybe someone else. Whoever it was, he knew far too much about Killian's whereabouts, and her plan was a perfect way to just disappear for twenty-four hours. At this point the only person she could trust was Peter Madsen, and he was a thousand miles away.

This was up to her. She'd be bringing Killian back to the U.K. in one piece, though she didn't mind if he was a bit battered in the process. But failure wasn't an option.

Mahmoud was still out, and she put her hand on his forehead. Cool to the touch, and his eyes flickered open for a brief moment, dilated, drugged, before closing again. He wouldn't be causing any trouble for quite a while, she thought, sinking back into her seat. In the meantime she could only hope Killian was half as capable as he seemed to think he was. Or else they were all going to end up in a fiery crash somewhere north of Algeria or deep in the Mediterranean.

Peter Madsen quickly wiped the memory off his PDA, deleting all trace of Isobel's message, and tried to ignore the peculiar sense of relief that washed through him. He still wasn't comfortable with emotions. He'd made peace with the fact that he loved Genevieve to an almost dangerous degree, but he was determined to stay icy and detached as far as his work went. Except that Bastien, the closest friend he'd ever had, had turned his back on what was most precious to him just to save Peter's life. And Taka had almost died for him as well. Even if he'd paid that debt back in full, it made ties that Peter couldn't break.

But his strongest ties, after Genevieve, were to Isobel. He could see her so clearly, she was like a mirror of his former self. The ice-cold control, the gnawing pain that was going to make her crazy or kill her if she didn't find a way to deal with it. You could only stay in this business a certain amount of time before you snapped. And Isobel was dancing on the razor's edge.

But she was alive, she had Serafin and she was headed to Spain. He'd make arrangements for them to take the car ferry from Bilbao—giving them almost twenty-four hours of breathing space out in the Atlantic. He still wasn't sure why there was a child to provide papers for as well, but Peter was nothing if not efficient. The papers would be awaiting her at a café just outside the city, and they'd be on their way to England by tomorrow evening.

She hadn't asked for transport *to* Bilbao, so he was leaving that up to her. Nor had she said anything about the mission—he could only assume it was still on, even if she'd had to go dark for a stretch of time. He didn't doubt Harry Thomason's word that Isobel had known Josef Serafin in another life—Harry didn't make those kinds of mistakes.

And Peter didn't doubt Isobel had known exactly what she'd been walking into—she didn't make those kinds of mistakes either. Serafin might be considered the most dangerous man on earth by certain glossy news magazines, but Peter would put his money on Isobel every time.

He flicked off the light switch, setting the alarm system. Overhead he could hear Reno—music that could only be Japanese hip-hop, for God's sake, and thumps and bumps. Either he had half a dozen girls up there on the floor and he was doing them one by one, or he was doing some sort of exercise. Or dancing. The thought of Reno dancing was enough to send cold shivers down Peter's spine. He preferred the notion of an orgy. In the few days Reno had been in London it was clear he was like catnip to the nubile female population. It was astonishing he was finding enough time to work on his English.

Peter headed downstairs, out into the darkened streets. Genevieve would be waiting up for him, and he intended to lose himself in her wonderful body tonight. She was already past her fertile time, she'd told him gloomily. So now they could fuck just for the sheer pleasure of it, something he was looking forward to. He didn't mind providing stud service on call for Genevieve—there were far worse things on his plate—but he was looking forward to having the two of them in bed with no agenda. Maybe even doing a few things that didn't make babies but provided shattering pleasure.

No, he was going to have a good night, and then sleep soundly. He'd put enough roadblocks in Thomason's way; their former boss wouldn't know Isobel had successfully completed the mission until she was safely back in London.

If Peter were a decent human being he'd have some pity for the old man. Thomason had been shoved out of the job and the world he'd controlled for almost two decades, replaced by a female, no less. He'd do just about anything to get back in power, and the only way he was going to do that was over Isobel's dead body.

Not that Thomason would dare go that far. Not from any moral qualms—it was his ruthless ordering of terminations that had finally been his downfall—but because too many people were watching him. However, he was entirely capable of sabotaging Isobel's mission so that he could step in.

Peter had made sure Thomason wouldn't know she was in Spain, or if she was even alive, until she could present herself in person, mission complete. And then maybe Sir Harry would get the message.

In the meantime Reno had provided a distraction. Thomason had been so horrified, he'd gone rushing off, presumably to do his best to get both Reno and his cousin Taka drummed out of the Committee. It wasn't going to happen, but it would keep Sir Harry occupied for a few days until Isobel came home.

And then life was going to get very interesting indeed. In the meantime, Peter had a woman waiting for him, and he'd stayed too long at the office already. He glanced at the shaded windows of the third floor flat and shook his head. Isobel was going to love finding out about Reno.

12

Killian might think he knew how to pilot a plane, but several hours later Isobel was far from convinced. It was still dark outside when they landed—or crashed, if she decided to be critical—and if he'd found an actual airfield she'd be surprised. They were in the middle of nowhere, hopefully in Spain, but she couldn't even be sure of that. Mahmoud had woken up for a few moments, long enough to try to stab her with a knife she hadn't realized he was carrying, and once she'd disarmed him he fell asleep again. Even the bumpy, jarring landing didn't disturb him, but at least his color, beneath the layers of dirt, was better than it had been.

Killian emerged from the cockpit, stepping over the blanketed body of their erstwhile pilot. "Not bad," he said.

"Not good," Isobel said. "Where the hell are we?"

"Spain."

"Thank God for small favors. Where in Spain?"

"Did you know your English accent is starting to slip, princess? You'd best be careful if you don't want people like Peter Madsen and Harry Thomason knowing all your secrets."

She didn't blink. "How do you know who works for the Committee? I would have thought you'd be too busy pillaging and ruining countries and conducting ethnic cleansings. Though you have done a singularly bad job of it, haven't you? One botched massacre after another. It's no wonder you need to turn to your enemies to keep you alive."

"I wasn't aware there was anyone left in this world who wasn't my enemy," he said. "And I've survived as long as I have because I find out what I need to know. Do you want me to tell you where Bastien Toussaint and his family are living? I can even give you longitude and latitude. What about Takashi O'Brien and his American wife? I'm not sure she's too happy with the Roppongi district of Tokyo—she'd probably be happier out in the countryside, but O'Brien has work to do. And then there's Madsen and his wife, and their cozy little house in Wiltshire, where she plays dress-up and tries to get pregnant. I know everything."

Isobel kept her face stony. "You must have an informant," she said. "I'll have to see about that when I get back."

"Heads will roll?" he murmured. "What I'm most interested in is why you seem to have had no sex life whatsoever. Don't tell me you're still pining for me despite my betrayal?"

"Everyone betrays you, sooner or later," she said

with devastating calm. "You weren't the first and you weren't the last. I admit killing you might have been a little traumatic for the stupid girl that I was, but I've learned to adjust, and I can kill quite easily now."

"I think that's a lie," he said. "I think you suffer the torments of the damned when you have to terminate someone. You're not a born killer."

"You think not? Perhaps you're right—in general I don't like to take lives, no matter how evil my target. But I can thank you for a major change in my attitude. For the first time in my life I'm really looking forward to killing someone." The threat wasn't veiled. He knew exactly what she meant.

And the son of a bitch laughed. "I give you free rein to try, princess. You should have realized by now I'm a great deal harder to kill than most people."

"I can rise to the challenge."

He wasn't the slightest bit daunted. "Let's get out of here. You can fill me in on your bloody plans once we're in England."

"We aren't going to get to England unless you tell me exactly where we are."

"Outside of Zaragoza. This little plane had more range than I realized, and I thought I'd get us as close to Bilbao as I could manage. Not the main airport—I didn't want to have to deal with air traffic controllers and customs. Besides, the Spanish air force is stationed there and I'd like to avoid them if possible."

"I imagine you would. What about rental cars?"

"Why rent when you can steal?"

"Because it attracts more attention?" she suggested with deceptive calm.

"Not if it's done right. The Citroën was stolen, you know."

She didn't bother to ask which Citroën. "You're just lucky you've gotten away with it so far."

"I'm still alive, aren't I? I guess that proves how lucky I am. How's Mahmoud?"

"He woke up, tried to stab me, then fell back asleep again."

"That's my boy," he said fondly. "Did you get the knife?"

"Despite all evidence to the contrary I'm not stupid," she snapped.

"I never thought you were. And the good news is you can ditch the burka. It would cause more attention than your own spectacular self."

She blinked. She was so used to pulling her protective coloring about her, sinking into the background, that she hadn't heard a compliment in years. She had spent most of her life doing her best to be unspectacular—an elegant, faceless woman of a certain age. "Hardly spectacular," she said dryly. "I do my very best to be quite ordinary."

"Let me give you a hint, Mary Isobel," he said, leaning toward her. "You're doing a piss-poor job of it right now."

He moved past her before she could reply, opening the door to the plane and scooping up Mahmoud's body effortlessly, expecting her to follow. She almost grabbed the burka just to defy him, but she was beyond such childish reactions. Beyond any emotion at all, wasn't she?

The sun was rising over the flat, stubbled landscape—they seemed to have escaped one kind of desert for another, but the dawn was still and empty. There were no buildings, no shelter, no vehicles to be stolen anywhere in sight.

But Killian was already moving, Mahmoud's little body clasped in his arms as he strode across the open field, his long legs covering the distance so quickly that Isobel had to run to catch up. He stopped near a copse of trees, laying the child down with surprising care, then turned to look at her.

"Keep an eye on him, dose him if he tries to kill you. I'll be back shortly. This is farmland—civilization can't be too far away."

"You think you're leaving me here? Think again."

"I can't steal a car with you and the kid in tow," he said reasonably.

"What's to keep you from just taking off and not coming back?"

"The fact that I need your help to get into England and start a new life. Remember, I was the one who contacted you in the first place, and so far you've done squat to help me. I'll give you a chance to earn your keep before long. Until now you've been nothing but an added inconvenience."

"So maybe you think you'll have an easier time of it without me."

"Abandon you, princess?" he said lightly. "Never."

She turned her back on him, heading over to stand by Mahmoud, because if she spoke another word she'd hit him. There was no violence in her system, only reluctant duty. Except when it came to him, and suddenly she was six years old and enraged.

One thing for sure, if he came back with a Citroën she was going to shoot him, point-blank.

She glanced down at the sleeping child. Isobel didn't have a maternal bone in her body. She didn't want children, didn't know what to do with them, and it would have been better all around if Mahmoud had simply been blown to pieces in the explosion. He'd been through too much in his short life to come back from it all and have any chance of normalcy.

She knelt down, brushing the matted hair away from his face, the gesture almost unconscious. He looked so young, so innocent. If she had a heart it would have broken for him, but she'd disposed of it years ago.

She pulled off the jacket she was wearing, bunched it up and put it beneath the child's head. And then she hunkered down to wait.

It wasn't a Citroën, it was a significantly ugly Opel, probably made nearby at the Spanish Opel factory, and she wondered if he'd gone out of his way to find something small and hideous. It was a bilious shade of green, two-door and tiny. Being cooped up with someone as tall as Killian was going to bring back all sorts of unpleasant memories. If she let it.

She waited until he'd put Mahmoud on the tiny backseat. He'd picked up her discarded jacket as well, and, after a brief glance at her, tucked it under the boy's head again. She climbed in, her knees practically up to her chin, and glared at Killian. "Couldn't you have managed to steal something a little more roomy?"

"The trick to stealing cars, my angel, is that you choose ones nobody's looking for. Steal a Jaguar and half the country's after you. Steal a rusted-out economy car and the police have better things to do. Stop complaining. You'll be back to your Saab soon enough."

She let the little shiver of ice slide down her back. "I'm no longer surprised by how much you know about me," she said as he put the tiny car into gear and headed out into the morning light. "But I wonder why you bother to remember such mundane details."

"Nothing about you is mundane. And I have a photographic memory. Everything is kept somewhere inside my head. Every word, every act, every touch, every taste."

"Stop it." Her voice was small and deadly.

"Yes, ma'am." His was deceptively docile. "We're heading for Bilbao, right?"

"Yes."

"And what time does our ferry sail?"

She hadn't told him it was the Bilbao to Portsmouth ferry, but it wasn't that big a leap on his part, once she'd said they weren't flying. "Late this afternoon. We have to pick up our paperwork by two."

"Good. We should make it with time to spare. If you reach on the floor behind you there's some food and coffee."

"I don't trust your coffee."

"I wasn't the one who drugged you last time—it was Samuel's wife, and while I didn't stop her, I didn't necessarily order it. If you'd promise to stop nagging me I'd have no reason to drug you."

She wasn't going to bring up the other time he'd drugged her, so many years ago. Because she remembered every touch, every taste, as well. She reached in back, finding the paper sack. A thermos of coffee, fresh bread, cheese and olives. No cups—she was going to have to share. Put her mouth where his had been. Maybe she'd prefer to be drugged.

She took a deep slug of the coffee, full of cream and just a touch of sugar, just as she expected, then handed it to him. If he recognized her distaste he said nothing, simply pouring a good half of it down his throat before handing it back to her. With any willpower she'd have put the stopper back in and done without, but right now she needed coffee more than pride, so she drained it, waiting to see if she was about to pass out. Or die. She wouldn't put poison past him.

She was rewarded with a ferocious growl from her empty stomach. "No drugs," Killian said, his eyes on the road. "Now eat something and hand me the rest."

She pulled apart the bread, reluctantly, for she could have devoured it all herself. Keeping a chunk in the bag for Mahmoud when he woke up, she handed the smaller of the two remaining pieces to Killian. The cheese was sharp and tangy, the olives rich, and she ate slowly, staring out at the countryside, ignoring the man beside her for as long as he'd let her.

"You have a mole in your office."

She jerked her head around. "Don't be ridiculous. I'd know if anyone was untrustworthy."

"The pilot was tipped off. Whoever paid Samuel took care of the plane, as well. You led someone to me."

"They found you on their own. What makes you think I had anything to do with it?"

"The pilot was chatty while he thought he had me trapped. Apparently he didn't read those überwarlord rules, where you never brag about your wicked deeds to the hero because he's likely to escape and make all hell break loose."

"You're not the hero."

"No, I suppose not. Nevertheless, the pilot knew to expect you and me, though they had no idea Mahmoud would be with us. The same source paid off both the pilot and Samuel, and the arrangements were made five days ago. Just after I contacted your office."

"Coincidence. If you'll remember I had nothing to do with our going into Algeria. If you'd followed my plans we would have flown out of Mauritania and been back in London by now. Someone must have been watching you."

"If we followed your plans we probably would have been dead several days ago. I still have sources, and you've got someone in your operation who knows too much."

"Don't blame me for your screwup. I trust my associates with my life."

"Fine," he said, his tone cool. "But I don't trust them with mine. Which is why we're taking the ferry from Santander, not Bilbao. I'm afraid it takes us into Plymouth, not Portsmouth."

She froze. "I don't want to go to Plymouth with you," she said coolly.

"I know you don't. Tough."

"And how do you expect to get the proper papers?"

"Already taken care of, princess. I'm not giving anyone else a chance to take me down until I'm safe and sound in London, where I assume you'll provide adequate protection. Where are you planning to put me up? I was thinking the Ritz-Carlton would be nice."

"And a little too visible, don't you think? We have a number of safe houses around the city, as well as out in the countryside. It might not be quite up to your exacting standards, but beggars can't be choosers."

"I'm hardly a beggar. We've got a business arrangement, exchanging information for services rendered. I expected to be handsomely compensated."

"You'll be well compensated," she said. Even though the words stuck in her throat. Harry Thomason would see that Serafin was well rewarded for his life of blood and death. At least her old boss wouldn't have any moral qualms about arranging for the notorious operative's future. He would see it as Killian did: a business arrangement, and all the blood spilled meant nothing. "Assuming the intel you provide is useful. We'll know if you're lying, and we won't be happy about it."

"And of course I want to make you happy," he said, his voice a low purr. Familiar. Unfamiliar. He'd talked to her in that low voice when they were in bed together, when she'd been drifting in and out of a daze that was half due to drugs, half to lust. She forced herself to look at him, to remind herself that he was a different person.

But in the morning light he looked far too much like the man she'd fallen in love with. His hair was darker, a little shorter, and there were lines bracketing his mouth and fanning out from his eyes. Somehow she thought they weren't laugh lines. His skin was burnished dark from time spent in a hundred deserts, and the stubble of his beard had gray mixed in, but all in all he looked the same. Dark, mesmerizing eyes. Sensuous mouth, full of lies. And elegant, deadly hands.

She looked away again, closing her eyes. He was Serafin the Butcher, she reminded herself. He was Killian, the assassin who'd lied to her, betrayed her and tried to kill her.

He was the only man she'd ever believed she was in love with. He was her worst nightmare, her first kill, her nemesis from beyond the grave. She only hoped he was right, and that there was a mole in the Committee. Because then Killian would be dead, truly dead this time, and all she'd have to worry about was the security of her organization. A minor detail, compared to the bleeding wound that was Killian's presence in her life.

Bastien had been sent to kill him five years ago, and it had been one of his few failures. They'd tracked Serafin down to a small country in South America, wealthy from drug trafficking and oil deposits. The prevailing government had been controlled by a dictator named Ideo Llosa, and Serafin, soldier for hire, had been his second in command and enforcer. Bastien's cover had been excellent—he posed as a dealer in specialized weapons, and Llosa had a problem with insurgents, rebels, and anyone who disagreed with him. Bastien was supposed to come in, make the deal for biological weapons, dispose of Serafin and Llosa and then disappear.

But instead he'd come back, admitting failure for what might have been the only time in his career, and Serafin had moved on, to continue his bloody deeds. Llosa had died anyway, brought down by an unknown assassin.

Looking back, Isobel had wondered whether that was Bastien's first sign of burnout. The first hint that he couldn't keep on in his machinelike capacity. It had been a growing problem. In the past, operatives were killed in the line of duty or disposed of by Thomason's brutal orders. No one was good enough to survive the amount of time it took to get burned out.

First Bastien, then Peter. Taka was getting close—it

was only a matter of time before he wanted out of active work. At least he'd sent one of his tamer cousins to train.

As for Isobel herself, she'd been on the edge of disaster for longer than she could remember, and yet she still kept on. As she intended to do, until something stopped her.

But why had Bastien failed, that one time? He'd been tight-lipped, never giving a reason, but Isobel knew him too well to accept that the task had been too difficult. Bastien had been made for impossible missions.

No, there was something more to the story, something to do with the ruthless, lying, amoral monster who drove through the Spanish countryside.

If she didn't find out soon, it might be the death of her. And she wasn't quite ready to die.

13

Mahmoud woke up about an hour into their drive, and Isobel was half tempted to jab him with Killian's syringe. The boy pulled himself into a sitting position, arguing loud and long in incomprehensible Arabic, devouring every piece of food that was left in the car, including the Diet Coke that had somehow been among the provisions. If she didn't know better she'd have thought Mahmoud was simply a variant of a cranky child, stuck in the back of a small car, demanding to know how much longer before they got to their destination.

But Mahmoud was as far removed from a whining child as a rattlesnake was, and Isobel kept her eyes forward as Killian talked to him. Didn't he know it was better not to engage with someone who was bad-tempered and irrational? But then, child-rearing would have been missing in his life, as it had been in hers. Or had it been for him?

Mahmoud had lapsed into a blessed, sulky silence. "Did you ever marry?" she asked Killian.

He slanted a glance at her. "Why do you want to know? Were you hoping I'd carry a torch for you during all these years?"

"Hardly. If you thought of me at all you probably wanted me dead. I'm just curious. Not much is known about the illustrious Serafin. Consider it part of your debriefing."

"Three times."

She refused to react. "Interesting," she said. "At the same time, or were they serial wives? What happened to them—did you get tired of them and have them killed?"

"I try not to kill the women I have sex with. I learned long ago that it tended to leave a disturbing aftereffect. Fortunately, you weren't so squeamish."

"So what happened to them?"

"Maria Number One was killed by a car bomb in Sarajevo. Maria Number Two decided she'd do better with the man I was working for. Maria Number Three was murdered. Not by me."

"They were all named Maria? Couldn't you have been more selective?"

"Maria's a very common name in third world countries. I think Maria Number Two is still around somewhere in South America, but since I was still married to Maria Number One at the time, that marriage wasn't legal. So in case you're wondering, I think I'm available."

She'd asked for it by bringing up such a stupid subject. Then again, the Committee needed to know everything they could about Killian-Serafin. If he had any ties, any connections.

"No thanks," she said, rolling down the window to let some cool air into the car. It was a damp, chilly winter day, but the tiny car was suffocating. "It sounds as if being married to you was relatively unhealthy. At least you didn't bring any children into the world."

"Why do you assume that?"

She wasn't expecting it. She'd managed an effortless calm through most of the time she'd been trapped with him, showing nothing but mild curiosity and annoyance. Her defenses, her weapons were powerful, and she'd learned the hard way not to let anything get to her. Vulnerability was a luxury she couldn't afford.

And she could only hope he didn't hear her sharp, painful intake of breath. "Where are they?"

"Not they," he said, his voice devoid of feeling. "Just one. Maria Number Three was five months pregnant when she was killed. Someone trying to get to me, of course, but she was in the wrong place at the wrong time."

Isobel had to look at him, to see whether he was really as unfeeling as he seemed to be. His face gave away nothing. "I'm—"

"If you say you're sorry for my loss I might hit you," he said in an even voice. "It was long ago, and it's of no importance. I was annoyed for a week or so, but then I moved on."

"Annoyed?" She could almost believe him. The legendary Serafin would be annoyed. But this wasn't the notorious monster sitting beside her. It was Killian. He'd overplayed his hand, trying to convince her just how ruthless he was.

"That may have been your first mistake," she said finally.

If he was worried he didn't show it. "I don't make mistakes."

"Are you serious? You've barely gotten out of your various career moves in one piece. If it hadn't been for you, three hundred ethnic Albanians would have been butchered. If you hadn't screwed up, Ideo Llosa would have wiped out entire cities. Your mistakes ruined the plans of some of the most vicious dictators of the last twenty-five years. And no one, not even Hitler himself, would consider the death of his child an annoyance. If nothing else, there's the factor of pride."

"Oh, I'm singularly devoid of pride. It gets in the way of doing business. And you can romanticize me all you want, princess. You can tell yourself I'm a cock-up who's mourning his lost love and their unborn child, if that's what makes you happy. Though I'd think you'd prefer me to be totally devoid of feeling."

"I'd prefer honesty."

He turned to look at her, and his smile was dazzling. "You may as well ask for the moon."

They arrived at the resort city of Santander sometime in the afternoon, dumping the car in a busy alleyway and taking off on foot. Mahmoud could walk, and he seemed singularly unhappy to be deprived of any sort of weapon, but he kept up with them, silent, glowering. Isobel kept silent as well—she'd already ducked into a public loo to text Peter with their new arrival plans, but she didn't dare wait long enough to receive a reply. She'd just have to hope things were still working efficiently at the London office. Thomason had been doing his best to interfere, but he was an ineffectual nuisance. He wouldn't be able to distract Peter from getting done what needed to be done.

The ferry terminal, in the center of town, was blessed with a cafeteria and a newsstand. She had to force herself to eat the food Killian bought for them, but Mahmoud had no qualms, devouring everything in sight. She had no idea where he'd pack it all in his slender body, but that wasn't her problem. She drank her tea and nibbled at the fruit and rolls, waiting for Killian to return.

Something wasn't right. There were too many heavily armed police with trained dogs wandering around, not to mention a number of camera crews. Isobel ducked her head as an earnest Spanish reporter stood in front of them and rattled off information into the camera. Too fast for her to translate; she really needed to work on her languages. The news crew moved on, and she ducked her head further when she felt the curious eyes of the police checking them out.

A moment later a newspaper was dropped in front of her and Killian took the chair beside her. "Trouble," he said.

She looked at the paper. There was a grainy photograph of their abandoned airplane, presumably with the dead pilot still inside, and another of what appeared to be wreckage. *Terroristas!* The headline was in screaming red.

She handed the paper back to him. "What's happening?"

"We're fine, if we play it cool. Someone bombed the ferry terminal in Bilbao. I expect they were looking for us, trying to slow us down. In the meantime, security is heightened all over the country, and they're on the lookout for Basque separatists. Our nice nuclear family should have no problem—I've got our paperwork and tickets. Mahmoud there is a war orphan we're taking to England for rehabilitation and an adoptive family. You and I are aide workers helping out."

She took a breath. "The bombing at Bilbao couldn't have anything to do with us. No one knew we were headed there."

"No one but your office."

"I told you, Peter's trustworthy."

"No one's trustworthy." Killian took her cup of tepid Earl Grey and drained it. "Madsen might not be the mole. Things just might not be as secure as you thought they were. Do you have anyone new in the office?"

"Just Taka's cousin," she said reluctantly. "I haven't met him as yet, but Taka's among the best we have. I have complete faith in anyone he'd recommend."

"But you haven't met the guy."

"No."

"So you can't be certain."

"I'll ask Peter—"

"You won't ask anybody anything. We're not going to have any problem getting on the ferry, and once we're at sea no one's going to bother us. In the meantime, why don't you give me your PDA."

"What PDA?"

"The one you're keeping in your bra. Maybe someone else wouldn't notice, but I happen to have a particular interest in your breasts. Give it to me."

"No."

He sighed. "Don't make me do this."

"Do what?"

He moved so fast even she didn't see it coming. He rose, hauling her out of her seat, into his arms, and his mouth came down on hers, the shock of it both elemental and shattering. He shoved his hand down her shirt, cupping her breast, his long fingers fishing the tiny PDA into his palm, as the crowded cafeteria erupted into spontaneous applause.

Isobel tried to fight him, but he was bigger and stronger than she was. And he knew all the moves she normally would have made, forestalling her, so that it looked as if she was pawing at him back, in the throes of a passion that couldn't be denied.

Then he released her, and she sank back down in her chair, pale, shaken, her shirt half-open, as the enthusiastic cheers continued. Killian made a mocking bow in the direction of the crowd, and sat beside her. There was no sign of the PDA.

"You son of a bitch," she whispered.

"You enjoyed it, princess," he drawled. "Don't pretend you didn't."

She wasn't going to grace that with a response. Her entire body felt suddenly electrified, fragile, ready to explode. "What did you do with it?"

"I tucked it down my pants. Feel free to search for it at your leisure."

She turned away from him, trying to control her rapid breathing. She wasn't going to do this. Wasn't going to go there. She was strong, cold, an automaton, decades removed from the stupid girl who'd fallen in love with a murderer.

But the longer she was with him, the more that fool returned, and she could taste him on her mouth now. And it was good.

Apparently he didn't expect an answer. "We can board now. We're not sailing for an hour, but I figure the sooner we get past customs the better. Are you ready?"

Mahmoud had been ignoring them, still shoveling food in his face, and he finished by reaching out and taking the last sweet roll on Isobel's plate. Even if his command of English was practically nonexistent he understood Killian's tone of voice, and he rose, tucking it inside his ragged clothing.

There was nothing she could do but follow. And

when Killian's back was turned, when no one from their appreciative audience was watching, she rubbed her hand against her mouth, to wipe the feel of him away.

It didn't work.

So he shouldn't have kissed her. He knew that, had known going in that he needed to keep his hands off her until he'd finished his mission. And then he could have her. Assuming she hadn't managed to kill him, as she was no doubt fondly fantasizing about.

He might lie to everyone else, but he never lied to himself. He had every intention of getting her into bed; after eighteen years he was still thinking about her. But he couldn't afford to rush it.

He'd needed her PDA, though, and it had given him just the right excuse. She wouldn't know that he'd been looking for that excuse since she first walked into the ruined house in Nazir.

It hadn't taken him long to get used to her new face. He'd seen photos of it often enough over the intervening years. Stephan Lambert had done an excellent job on her, and the ageless perfection of her classic features worked well in her line of work. Most people would never guess she was thirty-seven. But then, there was no one left from her past life. She'd been reported dead, her family in the U.S. had mourned and then gone on with life. No one had asked any questions.

Which was one reason why he'd chosen her in the first place, to act as his cover. Her connections were tenuous at best—there were no close friends, no doting family for her to get in touch with. No one knew she'd spent the last two weeks of her former life traveling around France with a seemingly harmless graduate student. There'd been no way to trace her, and no way to trace him.

She wasn't happy about the room he'd booked on the ferry; it came with a double bed and a banquette that opened into a twin, but he wasn't about to make her life easier by telling her about it. Particularly since he knew she was going to make him share the bed with Mahmoud, who probably had lice, while she took the single.

Too bad. They'd made it onto the boat with little problem, and he noticed there were shops on one of the upper decks. Killian could find them some clean clothes, at the very least. It was too much to hope they'd be able to get Mahmoud clean—nothing short of major sedation would get him near water. Killian would make Isobel deal with it once they got to England. In the meantime, they'd simply have to survive.

The ferry was beginning to pull away from the dock. The sunny day had turned dark and windy, from a storm coming in. It was late afternoon; they'd arrive in Plymouth in the middle of the next day. They were safe for now, and he could relax his guard. Marginally. There was no way anyone could have picked up on their change in direction.

He was a man used to all possibilities. There were any number of people wanting him dead, but he had no idea who had bribed Samuel and the pilot. Someone who had far too good an access to his plans.

Isobel might be setting him up, but he doubted it. If it was a simple termination she would have taken care of it long ago. Unfinished business, she'd call it.

Some of his enemies had resources that were limitless. They'd know he'd made it to Spain, thanks to the pilot, but there were any number of ways to get out of there, any number of airports, ferries or roads over the Pyrenees to France. It was unlikely they could check everything.

The Bilbao ferry office had been bombed; they would be expecting the three of them to show up in time for the departure and then be stranded. They, whoever they were, had no idea he'd forestalled them and made his own plans. They would only now be realizing he hadn't come to Bilbao, and the Santander ferry had already set sail.

"I'm going to take a look around," he said. "I think we're safe, but I always like to be careful. Stay here with Mahmoud and I'll be back soon."

"How about you stay with Mahmoud and I'll do recon?" Isobel asked.

"Because I don't trust you?" he suggested. "Besides, Mahmoud isn't looking well. He needs a maternal touch."

"I'm not the motherly type," she snapped, glancing at the boy. Mahmoud was curled up on the banquette, and beneath the layers of dirt he was turning a definite green.

"Just keep telling yourself that, princess. I think I'd

better find some Dramamine before we're both very sorry. Do you need some as well?"

"I have no problem with seasickness."

"That's right, this isn't the first ferry we've been on together, is it?"

"Go to hell," she growled, looking away from him.

He closed the door quietly behind him. She'd take good care of Mahmoud. She was trying very hard to be a major badass, but it was a lost cause. Even after all these years, and the changes she'd gone through, he knew her too well.

And as long as she hated him with such a fiery passion, all was well. She hadn't gotten over him. She'd never get over him.

Not if he could help it.

Bastien Toussaint sank back on his heels, staring at the piece of wood in front of him. There was an American saying—measure twice, cut once. He'd measured seventeen times and cut twelve, and the damned piece was still just a hair too big. He opened his mouth to let out a long, colorful string of curses, and then closed it again. The baby was asleep, strapped into the perchlike contraption Chloe used for him, and he tended to sleep through everything, including saws, hammers and loud music. A blessing, since their first child, Sylvia, had chosen to disdain sleep for most of the first year of her life. And at age four months the baby was hardly likely to notice the difference between a "blast it" and the string of much more colorful invective Bastien had been toying with.

But he couldn't bring himself to swear in front of his very young children. He was getting soft in his old age.

He rose, took the offending board back to the table saw and shaved one more sliver off it, then returned. It finally fit, needing just a few taps of the hammer to secure it into place.

Baby Swede was stirring, now that things were quiet. Ridiculous name for a Toussaint, but Bastien had gone along with it, because Chloe had wanted it. In honor of Stockholm Syndrome, she'd said. That unfortunate and highly unlikely scenario in which a hostage fell in love with her kidnapper. And he couldn't argue with that, particularly with a very pregnant, very cranky woman.

He picked up the sling, gently, but Swede opened his blue eyes to stare up at him with that solemn expression he'd been born with. He looked like him, a fact Bastien found disarming.

Chloe was in the half-finished kitchen of their rambling house, and she raised an eyebrow when he came in. "How's the Hundred Years War coming?"

"Carpentry takes time," he said. "You can't rush these things."

She simply shook her head, knowing him too well. The work would be done in his own time, and meanwhile she managed with only two interior doors, on their bedroom and on the working bathroom, plus a door on every closet in the house. No door to the bedrooms, but the closets were complete, and fortunately no one asked why, when there were no kitchen cabinets, and only plywood flooring and Sheetrock walls. He wanted to do it all himself, needed to. Every other weekend Chloe's family came up to help him, but in the end it was up to him to make the house secure. And he needed to do that, to make peace with himself.

Chloe moved past him, scooping up the baby and giving Bastien a fleeting kiss. "I know, dear," she said.

It was close to dusk, almost time for him to quit for the day. He reached out to her, to pull her back, when suddenly the power went out, leaving them in the afternoon dusk.

Power went out often enough up in the mountains of North Carolina, but there was no wind storm, and the day was calm. There were only two possible reasons.

Someone might have hit one of the power lines with his car—an accident.

Or someone knew that most of Bastien's elaborate security devices ran on electric power.

He froze, waiting for the familiar, comforting sound of the generator powering on. Nothing. The lights stayed off, just the one battery-powered emergency floodlight spearing into the room.

He was crushing Chloe's hand, and she hadn't made a sound of protest.

"Where's Sylvia?" he mouthed.

"Down for a nap." She could be as silent as he was.

"Take the baby and go to her room. Take her and get in the closet. Lock it and don't come out until I tell you to."

"But—"

"The closet's fortified, remember? You'll be safe."

"But you…"

He simply stared at her and three years fell away, and she was looking into the face of a killing machine. The man she'd probably thought she'd never have to see again.

She simply nodded, vanishing silently into the shadows.

Leaving Bastien to the hunt.

He didn't carry a gun—it upset Chloe, and his security system was top-notch. He hadn't counted on them hitting the generator, too.

He'd grown dangerously soft. Nonetheless, Bastien had no doubt he could get his family out of this. He'd gotten out of worse situations, and it had only been his own skin. No one was going to touch his wife and children.

No gun, but he could improvise. He could kill someone with a wooden spoon if he had to, but there were plenty of knives in the kitchen, tools in the unfinished library. He wondered if the men who'd come after him had been properly warned what they were up against.

He was almost insulted there were only three of them. The first was skulking around the back door, looking for a way in. Bastien cut his throat and took his gun.

It was a heavy pistol—something Dirty Harry would

use. It lacked finesse, but beggars couldn't be choosers. Bastien would rather not use it—the sound might frighten the babies, and even though Chloe had nerves of steel he didn't want to test them.

The second intruder was heading toward the stairs, and he was good, better than the first. The fight was short and savage, and Bastien broke his neck with a quick, ruthless snap.

One more. He was moving in the library where Bastien had just been working on the burled walnut paneling, fitting the pieces together with the painstaking precision that was driving Chloe crazy.

If the man moved fast enough he might make it up the stairs before Bastien could stop him. His family would be safe in that steel-lined closet, but the very thought of a killer getting anywhere near them made him furious.

He stepped out of the shadows, and the man spun around, firing, his semiautomatic sending a spray of bullets across the walnut paneling.

It was the last straw. One shot with the elephant gun in his hand and half the man's head was gone.

Chloe was going to be pissed. He didn't know how much they could hear, but he couldn't let them come down to this mess.

He worked fast, getting most of the blood and bone cleaned up, sprinkling sawdust from beneath the table saw over the mess once he'd dragged the bodies out. There was no disguising the bullet holes in the paneling, but at least he could spare his loved ones the worst part.

He hated to make them wait, in the darkness, not knowing, but in the end it was better this way.

He dumped the bodies at the edge of the woods, making sure no one else was wandering around. Just three of them to take him out. Whoever had sent them had made a very grave error.

He switched on the generator, then raced up the stairs two at a time. Chloe fell out of the closet, into his arms, pale but in control. Sylvia, his fierce and passionate young daughter, was for once perfectly calm, and Swede was asleep.

Bastien had blood on his clothes, but at least he'd washed the hands he put on his wife. She didn't flinch.

"I took care of him," he said, wanting to keep the body count down for her peace of mind.

"Him?" she echoed skeptically.

"Them," he admitted, regretting that he hadn't been able to question any of them, to find out who'd sent them. There was nothing on their bodies to give him any clue. "How long will it take you to pack?"

"With your help, maybe half an hour. Where are we going?"

"To get help. From the only people I trust."

Chloe looked down at her somber daughter. "We're going to visit Uncle Peter and Aunt Genevieve, sweetheart. Go get your favorite toys."

Sylvia moved over to her toy shelves with that unnerving calm, and Chloe looked up into his eyes.

"I'm sorry," he said, feeling helpless for the first time in the last brief, bloody hour.

She kissed him on the mouth, and if her eyes were bright with unshed tears, she ignored them. "I'm not," she said. "You did what you had to do."

He held her so tightly that the baby woke up with an annoyed squawk. Resting his forehead against Chloe's, Bastien let out a long, shuddering breath. And then he pulled away.

"Let's just go," he said. "We can buy things on the way to the airport."

She nodded. And ten minutes later they were speeding down the road, into the darkening night.

14

After two hours of Mahmoud puking, first into the toilet, then dry heaves into a trash bin, a towel and the rapidly emptied fruit bowl in the cabin, Isobel decided she wasn't going to wait any longer. The storm had picked up, the huge ferry was responding to the waves with enthusiasm, and night had fallen. No sign of Killian—with luck he'd been washed overboard, leaving her stuck with Mahmoud. Even a psychopathic child soldier was preferable to her nemesis, but not one racked with nausea.

He was too weak to fight her when she scooped him up. He was nothing more than skin and bones, and she cursed Killian under her breath. If he was going to keep the damn kid with him out of some twisted form of penance, he might at least see he was properly fed.

Mahmoud tried to punch her as she juggled him in her arms. He was probably seventy-five pounds—light for a human being, damned heavy if you weren't used to it. Isobel pumped iron, practiced yoga and ran. He was still a strain.

The nurse's office was located on a lower deck. The few people who were out and about weren't looking particularly happy with the rough seas, but they didn't pay any attention as Isobel carried her small charge onto the elevator.

When the door slid open Killian was there, and she stepped out, dumping Mahmoud in his arms and stretching her shoulders. "He needs a doctor."

Killian looked down at the bundle. "I take it he doesn't like boats?"

"You could say that." Mahmoud began retching again, dry sounds, and the few people who'd been waiting for the elevator got on quickly, moving out of their way.

The medical office was surprisingly empty, given the decided roll of the vessel. A woman in a white uniform was on duty, sitting behind a desk as Killian shouldered his way in. "Seasickness, I presume," she said in English, rising.

"He's been throwing up for the last three hours," Isobel stated.

"You should have brought him down sooner. He might be dehydrated." She looked them over. "Is this your son?"

"God, no," Killian said. With a British accent that made Isobel jerk. "We're Mary and Jack Curwen, aid workers from England, and we're bringing this poor child to his new family there."

"Set him down on the table."

Mahmoud was too sick to protest. He lay on the white-sheeted cot in misery as the woman looked him over. He made a feeble attempt at batting her hand away when she felt his forehead, but a sharp word from Killian in Arabic made him deceptively docile.

"I'll need to keep him overnight," she said. "He is dehydrated. He'll need an IV to replenish his fluids, and careful monitoring. Just fill out the paperwork and you can come get him in the morning."

Isobel glanced at Killian, expecting a protest on his part, but he didn't argue. "Fine," he said. "You'll call us if there's any problem?"

"Of course." The nurse gazed up at them, strong disapproval in her eyes. "You might at least have washed and fed the poor boy before bringing him onto the boat."

Isobel's sting of guilt was entirely unexpected. She was glad when Killian replied, sounding calm and reasonable. "We did feed him. Quite a bit, as a matter of fact. Which is why he's been so ill. As for bathing him, that's easier said than done. Feel free to attempt it—you might have more luck while he's feeling so ill. But I wouldn't count on it."

Killian went over to the desk, rapidly filling in the forms with lies, then glanced at her. "Would you rather stay with the poor lad, darling?" he inquired.

In fact, she was tempted. She didn't want to go back to that quiet little room with the double bed, where she'd be alone with him.

"Sorry, no visitors. I'll alert you if I have any problems. We arrive at noon tomorrow—come by around ten and he should be clean and ready to go."

"God bless you," Killian murmured, looking saintly. "Come along, my love. Let the nurse take care of this poor boy."

He whisked Isobel out of the cabin before she could protest, his hand under her arm, strong, almost imprisoning. At least she had several layers of clothing on and didn't have to feel his skin against hers.

"You want something to eat?" he asked. "At least one of the restaurants is open."

"Not particularly. Spending three hours with a vomiting child isn't conducive to building up an appetite."

"Then just a drink, while we get someone to clean up the room," he said, steering her into the elevator.

There were a thousand protests she could have come up with. The ferry was far from full; it was off-season, or he wouldn't have been able to book a room so easily. There'd be empty cabins available, as well as reclining seats for passengers who didn't want to spend money on a room. The last thing in the world she wanted to do was go back into that tiny cabin with him.

But she couldn't leave him alone. They were probably perfectly safe on this boat as it plowed across the stormy Atlantic, but there had already been too many mistakes. She wasn't letting him out of her sight until she could hand him over to the Committee for debriefing. It wouldn't come soon enough, probably by tomorrow night, but in the meantime she was just going to have to put up with him.

"All right," she said. "One drink."

Only one of the ferry bars was open, and there were a mere handful of people inside. Smoking.

She took the seat Killian handed her into, and waited until he brought back the drinks.

Seven months was the longest she'd ever gone without a cigarette. She'd done it cold turkey this time—no patches or gums or nasal sprays. And she'd never dare try hypnosis—she knew too many secrets that could have leaked out.

No, she gritted her teeth, snapped at anyone who came near her and went without cigarettes. She'd only gained five pounds that last time, and she'd done her best to make sure those pounds were solid muscle, turning in her nicotine addiction for an addiction to pumping iron. She thought she'd gotten to the point where she no longer even wanted one.

She'd been wrong, that time as well as now. She could smell the fresh smoke. That was one problem with Europe: it was too damn easy to smoke. In America they made it so inconvenient it was almost better not to bother. Though of course her rebellious streak always kicked in, making her crave them even more.

But this time she'd sworn it was for good, more than half a year ago. They were making life unpleasant. She was free of them. Her breathing had started being affected, the taste lingered in her clothes and hair.

So why was the scent of tobacco dancing over to her like something out of an old cartoon, undulating and beckoning? And why the hell had she stolen the mashed pack of cigarettes from the dead pilot's pocket?

A moment later Killian was back, carrying two drinks. He put one down in front of her, and she eyed it doubtfully. It was a gin and tonic, with one cube of ice and a slice of lime, not lemon. She'd been drinking them for ten years now—long after their time together. How had he guessed?

His own glass held unwatered whiskey. Scotch, probably. He hadn't changed in all these years, even if she had.

"They called maid service from the bar. Our room should be ready by the time we finish our drinks."

Our room. She didn't like the sound of that. She picked up her glass, taking a sip. Tanqueray gin, her favorite. Enough was enough.

"How do you know so much about me?"

His smile was lazy. "Tricks of the trade, princess. I'm surprised you aren't equally well informed. For what it's worth, I like single malt Scotch at night, dark beer in the afternoon. I don't like gin, hate vodka and despise martinis. If I drink too much I get short-tempered and lustful. In your honor I'm moderating my alcohol intake."

"Thank heavens for small favors. You didn't answer my question."

"You know perfectly well that you can find out

anything you want about someone if you know where to look. My life has depended on being able to access the right information at the right time."

"And how does knowing what I drink affect your life?"

"Let's just say I was curious."

"When did you find out I was alive? You thought I was dead, didn't you?"

"When did you find out *I* was alive?" he countered.

"I asked you first."

"Tough."

She took another sip of her drink. It was strong, and she hadn't had much sleep or much to eat. It wouldn't affect her judgment, but she needed to pay attention. "Five days ago," she said. "When Peter told me you wanted to be brought in. I went through some intel and saw a picture of you—of Serafin, actually. But I knew it was you. It must have been quite a shock to see me after all these years."

He said nothing, toying with his glass, and her eyes were drawn to his fingers. Long, elegant, clever fingers. Which had touched her. Brought her exquisite pleasure. Killed countless innocent people.

"When did you find out I was alive?" she asked again, annoyed.

His eyes met hers for a long moment. "I always knew."

She spilled her drink. Clumsiness had never been a particular failing, but his simple words shocked her so much that she jerked, and the glass tipped over, spreading gin and tonic and ice over the white tablecloth. "You're lying."

"And it was no shock when you appeared in Morocco. I knew there was no one else available but you. Bastien Toussaint's retired. Peter Madsen's still recovering from that shoot-out in California, Taka O'Brien is tied up in Japan, and the other agents are under such deep cover that even I couldn't find out where they were."

"Thank God for small favors," she muttered. "I still don't believe you."

"James Reddy."

So much for cool invulnerability. Isobel knew she was turning white, knew the shock was clear on her face, and she didn't give a flying fuck. How could he know about James? What goddamned right did he have?

She stood up, pushing the table back so hard that his drink would have spilled as well if he hadn't grabbed it in time. Ignoring the curious looks directed at her, she ran out of the bar and onto the deck, into the furious blast of the rain and whipping wind.

She kept going. The deck was wet beneath her feet, slippery, and the ferry was lurching like a majestic old drunk, but the railings were secure, and if she fell into the goddamned Atlantic she wouldn't care. She was muttering a litany of curses under her breath as she ran, knowing she was weeping as well, knowing that the rain would wash away all trace of her tears and he'd never see them. For a brief moment she could let herself go.

She ducked into an alcove, out of the direct fury of the storm, and reached in her pocket for the cigarettes. Her hands were shaking as she knocked one out, only to find it broken. She pulled another two, also crumpled, and dropped them on the deck, finally finding one in reasonably good shape.

No matches. No lighter, no nothing. She needed that cigarette so badly she'd kill for it, and she was stuck out in the middle of nowhere on this huge ferry with no matches and no one to beg one from.

She sank down on her heels, turning her wet face to the bulwark. Her hair was soaking, her clothes were drenched and it was cold, so cold. She was shivering, and she didn't care. She just needed a few minutes to pull herself together. Then she'd go back, pick up a pack of matches in the bar and face Killian with her usual cool dignity. She only needed a few minutes.

A second later the minimal light was blocked out, and rough hands were hauling up her. "Come on, princess," he said in a gruff voice. "You'll catch your death out here."

She could push him overboard, using the element of surprise. He was stronger than she was, but he wouldn't be expecting it, and he'd disappear into the icy waters. And right then it was the only thing she could think of that would stop the blaze of pain spearing through her body.

"Don't even think about it," he said, reading her mind. "If I go over that railing you're coming with me, and I know you don't want that. You're freezing to death already. Come on."

She wouldn't move. He'd pulled her upright, but he couldn't very well drag her the length of the boat, back to their cabin, without someone taking notice. She'd fight him with all the dirty tricks she was so good at and…

He knew all her dirty tricks. He disabled her struggles in a matter of seconds, wrapped his arms tightly around her and marched her down the long stretch of rain-lashed decking. She couldn't struggle, couldn't fight back. She could do nothing but move when he moved her, her feet obeying him, not her. She would have screamed at him, but common sense finally hit her. She couldn't afford to bring any unwanted attention to them. She had to handle him on her own. Even if, for one brief moment, she wasn't strong enough.

He pushed her into the elevator and the door shut, closing them in, alone together. He released her, and she tried to hit him, but he simply grabbed her wrists in one hand, so tightly that the bones seemed to grind together, and it took all her will not to cry out in pain. The elevator door opened, and he half carried, half dragged her down the deserted hallway to their cabin, unlocking the door and shoving her inside before he followed her into the darkness, slamming the door behind him.

"Grow up, Isobel," he said in a cold, merciless voice. "I knew everything about you, and you aren't the sort of woman who gets hysterical at the drop of a hat."

"I want a separate room," she said. "I can't be here."

"You *are* here. You took the mission, and it's not like you to flip out over trivialities. You're the Iron Lady, beyond fear or pain. So calm down."

She hated him. Hated him with a raw, bleeding passion she hadn't felt in years. Her armor had been pierced, and while she knew he couldn't tell she'd been crying, he still knew that he'd finally managed to get to her enough so that she'd run.

She wiped the rain from her face, disguising the tears. "I need a cigarette."

"These?" He'd somehow managed to get his hands on the crumpled pack of cigarettes she had been pursuing like the Holy Grail. "Forget it." And he crushed them in one hand.

It was the final blow. Isobel let out a shriek of rage and jumped him, trying to get her hands on what remained of the pack. Big mistake. A moment later he had her slammed up against the wall, pressing his body against hers, holding her immobile.

"Let's establish a few ground rules, shall we?" he said. "If you try to hurt me, you're just going to have my hands on you, and I know you think that's the last thing you want. So I know all about you—get over it. I haven't gotten to where I am due to faulty intel. I've made it my business to keep track of you since you ended up at Stephan Lambert's. I know you were recruited by the Committee shortly before Stephan died, and he didn't want you to work for them. I know you're smart and strong and ruthless."

"Everything I wasn't eighteen years ago," she said in a cold voice. He was touching her in too many places: his hips against hers, pinning her to the wall; his chest pressing against hers, so she couldn't breathe; his hard hands trapping her wrists so she couldn't fight back.

She'd forgotten how much taller he was. Perhaps not as tall as Peter, but enough so that at such close proximity she felt rattled. Which was exactly why he was doing it. She was aware of him, suddenly, strongly, when until now she'd been able to keep a mental distance.

"You were smart enough," he said, and she could taste the whiskey on his breath. "Just no match for me."

"That's not the case anymore."

She could see his faint smile in the dim light. "I agree. You're a perfect match for me."

She tried to kick him but her legs were trapped, tried to hit him but might as well be handcuffed. She tried to slam her head against his but he saw it coming, so instead she sank her strong white teeth into his neck.

You could kill someone that way. If you had the strength and the stomach for it you could rip out their carotid artery and have them bleed out in a matter of minutes.

She could taste blood, but a moment later he moved her away from him, holding her at arm's length, his eyes glittering in the darkness. "I should warn you that I find biting to be highly erotic."

She froze. He was between her and the door in their

tiny cabin, and there was no way she was going to be able to get past him, at least not now.

She took a deep breath, certain that only she could hear its shakiness, and he stepped away, no longer touching her. She could breathe again, the iciness of her skin slowly warming.

"So sit down, Mary Isobel," he said. "I'll make another drink and you can tell me all about yourself."

There was a banquette opposite the bed—the lesser of two evils. She sat stiffly. "I don't care for another drink, thank you. You'd probably just drug me."

"The notion is tempting, but I think I need you awake right now." He stretched out on the bed, seeming perfectly comfortable, and with anyone else she'd be able to escape. She already knew his reflexes were equal or superior to hers. She wasn't going anywhere unless he decided to let her.

She leaned back against the banquette, forcing her tight muscles to stop screaming and relax. If she stayed on high alert they might cramp, and she couldn't afford to let that happen. She had to be ready to run.

"All right," she said with deceptive calm. "What exactly do you want to know?"

The flash in his eyes was so brief she might have imagined it, if it weren't for the shard of fear that spiked through her body.

"Time to catch up on old times. I want to know what was happening to you during the last eighteen years. Were you happy with Stephan?"

"What the hell does that have to do with anything?"

"Humor me. I was quite surprised to hear he'd married you. I wouldn't have thought he was the marrying kind."

"If that's your way of saying he was gay, then yes, he was. He also considered me his masterpiece, and he was enamored of his finest work."

"That explains Stephan. It doesn't explain you. Why did you marry him?"

"I didn't have anything better to do at the time."

He ignored her caustic statement. "I imagine you were grateful. He saved your life, after all. I gather you were a pretty mess when he first worked on you."

"Yes."

"Yes what?"

"Yes, I was grateful. That's the only reason I fuck."

He said nothing, not rising to the challenge. "So you marry Stephan, became a proper French housewife for a while, and then join a covert group of operatives intent on saving the world from scum like me. I suppose I can take pride in motivating you."

"By that time I'd forgotten all about you. I don't remember much of that night, but I believed you were dead and that I'd killed you. Case closed. I met a great many people through my husband's work. It was nothing more than being available when they needed someone. I joined the Committee. When Stephan died I became a professional."

"Very professional. So what about James Reddy?"

"Shut up." Her reaction was so strong and instantaneous that she didn't have time to shield it.

Killian leaned back on the bed, apparently at ease. "I know you got over me easily enough, but James was another matter. Your one true love, I gather. Too bad he died so poorly."

"Shut the hell up," she said, feeling desperate. No one, not even Peter, had spoken that name out loud to her in more than ten years.

Killian sat up. "What's the problem, princess? Is that guilt rearing its ugly head? You didn't kill him—he died in a helicopter crash in Somalia."

He wasn't going to let it go. She could shut her eyes, cover her ears and start screaming, as she so desperately wanted to do. Or she could pull herself together.

She really didn't have any choice. Peter had been right to worry about her. If she was at the top of her game Killian wouldn't be able to mess with her head like this. She wouldn't feel as if she was about to explode.

She'd never had a problem with a mission before, no matter who or what it had involved. It made no sense that this ghost from her past would be making her crazy, unless she was a little off to begin with.

That was it. It wasn't him, it was her. She'd been under too much stress. All she had to do was get through the next day or so and she'd be safely back in her flat, where she could let herself go in privacy. For now all she had to do was keep it together so he didn't realize just how fragile she really was.

"I sent him to Somalia," she said, marveling at her ability to sound calm and detached. A cigarette would have done wonders for the image she was determined to project, but there was no way she was going to incite another wrestling match. "He got careless and he died. End of story."

"Then why are you carrying around such a buttload of guilt? He can't have been the only man you sent to his death. Not even the first man."

"I loved him."

She wanted to slap the slow smile off Killian's face. "Tragic," he said. "But you didn't marry him."

"We didn't need to get married."

"You didn't live with him."

How the hell did he know that? "That was unnecessary, as well. We had an understanding. And I still don't see why you're so interested in my ancient history."

"I'm interested in everything about you, princess. Including why a medium level operative like James Reddy would have made the kind of fucked-up mistake that got him killed. You shouldn't have sent him to Somalia in the first place—he wasn't properly trained."

"Goddamn it, how do you know…?"

"I know," Killian said. "Just accept it. Why did you let him go to his death?"

Hiding wasn't going to help. The only way out of this trap was to tell him the truth, calmly. "James and I were…close. Unfortunately, I wasn't able to have the kind of relationship he wanted, and he thought proving himself might change my mind. Instead he died. Badly. Not in the helicopter crash—he was still alive when they dragged him out of it. It took him anywhere from two hours to two days to finally die." She pushed her wet hair away from her face. She was getting it together, and she met Killian's gaze squarely. "It was unfortunate, and I felt needlessly responsible. We all have our weaknesses, our mistakes."

"Not me."

"Bullshit," she replied. "You've screwed up on just about every mission you've been involved in. It's no wonder half the world wants you dead. The other half wants to kill for the things you didn't fuck up."

"I'm not going to argue with you," he said lazily. "You see mistakes, I see alternative opportunities. And I don't have any particular weakness."

"Not even me?"

"Damn, woman, you're getting feisty on me," he said lightly. "Are you sure you want to go there?"

She didn't. She didn't want to go anywhere near the question of why he'd kept track of her over the years. Except that answer made perfect sense. "I assume you want revenge. A stupid, innocent girl got the drop on you and almost killed you. That must have hurt your pride, even worse when you found I'd survived, and spent my life doing a damn good job of interfering with monsters like you. I think you want to humiliate me, torture me and then kill me."

He looked thoughtful. "You don't seem to be troubled by any of those possibilities."

"I said it was what you wanted to do. Not what you were going to do. You need me, you need my resources, and by the time I'm no longer necessary I'll be well out of your way."

"I could always hire someone."

"You could have done that anytime in the last eighteen years."

"Maybe I wanted to see your face when you found out I was still alive."

"Well, you missed that particular treat. I was alone in my office when I realized the lousy footage of a war criminal was someone I thought I'd killed long ago."

"And how did you feel, Mary Isobel?" His voice was silky.

"Redeemed. Justified. Saddened that I hadn't done a better job. You were someone who should have been killed—I just wasn't good enough at the time."

"You are now. And you can't do it, because you need me as much as I need you. That must be incredibly annoying."

"Incredibly."

"So why couldn't you have the kind of relationship James Reddy wanted?"

She thought she'd distracted him from that line of questioning. The more she resisted, the more he'd dig, so she swiveled around on the banquette, drawing her legs up under her. "He was in love with me.

Hearts, flowers, all that bullshit. And I don't believe in love."

"So why didn't you just screw him and keep him happy? Most men will settle without going all emo on you. Most men would prefer it that way."

"James was a romantic. An idealist. He came into the business trying to save the world, trying to do the right thing. He died because of it."

"And because he wanted to prove himself to you. What would he have to do to make you love him?"

She answered him, because she knew he'd badger her until she did. "I did love him. Just not the way he wanted."

"Not sexually." It wasn't a question.

"I'm not discussing my sex life with you," she said.

His smile was cool and deadly. "We don't need to talk about your sex life, since it appears to be nonexistent after James Reddy. Maybe even before."

Isobel said nothing, trying to shut him out, that soft, insinuating voice other women would have found so seductive. Not her, of course. But other women.

He rose from the bed, and she braced herself for God knew what. He stood over her, too close, and she made herself look up at him, trying to judge him dispassionately. He'd been good-looking eighteen years ago. He was flat-out gorgeous now; she could admit it without emotion. His endless legs encased in faded jeans, the khaki shirt that was worn but clean, the face that somehow only looked better with age. Gray-blue

eyes she'd thought were green, warmer than the eyes of
a butcher should be. When he was in his twenties she'd
been passionately, devotedly besotted, thinking he was
so impossibly handsome he'd never look twice at her.

He had, but for his own reasons. And now, impossible as it was, he was even better looking, with a lean,
weathered, world-weary grace that would have melted
a heart of stone.

But hers was made of ice, and all the lazy charm left
her inviolate. He was just a man. A bad man, to be sure.
But just a man.

He leaned over her, his hands braced against the
bulkhead, trapping her, and he moved his mouth to her
ear, whispering. "What are you so afraid of, Mary
Isobel? You're the Iron Lady, the Ice Queen, nothing
frightens you. And you're sitting there like I'm about
to stab and rape you."

She wouldn't look at him. He was too close, invading
her space so thoroughly that he was almost inside her.
And she didn't want to be thinking about that.

She wasn't about to fight him, push him away, try to
take the upper hand as she could have with just about
anyone else outside of the Committee. Because it would
give him an excuse to put his hands on her, and if he
did, she didn't think she could bear it.

"So tell me," he whispered, his voice low, beguiling.
"What are you afraid of?"

"Absolutely nothing."

He smiled. "I'd almost believe you, if I didn't know

you so well." His mouth brushed her ear, and she felt a shiver run through her body. "So why didn't you love James Reddy the way he wanted to be loved? Why did he feel he needed to prove himself to you so badly that he ended up dying stupidly for it? He wasn't a stupid man, but he died for no good reason, because of you."

"Shut up," she said, fierce.

"Just answer the question, princess." His breath warmed her ear, tickled it. She was cold, wet from her run on the deck, and she hadn't even realized it. Cold from the center of her being, radiating out in icicles. "Answer the question and I'll leave you alone. What was the problem between you and James? Exactly what was the sexual dysfunction Dr. Kellogg diagnosed?"

It had gone beyond any reasonable control. There was nothing she could hide, nothing she could hold back, and the fact that it had gotten this bad, reached such a devastatingly naked level, almost made her stronger. Of course he knew.

She jerked her head up. "To use the old-fashioned term, I'm frigid. If you were able to get into my records to find a diagnosis, I'm sure you could find out that much, as well."

His expression was cool, assessing. As if he wasn't exposing her mercilessly. "My contacts got into the insurance records, not the doctor's notes. Trouble having an orgasm, princess? Some men simply don't know how to provide one. You didn't seem to have any problem with me, but then, you were drugged most of the time. Maybe you're just too uptight to have sex unless someone else is in control."

She was the past the point of caring. "Total lack of sexual interest or desire, Killian." It was the first time she'd called him by name, and the sound of it was strange, intimate in the small cabin. "Presumably as a result of the trauma I suffered the night I killed you. They suggested I take testosterone as one way of creating a libido, but I figured I was aggressive and dangerous enough without added hormonal help. I'm exactly what you said—an iron maiden, an ice queen, and totally devoid of sexual feelings. Not even for a good, good man like James Reddy. And I prefer it this way, even though I still mourn his death. It's one less vulnerability I have to deal with."

Killian moved back, and the faint smile on his face would have bothered her if she wasn't already past that point. "You have other vulnerabilities," he said. "Including monumental self-deception. You're lying to yourself, and you have been for years."

"Oh, that's right, I've just been waiting for your touch. Mourning your loss all these years, unable to love anyone else. I never realized I was such a tragic heroine. I'm so glad you pointed that out to me. Now I should be able to heal and live a full, rewarding life." She smiled sweetly. "Killing people like you."

He moved to the door, and she had a brief, hopeful moment where she thought he might leave her. But then he simply double bolted the lock, so it would take her longer to escape, longer for someone to come in and save her. Save her from what?

"So you haven't responded to gentle, adoring men, Isobel?" It was the first time he'd used her new name, and the atmosphere in the cabin was suddenly charged with something strong and inescapable. "So let's see if you like violence." And he reached for her.

15

She didn't hesitate. She was too good at what she'd done for years, and she was motivated. The last time she'd had sex was the night James had left, the night before he died. She'd made herself do it, had put on her best performance, but James wasn't fooled. She hadn't tried again.

She wasn't going to let *this* man touch her.

She surged up from her seat, breaking his hold, shoving him back against the wall. She had the short blade of the pocketknife against his throat, against the bloody mark her teeth had made, and she couldn't afford to hesitate. One sharp, deep slice and he'd go fast. Covering her in blood.

His eyes were half-closed, that damnable smile still on his face. "What's stopping you? You know how quick and easy it would be. I won't stop you."

She froze. He reached up and took her hand in his, pulling the knife away, making her drop it on the floor. "Show me how much you hate me," he whispered against her mouth. "Prove it to me."

She hit him, both of her fists raised, beating at his chest as he imprisoned her in the circle of his arms. She was striking him, scratching him, tearing at his clothes in a silent, deadly rage, and she could feel his skin beneath her hands, hot, sleek skin. He picked her up, wrapping her legs around his waist as he fell back against the door, the light switch, plunging the room into inky darkness.

And Isobel was gone, swallowed up in rage and darkness and heat, and she was the one who pulled his head down to hers, she was the one who kissed him, openmouthed and full.

He turned her, and they fell crosswise on the bed, and he was tugging her clothes off her body, yanking at them, and it hurt, and she wanted it to hurt. She hated herself, hated him.

She heard the rasp of his zipper in the darkness, his muffled curse, and she caught her waistband in her hands and shoved her jeans down her legs, kicking them free. He arched over her, pushing her legs apart, resting against her, heavy, hard, pressing against her.

"I hate you," she whispered.

"I know," he said. And slammed into her, so fast and hard that her breath caught, and she waited for the pain and tearing.

Except she was wet. Her body had welcomed him, even as her mind rejected him, and she wrapped her legs around his hips, trying to pull him in deeper still, scratching at him, clawing at him, trying to get more of him. He caught her wrists, slamming them down against the bed, holding her still as he moved. Thrusting deep, so deep that she cried out, so deep that she needed more, and she couldn't breathe in the velvety darkness, trembling, shaking, fighting it, fighting him.

She wasn't strong enough. Everything was gone now—only the darkness and their sweat-dampened bodies remaining, and she didn't want this, didn't want to…

The first wave hit her with such force that she cried out. He released her wrists, putting his hand over her mouth to muffle the sound, and she bit him again, tasting blood, as her entire body arched into a silent, endless scream of such intensity that everything exploded. No enemies, no boat, no bed in the middle of the ocean. Just elemental, hot, sweaty sex, and she couldn't stop, as wave after wave of climax washed over her.

He rolled off her, and she could hear the hoarse roughness of his breathing.

She opened her eyes in the inky blackness, because it was safer that way, because bad things could hurt you if you closed your eyes.

Her face was wet, and she knew she was crying, but for some reason it didn't matter. She lay next to the man she hated most in the world, a butcher, a monster, the man who had just destroyed her, and she tried to catch her breath. She had to find the knife. Now she had a reason to kill him. Nothing would stop her this time, no weakness that she hadn't realized existed. She could kill him now, and the longer she delayed the worse it would be.

A final shudder racked her body, and she squeezed her legs together, arching her hips, and shame swept through her. *The knife,* she thought, letting her eyes drift closed once more. *The knife...*

He hadn't climaxed. He lay beside her, listening to her as her murderous little soul relaxed into an exhausted sleep, and considered his rebellious body. It was pitch-dark in the room—she wouldn't have been able to see he was still painfully erect, practically vibrating with need. But something had made him pull out at the last moment. Something had stopped him, and he wasn't sure what.

He considered finishing then and there, lying beside her in the darkness, breathing in the rich scent of her arousal. He could probably do it without touching himself, but he wasn't going to. He could head into the bathroom, into the tiny shower, and take care of it, but he wouldn't do that, either. He was going to lie in the torn-up bed next to his worst enemy, and think about how he wanted to be inside her again. And again. And again.

He should have gotten rid of Mahmoud days ago. Another man, the man he used to be, would have. The man he used to be would have fucked Madame Lambert into a compliant stupor by now, or he might not have touched her at all. But Killian wasn't the man he used to be. And he didn't even know who that man was anymore.

He wanted to turn and wrap his arms around her, pull her close. She was asleep—he could tell by her breathing—and she wouldn't fight him, at least not for long. And he could put his head in the crook of her neck, taste her skin, and erase all the deadly years that had come between them.

But he wasn't going to. He was going to spend the rest of his goddamned life with a hard-on, but he wasn't going to touch her again. She was bad for him, and always had been. Crazy and bad, making him think things he couldn't afford to think, making him a little crazy, too. He'd watched her from afar the last eighteen years, always knowing where she was, waiting, listening. He'd squandered his employers' money and intel-gathering resources keeping track of her. Not that it mattered—his employers had money to spare, and he surely wasn't getting as rich as he deserved for all his hard work.

He was hoping he'd be able to leech some money away from this current job before it was over. Shutting down the Committee was a complicated business, but he was well on his way to success. He'd already broken the acting head, and after Toussaint's defection and Madsen's injury, they were sadly understaffed. It wouldn't take that much to finish them off.

Frigid. He let out a silent snort of laughter. What exactly had she been doing with herself during the intervening years that she'd managed to convince herself of such an absurdity? She would have had training in sexual techniques as part of her initiation into the Committee. No undercover operative could afford to be squeamish about such an effective weapon. And

Stephan Lambert would have been certain to have given her a workout. While he was openly gay, he was also broad-minded, and could count any number of beautiful women among his former lovers.

So what had turned Isobel off so completely that she'd shut down all her physical responses? The logical answer, absurd though it was, was that she'd been waiting for him.

He wasn't sure how he was going to use that knowledge. It was a useful weapon, but for the time being he'd keep it in reserve. He'd done what he needed to do, thrown her so off balance that her effectiveness would be compromised. His first step to taking down the Committee. It was enough for now.

He got out of the bed, heading for the shower. She stirred in her sleep, making a soft, protesting noise, and it took all his determination not to finish what he started. The feel of her, the taste of her, hadn't changed. The way he wanted her hadn't changed.

His self-control hadn't changed. She was still the means to an end. And he couldn't afford to forget it.

Isobel was alone when she woke up. She pulled herself into a sitting position, looking at her hand. It was shaking. Her whole body was shaking.

She stiffened, forcing the trembling to vanish. It was late morning, and they were due to land in the early afternoon. It was time to get on with her life.

She hurt. Her entire body ached, as if she'd run for

a very long time. The only part of her that didn't hurt was between her legs, and that held its own particular fury.

There was nothing of him to wash away. He couldn't have used a condom—it had happened too fast. And she couldn't remember him climaxing. She'd been too caught up with the overwhelming sensations to even think about the man who was providing them. Didn't want to think about him. She'd been swept away, and he hadn't even come.

She washed thoroughly, including her hair. The auburn roots were just beginning to show beneath the blond; she'd need to get to her hairdresser as soon as she got back. That, and see how the new recruit, Hiromasa, was doing. She'd pass Killian off to Peter, or perhaps to someone else the Committee provided. Harry Thomason had never been a particularly effective interrogator—he tended to let his inherent violence get in the way. And violence wouldn't work on a man like Killian.

She wasn't going to think about it. There was a pile of fresh clothes on the banquette, clearly for her, and while she would have liked to ignore them, her own clothes, torn and stained, were an even greater reminder of something she was determined to forget. It had happened; she couldn't change that. But nothing on this earth could make it happen again.

She was sitting on the banquette, cross-legged, making a list on the pad of paper she'd found in the little desk. She was crippled without her PDA. She looked up when he walked in, steeling herself.

"I need my PDA," she said, her voice flat.

He gazed at her for a long moment, standing in the open door of the cabin, and she felt a moment's fear that he was going to talk about what had happened in that room, on that carefully made bed.

But he didn't. "When we get to London," he said. "I don't trust your people."

"I do."

"But I've got the PDA," he said. "We need to go pick up our little orphan or the nurse might report us for abandoning him."

Dealing with Mahmoud would at least provide a distraction. She pushed herself off the banquette, half expecting Killian to touch her, to say something. But he could have been a polite stranger, moving out of her way, walking beside her, but not close, as she headed for the elevator and the infirmary.

Last night's storm had vanished, leaving the water calm as the huge ferry plowed through it. People were out on the decks, children were playing in the sunshine despite the chill, lovers were kissing. They lived in an alternate reality, she thought numbly. One she could never find again.

Mahmoud was sitting up, looking disgustingly healthy and surprisingly clean. He was wearing shorts and a long-sleeve T-shirt and sandals, his hair was washed and combed, and he looked oddly like a child, not the savage creature he really was.

"You were able to get him washed…" she said,

grateful, and then her words trailed off. The nurse was filthy, bruised, her hair a tangle, scratch marks on her arms. She wouldn't have looked worse if she'd met Mahmoud on the battlefield.

She glared at Isobel. "He's stronger than he looks."

"We warned you," Killian said mildly in that perfect Oxford accent. "Come along, my lad. We'll be docking in a few hours, and I imagine you want to fill that empty belly of yours."

"Just clear liquids and a little toast," the nurse warned.

Killian looked at her. "I'm not about to get in a wrestling match with him in public. I expect he'll eat what he wants, and his new family can deal with his stomach. If he starts throwing up again it'll be someone else's problem."

"Serve the little brat right," the nurse muttered, clearly devoid of charity that morning.

Killian said something in Arabic, and Mahmoud slid off the cot to follow him out the door. At the last minute he turned and directed a string of words to the nurse that sounded far from complimentary.

"He's thanking you for your kind assistance," Killian translated helpfully. He was clearly lying.

"Hummmph."

And to Isobel's shock, Mahmoud grinned—a normal, naughty-little-boy grin. He caught her expression of surprise, and it vanished immediately, turning him back into the sullen little creature she was used to. But at least he was clean.

Killian was right—Mahmoud ate enough for the three of them, finishing the practically untouched food on her own plate, scarfing down Killian's last piece of toast. Isobel could only hope he wouldn't get carsick once they landed in Plymouth. It was a long drive to London, and she didn't fancy being trapped with a puking child. Whoever came for them would probably bring the Bentley—elegant and stately and armor-plated. Just in case. If Mahmoud started heaving again she'd put him in the front seat with Peter. She'd suffered enough on this particular mission.

At least it was almost over. Last night hadn't happened; it was locked in a little box and thrown overboard into the icy blue-green Atlantic Ocean. She'd pass Killian on to Peter, go home and break something.

They ate in silence, Killian perfectly at ease, leaning back in his chair drinking coffee, and watching as they pulled into Plymouth harbor. "We'll be one of the first off the ferry," he said. "We need to get through customs and be on our way. I've got a couple of ideas for transport to London, but I need to check out the lay of the land."

She really didn't want to speak to him. But she was being silly—anything that had happened was immaterial, imaginary. "I've already arranged for someone to pick us up."

"What?" She hadn't seen that cold anger before. He usually covered everything with an easy charm that made her crazy. "You couldn't have. I took your PDA."

"I called before you groped me in the cafeteria," she

said, ignoring the fact that she was bringing up a subject that could lead to dangerous places.

He swore, in half a dozen languages. "You've been in the business long enough not to have made such a stupid mistake. Unless you're trying to get me killed. In which case you could have tried it long distance."

"Maybe I want to be in at the kill," she said in a silky voice. "Don't be paranoid."

"Paranoia keeps me alive. I thought you were smarter than that."

She was impervious to his anger or his insults. "I took you seriously. Peter Madsen is the only one who knows we're coming in, and whether you realize it or not, there are some people in this life that you can trust absolutely. The Committee has survived numerous attempts at infiltration—we're invulnerable. And even if someone managed to get in, Peter would know."

"Whether you realize it or not, there's no one in this life like that," he shot back. He pushed away from the table, and Mahmoud uttered a protest. Killian's response was short and sharp, and Isobel decided not to argue.

"Why don't you give me back my PDA and I'll find out what arrangements have been made?"

He shoved his hand in his pocket and handed the tiny thing to her. "We're screwed, anyway. We might as well find out what we're up against."

She started to move away from the table, but he stopped her. "Where do you think you're going?"

"I'll get a better signal from outside—"

"You'll call him while I can listen. No texting."

She sat back down again, pushing buttons on the compact machine. Peter answered immediately.

"We're coming into Plymouth," she said. "My friend thinks we've got a problem in the office."

"Unlikely." Peter's voice on the other end was cool and detached. "In any case, I sent Morrison to fetch you in the Bentley. I need to stay here. You should be safe enough."

"What's Morrison doing home from Germany?"

"There are problems. We'll talk when you get our friend back here."

"What kind of problems?"

"I'll be waiting for you." He broke the connection, and Isobel looked up at Killian.

"You may be right," she allowed. "Something's going on, and Peter wouldn't be more specific. However, Charlie Morrison is just about as good as it gets, and he's the one coming for us. The Bentley is armored—if someone decides to follow us it'll take a rocket launcher to stop us."

Killian said nothing. For a moment she gazed at him, seeing him clearly in the bright light of day. Other women were noticing him, too. He was the kind of man women looked at, wanted. His gray-blue eyes were cool and flinty as they stared at her, his strong, lean body deceptively relaxed, his mouth…

She wasn't going to think about his mouth. It hadn't

happened. She could arrange reality to what was bearable. It *hadn't* happened.

He could have no idea what was going through her mind; she was too good at dissembling. And he seemed less than interested. He was surveying their surroundings with a casual air that belied his high level of alertness. She was just as cautious. If anyone made a move, she'd flatten Killian, taking him out of the line of fire. She'd come this far, and wasn't going to let anyone get to him.

But the passengers from the ferry seemed more interested in disembarking than watching the odd-looking family. Killian managed to get them to the front of the line, and, despite their lack of luggage, the customs officials barely glanced at their forged papers. It was a security breach that could cause trouble in the future. She'd have Peter pass on the word, Isobel decided. It could keep Thomason busy.

The terminal was new and clean, and it took a sharp reprimand to keep Mahmoud from the cafeteria. Killian had them walk straight through the crowded building. There were short- and long-term car parks surrounding the facility, but he kept going, expecting her to follow him with Mahmoud taking up the rear.

She recognized the Bentley from a distance, and beside it, Morrison's sturdy body dressed in a chauffeur's uniform that would have infuriated him. His father had been a chauffeur, and he had class issues that flared up at inconvenient moments. She knew how to handle her people, and once they were heading out on the A38 she could soothe his ruffled feathers.

"There he is," she said.

Morrison caught her eye and nodded almost imperceptibly, climbing back into the heavy car, preparing to come pick them up.

The blast hit them like a heat wave, several seconds ahead of the noise, and Isobel barely had time to fling her arms around Mahmoud, throwing him to the ground and covering him as debris rained down on her.

Not that the little beast was grateful. He was using all his deceptive strength to try to dislodge her, but despite her unimpressive weight she could flatten a full-grown man if she needed to. A tiny twelve-year-old was no problem.

Noise and smoke were everywhere. She could hear people screaming, crying, the crackle of fire, but she was busy trying to keep the squirming kid out of harm's way when strong hands caught her shoulders and yanked her to her feet.

Her back stung, but she couldn't afford to pay attention and keep hold of Mahmoud at the same time.

"I'm fine, thank you," Killian said mockingly. He had a cut over one eye, oozing blood, but apart from that he seemed to be in one piece. "Let's get the hell out of here before the police show up."

"Morrison…" She tried to look past him, but Killian blocked her.

"You don't need to look," he said.

"Oh, bite me," she snapped. "You're forgetting who you're talking to." She pushed him out of the way, then paused.

It wasn't pretty. The Bentley had exploded, sending shrapnel spraying through the crowd. There were at least seven people down, and she could thank heaven it was the off-season, or the body count would be far worse.

She recognized what was left of Morrison by the uniform. He'd been a good man, loyal and brave. He would have hated to die dressed like a chauffeur, she thought, dazed.

Killian had an iron grip on her arm, and the pain pulled her back into reality. In turn, she grabbed Mahmoud's hand, hauling him after her. The place was in chaos, but ambulances and police were already on their way, and the sooner they got out of there the better.

They ran. Into the heart of the city, past people rushing in the opposite direction. "Hold on a minute," Killian muttered, pulling them toward a tea shop. He yanked off his jean jacket. "Put this on."

She wasn't wearing anything of his, particularly something still holding his body heat. "Forget it."

"Put it on," he said. "Or people will see the blood on your back."

She didn't question it, didn't think about it. There wasn't time. She took the jacket from him and pulled it on. She didn't wince at the pain in her back, simply pulled the damn thing close, ignoring the crazy fact that it felt as if he was putting his arms around her.

Mahmoud said something, and she glanced down at him.

"Mahmoud says you're a warrior woman," Killian translated. "Worthy of being a suicide bomber."

"Charming," Isobel responded, chilled. "Tell him I'm flattered."

"Later," Killian said. "Keep your head down."

She stopped thinking at that point. The sunny day had vanished, and a cold rain began to fall. All she could do was follow him, the child trotting beside her, and hope Killian wasn't leading her into a trap.

16

Harry Thomason lit a cigar, leaned back in the leather chair that had cradled the backsides of generations of English civil servants, and contemplated the goodness of life. The glass of whiskey in front of him was just the right blend—no single malts for him, thank you very much. He was a traditionalist, and he liked his whiskey blended, his cigars Cuban and his power absolute.

A street rat like Peter Madsen didn't belong in a gentleman's club like this, he thought. In these sorry times Peter could probably get membership, but at least they drew the line at a bitch like Isobel Lambert. Sooner or later some idiot in the government would try to change that, as well. But by then Sir Harry would have regained enough power to see that sort of bullshit never happened.

The first thing he was going to do was get rid of that Oriental freak Madsen had brought in. Were they out of their minds? Takashi O'Brien had been bad enough—

there was no room for third world operatives in their line of work. He'd proved useful, there was no denying it, but it would have been just as well if Van Dorn had finished him, and he could have been replaced by any one of the shadow agents Thomason was still running.

He should probably dispense with Madsen, as well. The fellow knew too much. Harry had picked him up in the first place, trying to murder an MP's son, no less. A bloody, violent little brat who'd cleaned up well enough, he'd now outlived his usefulness. Besides, he was unfit for duty, a cripple, and only a sentimental fool like Isobel Lambert would keep him on. Maybe he could just be retired out to that place in Wiltshire with his obnoxious American wife. Then again, Peter never did listen to warnings.

At least Bastien Toussaint and his family would be gone. He'd always been a thorn in Harry's side; had it not been for Toussaint he never would have been replaced. The knowledge that he had, at last, made it right, was sweet indeed. Sending three of Stolya's men was probably overdoing it, but he didn't like to take chances. Word hadn't filtered over to this side of the Atlantic, but it would soon. It was something he was looking forward to.

He took a sip of the whiskey, letting it roll around on his tongue, blend with the taste of the cigar. It had been a frustrating few days, but he'd learned to be patient. Good things seldom came without drawbacks. The Serbs had screwed up the information he'd carefully leaked, and Serafin and the bitch had gotten away. The pilot had screwed up, as well—they'd found the plane and the body on an airfield just outside of Zaragoza, with no sign of his passengers.

But by now it should be finished. The incendiary device on the Bentley had been precisely timed, set to blow the moment the ignition was turned a second time. Just when Serafin and Isobel and the child they were dragging along with them got in the car.

Let it never be said that Harry wasn't a practical man. He had no idea what had happened in Isobel's past, how she had come to know a man like Serafin. And now he never would, because they would all be gone in a cloud of smoke and shrapnel and blood. He could live with that. The Committee had lost too many good operatives, and Stolya would see that Madsen would provide no difficulties. A tragedy involving Peter and his new wife could go either way—a sad accident or a preemptive strike from an unknown enemy. In either case, they would have to turn to him, with Isobel dead in a car bomb blast.

Things were far too lax. In Harry's day, someone like Hiromasa whatever his bloody name was wouldn't have gotten as far as London. In his day, a woman would never be put in charge of a job only a cool, practical man could accomplish.

And Thomason had every intention of getting back there, where he belonged. Back to the good old days, where enemies were straightforward, where you trusted no one, and any inconveniences and anomalies were wiped out. The ends justified the means.

He leaned back and closed his eyes. He was going to be a busy man the next couple of days, once the word about the car bomb came through. His cigar had gone out, and he relit it, drawing in a deep, mellow stream of smoke. He'd be ready.

It felt like they walked for miles through the busy streets of Plymouth. The smell of the car bomb lingered in the air, mixing with the scent of diesel fuel and the distant tang of the ocean. A cold, light rain was falling, and Isobel kept her head down, huddled in Killian's jacket.

Mahmoud seemed impervious to the cold, scampering along after them like a child on holiday as they moved through the streets. It was hard to believe he was keeping Killian in his sights because he wanted to murder him, but Isobel didn't doubt it. She wanted to murder him as well, and she wasn't letting him get too far ahead.

She shouldn't be letting him take charge—there was no reason to trust him, and now that she'd gotten him into England, he could just take off. If he had any sense, he'd kill the two of them first—or, at least he'd try.

Right then she wasn't sure she could stop him. Her back was on fire; she was cold and wet and numb. She needed to pull herself together. She needed to find out who the hell had put the hit out on them. But for the time being, all she could do was trudge after him, wishing she still had her burka.

At one point he pushed them into an alley and left them, and she and Mahmoud had no choice but to stand there, shivering, not looking at each other. She should be hoping Killian hadn't abandoned them for good, striking out on his own, but in fact she would have welcomed his disappearance. Enough was enough. She wanted him gone, she wanted him dead, she wanted her life back. If he didn't return she'd get back to London on her own, with or without Mahmoud dogging her heels.

For forty-five minutes she stood there shivering, though her back was on fire. Her fingers were numb, her feet soaked, but Mahmoud just kept waiting, expressionless. And then he perked up, hearing something she was too miserable to notice.

"Serafin," he said. The first word he'd spoken directly to her since the deserted village in Morocco.

He was right. The bright blue Jaguar was gorgeous and striking, and Killian was behind the wheel, looking impatient. He pulled up at the end of the alleyway and lowered the window.

"Get in the front seat, princess," he ordered. "Mahmoud will ride in the back."

The boy seemed to know the drill, for he'd already scrambled into the backseat and slammed the door behind him.

"Isn't this rather a conspicuous car to steal?" Isobel said, stalling.

"I didn't steal it, I rented it. The leak's on your end, and they don't know the names we're using."

"And if the leak's on *your* end?"

"Then we're toast. It'll make the day more interest-ing. Do you want to put some money on it? I'll give you excellent odds."

"I think life or death are high enough stakes," she said. "I can sit in the back with Mahmoud."

Killian just looked at her. "It happened," he said flatly, and she didn't bother pretending she didn't know what he was talking about. "Get over it, and climb in the front seat. It's already growing dark, and at the least they have our descriptions. We need to get the hell out of here."

She was a practical, unemotional woman. He was right, and she was cold. She got in the front seat, closing the door behind her, and he took off into the twilight, driving fast and well.

She heard a rustling sound, and looked back to see Mahmoud already chowing down on a bag of crisps. "You stopped for food?"

"I stopped for supplies. Take off my jacket and lie down."

"Fuck you."

"Take off the jacket, Isobel," Killian said. He didn't sound patient.

"I'm not…" She leaned back against the seat, then jerked erect as fire spread through her.

"You heard me. Take off the jacket and lie down."

"There isn't room."

"Put your fucking head in my lap," he snapped. "And

stop playing games. I need to get you cleaned up and we can't afford to stop. Take off my jacket before you get any more blood on it, and lie down. Unless you have a damn good reason not to."

She had a million reasons not to, and she wouldn't admit to any of them. She pulled the jacket off gingerly, trying to ignore the tiny shards of pain that sped through her body, and put it in her lap. Even in the dusky interior of the car she could see the blood.

"The shirt, too," he said.

It was the T-shirt he'd bought her on the ferry, the one with Ibiza Is for Lovers emblazoned on the front. She pulled it over her head, carefully, not making a sound as her flesh screamed in pain. The back of the shirt was shredded, stained with more blood.

"I haven't lost that much," she said, not moving closer. "I'll be fine until we reach London."

"You have a dozen or more tiny pieces of glass sticking out of your skin, Isobel. Put your face in my lap or I'll make you."

He was the man who'd fucked her and hadn't come. He was the man who'd used her, tricked her, treated her as one more weapon in his destruction of the world. He wouldn't give a damn if her face was in his crotch, and neither would she.

"You could have gone for a bench seat," she muttered, lying down, putting her head on his thigh beneath the steering wheel. She could feel his heat, bone and muscle. She already knew how strong he was;

he carried Mahmoud's slight weight without seeming to notice, and he could probably haul her around as well. She lay there, balancing tentatively, ignoring the fact that she was wearing jeans and a bra and nothing else. He didn't care.

Mahmoud chose that moment to lean over the seat and make an observation, and Killian laughed, damn him. "Don't translate," she said between clenched teeth. "Just get the damn glass out if you think it's so important."

He put his hand on her head, silencing her. It was getting darker, the roads were crowded and he couldn't afford to watch—he had to keep his eyes on the road. One hand was on the steering wheel, the other left her head to drift gently down her raw back.

"Got one," he murmured, and one tiny spike of pain lessened as he pulled the shard free, dropping it in the space usually used for coins. "Hold still."

"Couldn't Mahmoud do this?" she said. The hand moving across her back, so gentle, was worse than her face in his crotch. She didn't want gentleness from him.

But then, he'd offered her violence last night and she'd taken it. Without argument.

"Stop thinking," he said. "If you tense your muscles, it'll be harder to pull the glass out." Another piece gone. She was holding her breath, and she forced herself to let it out, concentrating on calming exercises. It wasn't the pain, it was the position that was making her tense, but in the end the effect was the same. She knew how to slow her breathing, how to make herself relax no matter what the circumstances, and she brought all her resources into play, relaxing, softening her body, sinking into the seat. Sinking against his hard, hard thigh.

"That's better," he murmured. She could hear the steady swish of the windshield wipers, the hum of the tires, the sounds of traffic. She closed her eyes, giving herself over to the dubious ministry of his hands as he plucked shards of glass from her skin.

"Why did you save Mahmoud?" Killian's voice was so low she almost didn't hear him.

"Instinct," she muttered sleepily. "I certainly wasn't about to save *you*."

His laugh vibrated through his leg, through her body. "Of course not. Mahmoud's grateful."

She couldn't be relaxed and hostile at the same time—that much multitasking was beyond her at the moment. "Sure he is," she murmured. "I wouldn't trust him not to thrust a knife in my ribs if I got between him and what he wanted."

"True, but he'd feel bad about it." Another piece gone. She'd lost count. She could open her eyes and look at the little pile of glass shards in front of her, but she didn't want to. One thing she'd learned over the years was to give in when there was nothing she could do about a situation. Killian was heading to London— he'd have no reason to do otherwise, and self-preservation was his number one priority. She could let go of that responsibility for the time being. He was probably just picking the stuff out of her back because he needed her in good working order, in case someone else tried to hit him. That, and the fact that it humiliated her, were two strong motives.

And her only defense was not to feel humiliated. "Are you almost finished?" she asked in a deliberately caustic tone.

His fingertips danced across her abraded skin, as gently as a whisper. "I think we've got most of them. I have a suggestion while you're in that position."

"I'll bet you do." She tried to sit up, but his hand came down on her neck, no longer gentle at all.

"Stay put," he ordered, his voice flat.

"If you think I'm—"

"Someone's following us," he said. "Right now it looks as if I'm alone in the car, and we'd better keep it that way."

She couldn't argue with his logic. He loosened the pressure on her scalp, and she lay still, listening as he spoke to Mahmoud. The first thing she was going to do when she got back to London was take an intensive training course in Arabic. It was maddening not to know what was going on. And given the state of the world, she had no doubt she'd be needing it sooner rather than later.

Assuming she continued to go out into the field. She'd had no choice in the last year or so. When Thomason had been in charge he'd simply delegated, probably due to the fact that he never liked to get his hands dirty. He had people to enforce his decrees, but he himself was no operative. He'd come in at an early age, a London bureaucrat with connections, and he'd never had to do anything more than give orders and exercise power.

Absolute power corrupts absolutely. She wasn't convinced that Sir Harry Thomason was, in fact, corrupt. It was a possibility, but a remote one. He cherished the life of an English gentleman a little too dearly. He was just a useless old man with nothing to do but harass Peter with petty annoyances. If that was the worst thing she had to deal with, then she could count herself lucky.

And now they'd lost another agent. Morrison had been one of the oldest and best operatives they had, and now he was gone. At least it had been quick for him. As soon as she got to London she'd have to make arrangements for his body to be collected and properly buried.

It was easier to think about Morrison than what she was doing at the moment, a fact that should have shamed her. But it didn't. She could grieve Morrison's loss, but her practical side forced her to consider how they were going to make do. Hiromasa was just going to have to come on board sooner than expected. She only hoped he had Taka's ability to blend in.

Killian's hand had moved from the back of her head to her neck, underneath her loose hair. The heat was on full blast, and even wearing nothing but her bra, she felt warm, almost drowsy. If she didn't know better she'd suspect him of drugging her again. But he simply hadn't had the chance.

No, it was just a matter of coming down from being on high alert. She knew she was safe, for at least a few moments. She was warm, and though her back felt raw, it would heal. The Committee had all sorts of expensive concoctions that could speed up the healing process. In general, she healed quickly anyway, but she needed to be at the top of her game until she finally managed to get rid of the man whose hard thigh lay beneath her head, whose long fingers were slowly, absently stroking the soft skin at the nape of her neck. He probably didn't even realize what he was doing, she thought. He was concentrating on his driving, accepting the fact that she was momentarily quiet. She could be anyone beneath the slow, hypnotic stroke of his hand.

"Mahmoud wouldn't even notice," he said in a low voice laced with amusement. "You could just unzip me...."

She put her hand on his thigh to shove herself up, and to hell with anyone who might be following. But he was too fast for her, grabbing her hand and placing it against the hard flesh straining against his zipper. He had an erection. Why? There was nothing he wanted from her, nothing he'd wanted last night except to humiliate her, to prove his mastery, to prove—

"Shut up," he said.

The only way she could pull her hand free was to bite

him, and that was one thing she wouldn't do. "I didn't say anything."

"You were thinking."

"That's out of your control, Killian," she said. "Sorry about your problem, but I'm not doing anything about it."

"I don't have a problem."

"What's this?" She couldn't pull away, but she could move her fingers, and she brushed the length of him beneath the heavy denim. He didn't react, but then, she hadn't expected him to.

"Unfinished business. We'll take care of it later. In the meantime, you can just lie still and be quiet. Look at it this way, you'll be putting me through exquisite torment. Won't you enjoy that?"

"I doubt it's torment. I wasn't fighting last night. You missed your chance."

"There are always more chances, princess," he whispered. "I had a crisis of conscience."

"You have no conscience."

"Not much of one, I'll admit. But it does seem to appear when you're around. I wasn't going to kill you, you know. You didn't have to shoot me."

"You could have fooled me."

"Oh, I did. Over and over again. You still are completely blind when it comes to me, aren't you?"

"No. I see you far too clearly, as the sick, murderous bastard you are. It doesn't matter how hard you try to be charming, I know you're an ugly piece of work in pretty packaging. I won't kill you, but I'll dance on your grave when someone finally manages it."

He laughed, sounding almost lighthearted. "How sweet. You still love me, don't you? I wouldn't have thought it possible, but you always were a stubborn woman. Lousy judge of character."

"I can change my mind and kill you."

"Of course you can. But you won't. It doesn't matter what you think I am, what you think I've done. You're in love with me, and you will be until the day you die."

She shoved at him, and he let out a small sound of pain as he released her. "Careful there, Isobel. You really wouldn't want to damage me."

She sat up. The highway was empty—no one was following them. Probably no one had been following them for the last hour; he'd just used it as an excuse to humiliate her.

She opened her mouth to tell him all the things she wanted to do to him—hurt him, kill him. But the words didn't come.

Because he knew her too well. Better than she knew herself. She was the Ice Queen, the Iron Maiden, and she wasn't going there.

"Shut up, Killian," she said, reaching for her ripped shirt. In the darkness he wouldn't know how rattled she was. He might guess, but there was no way he could know for certain he'd managed to get to her. "Shut up and drive."

And he did.

17

Things were not going according to plan. Then again, things seldom did, and Killian was used to adjusting at an instant's notice. But something wasn't feeling right about this situation, even taking into account the expected complications and snafus.

He had a simple enough job. The Committee was to extract him from North Africa, bring him to London, where he would supposedly be debriefed on his years spent in the service of some of the world's most notorious dictators, warlords and terrorist organizations. While he was feeding them false and useless information, he'd be doing his own part to bring the Committee to total ruin. By the time he vanished, the Committee would be disbanded, leaving the way clear for his people to take over. It should be easy enough to accomplish—his cover was so impenetrable that no one even suspected there was more to him than there appeared to be. He'd always been particularly good at that. People believed what he wanted them to believe.

But someone was killing off members of the Committee, and that body count had nothing to do with his job. At least, he hoped it didn't. If someone else was assigned to the same task and they hadn't bothered to inform him, he'd be beyond angry.

But the attack on the Committee seemed to be coming from somewhere else entirely. It was direct and bloody, and if he just stayed out of the way he might not have to do anything at all. Whoever was intent on bringing down the organization was doing a very effective, if violent, job of it, and his employers wouldn't care just how it happened. No one in his line of work was particularly squeamish about body counts, as long as the outcome was the required one.

He could pull over and disappear into the night, leaving Isobel with Mahmoud. She wouldn't thank him for that, and sooner or later he had no doubt that Mahmoud would track him down and kill him, if he had to wait ten years to do it. The boy was on his own mission—one from God—and Killian had to pay.

As far as his intel went, the current roster of active Committee agents was very small. Takashi O'Brien was tied up in his late grandfather's business in Tokyo. Peter Madsen was little more than a bureaucrat, sidelined with a bad leg. Morrison was dead, and MacGowan had disappeared, which left Jeffreys in Thailand, and perhaps one other.

And Isobel. Sitting beside him in the front seat, her bloody shirt covering her poor back, staring out into the night as he drove down the A35. If someone was targeting Committee operatives, she'd be high on the list.

"Did you ever consider that they might not be trying to kill me?" he said, breaking the thick silence.

She turned to look at him. "Everyone in the world wants you dead," she replied after a moment. "Have you done anything to change their mind?"

Such a sweetheart. The hostility was coming off her in waves—waves of heat, nothing like the ice she'd encased herself in. "Oh, I'm sure most people want me dead," he said. "I'm just wondering whether these current attempts are directed at me. Or whether someone's trying to get rid of *you,* just as they got rid of Morrison and MacGowan. Or do you think it's just a coincidence? Bad timing?"

"I don't believe in coincidences."

"Neither do I."

She pulled out her PDA, but he took it from her hand, opened the window and threw it out onto the rain-wet highway. "Your security's been compromised," he said.

"Do you have any idea how much that piece of equipment cost?"

"Do you have any idea how little I care?" He reached into the side pocket of the car door, handing her the cheap mobile phone he'd picked up. "Use this. I doubt whoever you call will be secure, but at least they won't be able to track us."

"I have a number for Peter."

"Madsen's probably dead by now."

He wasn't able to rattle her. "Peter's very hard to kill," she answered calmly.

"So were Morrison and MacGowan." The traffic was heavier now, and it was making him edgy. They were about to get on the M3, and on the highway he wouldn't be able to tell whether they were being followed. Right now his usually reliable instincts were shot all to hell. He could thank Isobel for that. He could still feel the warmth of her skin, still taste her mouth. She was a dangerous distraction, one he couldn't afford. But he'd asked for her, and now he was paying the price.

If he was the professional he prided himself on being, she'd have been left behind in a closet on the ferry. Though it might not have made a difference—security would have found her by now, setting up an alarm, and he wouldn't be that far ahead of the game. Besides, he needed her to get into the Committee. Unless someone else, someone with the same agenda but different rules, took it down first.

She was texting, and in the faint glow of the tiny screen he could see her face. She was frowning, biting her lower lip as she concentrated, and she had no idea he was watching her as well as the heavy traffic. She sighed and turned the machine off.

"Do you think I need to toss this one, as well?" she said.

It was the first time she'd asked his opinion in an equable tone. Maybe she was beginning to realize they might be in more trouble than she'd thought.

"If you've turned it off they shouldn't be able to trace it. Just turn it on if you need to use it again. What's up?"

"Change of plans. We had a safe house in Golders Green all set up for you. Very secure—there's no way in hell anyone could get in there."

"But someone did?"

"No. We've had to put someone else there, and you're too volatile a contact. We don't want to risk her life."

"Her?"

"Peter's wife. You're at least half-right—someone's targeted the Committee, and we're all at risk. Personally, I think it's simply because people are determined to get at you, and we're in their way, but in the end it doesn't matter. Peter's wife can't stay in their home in the country, so he brought her in and put her in the Golders Green house. And we're not going to risk putting you there as well."

"Who don't you want to risk, me or Genevieve?"

"Genevieve," Isobel said flatly. "I'm not even going to ask how you know her name—you'd just lie. At this point I don't give a rat's ass whether someone blows you to pieces or not."

"You should. You're with me. Unless you have some romantic notion of dying by my side."

Her low growl was absurdly sexy. He'd made the worst mistake of his life last night. Not fucking her—that had been smart and well-planned, throwing her entirely off balance. But not finishing. Coitus interruptus might be fine for sharpening the senses, but some of his senses were entirely meshed with hers. It wouldn't have made any difference if he'd come. And he'd be feeling a hell of a lot less distracted.

Maybe. Or maybe not. She'd always had the ability to distract him; through the last eighteen years he hadn't been able to let go of her. If he'd climaxed inside her body he'd just be wanting to do it again.

"All right, no Romeo and Juliet fantasies," he said lightly. "Nevertheless, keeping me alive would be the smart thing to do. Once I'm dead, what's to stop them from wiping you out entirely?"

"Wrong. Once you're dead they'd have no reason to come after us. Problem solved."

"And you without a gun," he murmured. "I don't think you'd get very far in hand-to-hand combat, but I'm more than happy to let you try."

"Just drive."

"Where?"

"Head north of London. Peter will meet us."

"And he'll have a gun," Killian said. "Are you going to shoot Mahmoud, too? Because he's going to be pretty pissed off if you kill me before he has a chance to do it."

"No one's killing anyone, no matter how tempting," Isobel said.

"At least not tonight," he said.

And Isobel said nothing at all.

* * *

"Get up."

Reno ignored the voice. The plump blonde lying next to him squealed, jumped up with the sheet wrapped around her, leaving him stark naked in the bed, and ran out of the room. Reno turned over, slowly, to look up into Peter Madsen's ice-blue eyes.

"What's up?" For a moment he wondered whether Madsen would put his hands on him. It would be an interesting battle—Reno didn't underestimate his opponent for one moment, despite his bad leg and the ten years age difference between them. There was no guarantee of the outcome, and Reno tended to fight dirty. He expected Peter Madsen did, as well.

"Get out of bed. And get rid of the girl. Who is she, by the way?"

Reno shrugged. "Just someone with a taste for the exotic," he said. "There are more of them around here than I can count. In English or in Japanese."

"Did you ever stop to consider that sleeping around might compromise our security?"

"I know what I'm doing," he said lazily, climbing out of bed. The girl emerged from the bathroom, fully dressed, beet-red. Was that one Lucy? Or Angela? He'd lost track.

"Uh…I'd better be going," she said, not meeting anyone's eyes.

He half expected Peter to stop her, but Madsen simply stepped back. "See you," Reno said unhelpfully.

In fact, he didn't expect to see her again. The novelty of English girls was wearing off.

He pulled on his discarded black jeans, zipping them, then turned to look at Peter with his usual innocent expression. He'd already gotten rid of the condom and washed off, hoping his activities would arouse his somnolent bed partner and send her on her way, but it had taken Peter to roust her. He never liked sleeping with them. "So what's the big emergency?"

"We've been compromised. Isobel almost walked into a trap at least three times in as many days, and we've just lost another operative. And I asked myself, what has changed around here recently that might have compromised our security?"

Reno reached for the black silk shirt he'd been wearing. He was growing very fond of the quality of clothing he'd been finding in London—rich silks, creamy leathers, angel-soft wools. He pulled it on, stalling for time. "So you think I'm a plant," he said. It was not a question. "You think I set Isobel up. So why am I still alive?"

"I'm not convinced of anything. And out of respect for Taka I'm keeping an open mind. Did you sell us out?"

"If I said yes, you'd kill me."

"Yes."

"If I said no, you wouldn't believe me." He slid his feet into the leather motorcycle boots he loved.

"Try me."

Reno tucked his shirt in, reaching for his sunglasses. "No, I didn't sell you out. I may not want to be here, but I don't betray family, and by extension, you're family. You matter to Taka, and Taka matters to me." Reno met Peter's gaze calmly. He'd taken out his tigereye contact lenses, and there was nothing between them, just ice blue gazing into cold brown.

And then Peter nodded. "I believe you."

He'd managed to shock Reno. "You shouldn't just take my word for it," he said.

"I have good instincts. And I already called Taka."

"Good," he said. "I would have done the same. So why did you wake me up? What time is it, anyway?"

"A little after midnight. We have to go pick up Madame Lambert and Josef Serafin. They've been driving around for hours now, until I could set this up."

"It sounds simple enough. Why do you need my help?"

"Why do you always ask questions?"

"Taka told me to. That way you learn things."

"What if people refuse to answer?"

"You can learn as much from what they don't say as what they do," Reno said in as maddening a tone as he could manage. He'd been working on it for a while, and it came naturally to him. Unfortunately, Peter Madsen wasn't the best subject to try it on.

"You're going to find out, anyway. There's a hidden apartment behind the offices, just below this one. It's totally soundproofed and blocked off, but we're going to have to keep Serafin there for the time being, until we find out who's been coming after us."

"Us?"

"Someone's targeting Committee operatives, which includes you, so no more sex."

Reno simply snorted. It hadn't taken him long to get tired of it; he wasn't going to find what he was looking for here, and substitutes weren't fixing the problem. He wasn't about to admit that to a hard-ass like Peter Madsen, though.

"Whatever," he said, one of his favorite English expressions, right up there with "holy motherfucker." "I thought he was going to the safe house."

"Genevieve's there."

Peter wasn't quite the Iceman he thought he was, Reno observed, keeping his expression blank. "Why?"

"We've lost three agents in the last two weeks. I've warned Taka, and there's no way Madame Lambert's going back to her apartment. Golders Green is safe enough for Genevieve, but I'm not putting someone like Serafin anywhere near her. The more scattered the targets the better our odds."

"And what did your wife say to that?"

"None of your business," Peter said, looking harassed. "She wasn't happy. If she didn't have some kind of stomach bug I wouldn't have been able to make her."

"Stomach bug? You're certain no one's poisoned her?"

"Son of a bitch," Peter muttered, opening his phone and texting quickly, then clicking it shut again. "You ready?"

"Ready for what?"

"For your first assignment. To meet Serafin the Butcher, the most dangerous man in the world."

"Sounds like he's got a good PR firm," Reno said. "And I've been ready for days."

Peter didn't look happy, Reno thought. But then, he hadn't looked particularly pleased since he'd first set eyes on Reno at the airport. It must gall him that he'd have to put him to work. Which was just an added bonus for Reno, banishing the last of his temper at being awakened so rudely. Besides, he'd gotten rid of Lucy or Angela, so everything was fine.

"Just follow orders and don't make the mistake of thinking for yourself," Peter said in a tight voice. "Serafin's an unknown quantity, and God only knows what's been happening to them."

"Unless Madame Lambert has changed, she probably has him on a leash and collar," Reno said.

"You're young," Peter said dismissively, annoying him. "You shouldn't take people at face value."

"You mean Madame Lambert isn't a coldhearted bitch who could take down an army single-handed?"

"Meaning Isobel Lambert isn't as invulnerable as she likes to think she is. None of us is."

"Not even you?" Reno asked mockingly.

"No, kid. And not even you."

The Kensington streets were empty when they stepped outside the white stone building that looked just like all the other white stone buildings. It had taken all

Reno's concentration to recognize it in the first couple of days—whoever had built this upscale area of London hadn't had much imagination. The street was lined with parked cars, and he picked out the milk truck immediately, heading for it.

Peter was at his side. "How did you know?"

Reno smirked. "Taka sent me here for a reason. We're picking up two people, one who might put up a fight, and a small car would be too dangerous. People are less likely to pay attention to a commercial van, and a milk van is more likely to be out very early in the morning making deliveries than any other company. I don't suppose you're going to let me drive?"

"Your first time in England? I don't think so."

"We drive on the left-hand side of the road in Japan, too, and London's nothing compared to Tokyo. Besides, that's probably a standard shift and you've got a bad leg. You'll put us in danger." He held out his hand for the keys.

Madsen looked at him for a moment. "You don't waste time on tact," he said. "I like that." And he dropped the keys in Reno's hand, climbing in the passenger side.

They were already leaving the city when his mobile beeped. Peter flipped it open, then sat there reading the screen, an odd expression on his face.

"Something wrong?"

"Concentrate on your driving," Peter said finally, snapping the phone shut. "I had the nurse take a look at Genevieve. She hasn't been poisoned, and she doesn't have stomach flu."

"So?"

"She's pregnant," Peter Madsen said in a voice of utmost doom.

And Reno, heartless creature that he was, laughed.

18

Killian opened his eyes very slowly, not convinced that he actually wanted to see where he was. The room was dark—no natural light whatsoever, and the artificial light was muted. He was lying in a bed, his hands tied to what presumably was a bedpost, his feet bound together with some kind of cording, and someone had stuffed a gag in his mouth. And he was in a very bad mood.

It had been a long time since someone had gotten the drop on him. More than a decade, maybe two, since he'd lost focus long enough that he was no longer calling the shots. The last thing he remembered was pulling over to the side of the road, though he wasn't sure why. He'd thought Isobel was thoroughly demoralized by the incident on the boat and she'd been pissed as hell to have to lie with her head in his lap. He'd assumed she wouldn't want to get near enough to him to try to take him out. He'd underestimated her.

In the end, it hadn't taken much. He could still feel the faint sting at the side of his neck, and he must have gone down hard. Someone had pulled his clothes apart, obviously looking for weapons, and he lay on the bed with his shirt open, his jeans unzipped, barefoot and pissed off.

How the hell had she managed to get something to knock him out? He'd been all over her body the night before, and there was no way she could have hidden something. It must have been when she insisted on a rest stop. He couldn't very well follow her into the loo at the petrol station, tempted though he might be. And she'd come right out again. He was disgusted with himself, letting her sucker him. First she'd shot him, then eighteen years later she'd tricked him. He was beyond annoyed.

Isobel wasn't strong enough to have dragged him to wherever they were if he was unconscious, therefore she must have had help. He was slowly assessing his surroundings—one smallish, dark room with the bed in the middle, and he could just see the faint outlines of a shuttered window. Not much light coming through, but it probably wasn't daytime yet. He hadn't been out that long, which meant they must be somewhere in or near London.

He wondered how Mahmoud was doing. He wouldn't have taken Killian's abduction well, for despite his elaborate and oft-voiced plans for Killian's eventual torture and murder, the boy was fiercely protective. He would have put up a hell of a lot better fight than Killian's own piss-poor performance.

He jerked at his hands, but the ropes were thin and

tight, and Isobel's friends had found just about every weapon he carried. Not that that would stop him; it just might slow him down a bit. He lay still, listening for anything that might give him a clue as to his whereabouts.

He had no doubt Isobel had called for reinforcements; anyone else would have killed him by now. Probably why he'd been so lax—most people simply wanted to kill him, and he was good at avoiding just that. A simple kidnapping was unexpected.

There was at least one other room beyond the small bedroom, and the light emanating from it was dull and yellow. He could see blankets on the wall—for soundproofing, he assumed. He tried to spit out the gag, but someone had put tape over his mouth. He had no choice but to wait until his captor made her appearance. In the meantime, he could work on the ropes that bound his wrists.

He knew she was there before he saw her, before he heard her. It was a sixth sense he'd developed over the years, and when it came to her it was fine-tuned. He turned his head to meet her calm gaze in the shadowed room.

She'd changed her bloody shirt, presumably taken a shower. Her hair was pulled back in an elegant knot at the base of her neck—part of her armor. She looked elegant and unapproachable, the Ice Queen, the Iron Maiden. Madame Lambert—a lifetime removed from Mary Isobel Curwen. She'd probably thought that girl was gone forever. Until he'd reminded her last night on the rumpled bed in the ship's cabin.

His eyes met hers, and her faint smile was flinty. A bit too sure of herself. "I suppose you want me to untie you?"

Since he wasn't able to reply he simply looked at her, daring her to move closer. She was a smart woman—she knew how dangerous he could be, and she skirted the bed, keeping out of the way of his long legs. Even tied together at the ankles they could sweep her, knock her onto the bed. He could break her neck in a matter of seconds if he wanted to.

He didn't want to. She came at him sideways, away from his legs, reaching down to pull the duct tape away.

He didn't even notice the pain, spitting out the rag someone had put in his mouth earlier. She turned, and handed him a bottle of water. "You're probably thirsty. The drug I gave you tends to make your mouth dry."

"No, I think that was caused by the sock someone stuffed in there," he said. "Your work?"

"Peter's."

"What made you think you'd have trouble getting me to come with you? Haven't I stuck with you for the last few days?"

"I thought it would be better if you didn't know where you are. That way no one can torture it out of you."

"I wasn't planning on being tortured," he said in his most amiable tone. "So why the bondage? If you wanted sex games all you had to do was ask."

She didn't even blink. However close he'd gotten to her before, she'd managed to recover. Now appeared immune to him, immune to their history. "It seemed better to keep you immobile until we were sure you were going to cooperate."

"I'm the soul of cooperation, princess. Is Madsen in the other room?"

"He had to go check on the safe house. I told him I could handle you without any difficulty."

"Oh, really? That remains to be seen. In the meantime, untie me and tell me where the hell Mahmoud is. You didn't have to kill him, did you?"

"Unlike you, I don't kill children. Or maybe you don't consider fifteen-year-olds to be children—not to mention twelve-year-olds."

For a moment he had no idea what she was talking about. "You mean Mahmoud's sister? Since she was pregnant, I considered her an adult."

"And therefore you shot her. What was she doing, coming at you with a burning pike?"

"You want some nice, noble excuse for it? I'm not giving it to you," he said. "I put a bullet in her forehead and she died instantly. You don't need to know anything more, as long as you realize what I'm capable of doing."

"I know all the horrors you've been capable of doing over the last two decades," Isobel said in a low voice.

"Where is Mahmoud? Because he's not going to like having me out of his sight, and you need to be careful. He can be a brutal little bugger when he's thwarted."

"He's fine. Reno's keeping an eye on him."

"Who's Reno?"

She sighed. She didn't seem any closer to freeing his wrists, but he wasn't concerned. Even tied up he could take her down when he was ready. "Reno is our newest recruit. Takashi O'Brien's cousin."

"Reno's not a Japanese name."

"His real name is Hiromasa Shinoda. Apparently he took his American name from a video game character."

"That doesn't sound like Committee material."

"He's not. But beggars can't be choosers, and he had to get out of Japan. In the meantime he'll be able to keep Mahmoud out of trouble."

"Untie me."

She looked at him. "I'm not sure I trust you."

"Of course you don't trust me. But you've brought me here, as originally agreed upon, even though I'm missing a bit of the liberty I expected, and this is a far cry from the Ritz-Carlton. However, given that your organization is going down the toilet, fast, I can be open-minded. Untie me, get me something to eat and I'll start telling you all the things you ever wanted to know about third world violence in the new millennium."

"You think I'm going to cook for you?"

"I think neither of us has eaten in quite a while, and I'm guessing this is an apartment complete with a kitchen. I'm also guessing that since we're holed up in here, we probably have plenty of supplies. I'll take coffee or Scotch, depending on what time of day it is."

"It's just before dawn."

"That makes it tough. It's either the end of a very

long night or an early start. Tell you what—make me some coffee and put some whiskey in it. That way I don't have to decide."

For a moment she didn't move. "All right," she said finally. "Stay put."

"And where would I be going, princess?" he taunted.

The moment she was out of sight he finished untying his right wrist, then made quick work of the other ropes. It was an old trick he'd learned long ago, a way of compressing his wrist bones that made him able to get out of almost any kind of restraint. He was a tall man, but his bones were thin and narrow, and that fact had saved his life more than once.

He was tempted to stay there until she came back, then pull her down on the bed and finish what he should have finished last night. The sight of her, the smell of her was driving him crazy, and he hated the way she tucked her hair in a bun, like some sexless bitch.

She was far from sexless. He'd made her wet last night, and she hated him for it. She'd been so damn proud of her frigidity, and it had come crashing down at the touch of his hands. There were women who could climax just from having their breasts touched, just from being kissed. He was willing to bet Isobel was one of them.

No wonder she'd thought she was frigid. She'd forced herself into a suit of armor made of dry ice, letting nothing come near her. Because she'd explode too easily if it did.

He was going to make that happen. First he needed to find out exactly what the hell was going on with the Committee, and why the operatives were being picked off one at a time. Was he right—had they really been after her all the time, and not him? And how was an untried Japanese kid with a fake name going to protect Mahmoud when some very powerful, very dedicated people seemed determined to take the notorious Josef Serafin out?

He pushed himself off the bed, pulling his shirt back around him but not bothering to button it, zipping up his jeans reluctantly. Had Isobel been the one to search him so thoroughly? He'd hate to think he'd missed it.

There was a small living room, a dining room with a laptop set up on the table, and a tiny kitchen. Her back was to him, but her voice was calm and accepting. "It's really hard to keep you shackled, isn't it?"

He moved into the kitchen, crowding her. On purpose. "Just about impossible." The windows were boarded up, allowing in no light. "I take it this isn't your apartment."

"You think I'd take you to my home?"

"Hope springs eternal. This seems like the kind of place you'd live. The perfect place to do eternal penance."

"My flat is very large, elegant and airy," she said, pouring boiling water into the coffee press. "And I have absolutely nothing to do penance for."

"Not anymore. You didn't kill me."

She turned around to glare at him. "I never regretted killing you. Only that I'd been such a fool in the first place."

"You were out of your league, princess. There was no way you could even guess how well you were being played. I've got skills you wouldn't even imagine, and you were nothing more than a kid, infatuated with me, just as I planned for you to be."

To his amazement there was a faint stain of color on her pale cheekbones, the only clue to her rigidly repressed emotions. When she looked at him her eyes were clear and cool. "As you say, I was young and stupid. I'm neither of those things now."

"I didn't say you were stupid. Just vulnerable."

"Trust me, I'm not currently vulnerable."

He didn't move. "Trust me, you are."

She'd managed to will the color away from her face, and when she turned she was the picture of calm efficiency. "I suggest we start the debriefing process as soon as you've had your coffee. I'll admit things aren't going as planned, and we shouldn't waste time if we can help it."

"I thought Madsen was going to do the questioning."

"He's got other things to deal with." Her voice was flat and unemotional.

"Like what?"

"Like none of your damn business. I don't have anything better to do at the moment."

"I thought you wanted to get back to that elegant and airy apartment of yours."

"I do. Unfortunately, the people who are after you are far too determined, and it's not safe. Given their recent track record they would probably figure out where I live quite easily. We need to conserve manpower."

"You still think it's me they're after?" Killian took the coffee press from her. "Don't you think the Committee has more than its share of enemies? Why take out MacGowan? He was in Central America, and he had nothing to do with me."

She slammed the mugs down on the table. "How do you know everything about our operations? We don't even know if MacGowan's dead. He may have just gone to ground—his cover was so deep no one should have broken it. Did you set him up? He was a good man...."

"I don't give a rat's ass what your operatives are doing, as long as they aren't interfering with me. The fault lies in your operation. If I could get that kind of intel, then so can other, less benevolent people."

"'Benevolent?'" she echoed.

"I'm not the worst man in the world."

"Prove it."

"You're still alive."

She stared at him. "Drink your coffee," she said finally. "And then we'll get to work."

"Breakfast first."

He was usually a good judge of how far he could push someone, and he knew Isobel far better than she would have wanted, but he might have gone overboard. And then she blinked, and like the shutters covering the windows in this small space, her emotions and reactions were shut down, blanketed. "You'd better be worth all this trouble," she said. "Good men have died for you."

"The truth is, many good men have died because of me," he said. "I don't let it bother me. If you were as cold as you want to be, it wouldn't bother you, either."

"If it didn't bother me, I wouldn't be in this line of work. I don't like good people being killed. I don't like bad people getting away with it."

"So it really must gall you to have to keep me alive."

"Believe me, it does."

He moved closer, deliberately crowding her again in the limited space. She stood her ground, simply because she had no place to go, and he leaned down and breathed in her ear. "I promise you can be the one to kill me if it comes to it. Does that make you happy?"

"Deliriously," she snapped.

She smelled like coffee and soap. She smelled like Isobel, and he wanted to take her up against the kitchen wall, no preliminaries, nothing but fast, hot sex. He let her see it in his eyes, and her own flared with sudden awareness. And then he stepped back, leaving her with the illusion of safety.

"I like my eggs scrambled," he said. And he walked back into the living room, smiling when he heard her drop something. Chaos, lust, confusion. His job here was done.

* * *

The house in Golders Green was small, older, seemingly ordinary. The reinforced, lead-lined door looked as if it was made of wood; the windows were shatterproof and as close to bulletproof as technology could get. There was a highly developed sensor system around the perimeter that could pick up any trace of explosives, and there were three escape routes underneath. It was a fortress inside an ordinary white house, and as Peter passed at least three invisible security checkpoints he told himself Genevieve was safe. He wasn't so sure about his own sorry ass. She was going to be majorly pissed off, and Genevieve Spenser was not someone you pissed off lightly.

It had been one hell of a night. Cleaning up the mess of Morrison's murder left no time to mourn his old friend. The man known as Serafin was unconscious by the time he and Reno reached Isobel, but the child in the backseat was both unexpected and a pain in the ass. To Peter's amazement, Reno had taken charge, subduing the brat just by the tone of his voice, while Isobel and Peter dragged Serafin's unconscious body into the car they'd bought and drove back to the apartment.

By the time they reached Kensington, Reno and the kid—Mahmoud was his name—were in curious accord, probably due to the iPod Reno had handed over. Peter hated to think what sort of Yakuza gangsta rap Mahmoud was listening to, but at least it kept the boy quiet while they lugged Serafin up the camouflaged back staircase to the hidden apartment behind the offices of Spence-Pierce Financial Consultants, Ltd. As long as Mahmoud knew Serafin was on the floor below, he went along with Reno peacefully enough, up to the stripped-down apartment Reno had turned into his home with a flagrant disregard of property. When Peter left them, Reno had switched on the state-of-the-art video game system, and Mahmoud's sullen eyes had lit up. At least that was one thing Peter didn't need to worry about.

Isobel was more than capable of dealing with someone like Josef Serafin, no matter what their history. Peter had taken one look at her, the blank expression in her eyes, and knew she was almost at the end of her endurance. But then she'd pulled herself together, as she always did, taking the news of MacGowan's disappearance with no more than a flinch.

Peter had tied Serafin to the small bed in the apartment, and hoped to God Isobel had the sense to leave him there until he could get back. He never would have thought it, but the indomitable Madame Lambert was vulnerable. Younger than he'd ever realized. And running out of reserves.

In the meantime, he had someone even more terrifying to face. His angry wife, who didn't even know she was, finally, pregnant. The nurse who had checked out her stomach flu had worked for the Committee before, and knew better than to say anything to anybody—even the patient—until given permission.

Peter had no illusions that his wife was suddenly going to become docile and complacent. Genevieve was a warrior woman, and if she had a child to protect she could take on the Russian army.

He passed the fourth checkpoint, punched in the code on the keypad and pushed open the door to the house, entering a long, narrow hallway with a row of closed doors on either side. Then he froze.

Somewhere in the depths of the house, a baby was crying, and for a moment he thought he'd somehow walked into the wrong building, the wrong life.

One of the doors opened, and if Peter weren't so disoriented, the man who stepped into the hallway would have already been dead.

"You're getting slow in your old age, Madsen," Bastien Toussaint murmured. "You'd better come in and explain a few things to your wife."

Peter shoved his gun back in the shoulder holster. "What the hell are you doing here?"

The crying noise had stopped—clearly the angry infant had been given what it wanted. Peter imagined a future filled with such moments, and told himself he should be miserable, but he couldn't summon up much of anything.

"Safest place to be," Bastien said. "Come in and meet Swede."

"Swede?" God, not another person crammed into the tiny house.

"The new baby. We're all here, in one piece, and we're

going to stay that way while we find out what the hell is going on. Three men tried to get to us in the States."

"And you couldn't find out who sent them?"

"They died too quickly," Bastien said with his impenetrable calm. "I decided not to wait around to see if someone else was going to show up. Where's Madame Lambert?"

"In trouble," Peter replied. "More than I've ever seen her."

"Then we'd better see to it. Chloe will keep Genevieve calmed down. I don't think you have the time to deal with her at the moment. A pregnant woman is a dangerous thing."

"How did you know she was pregnant? I don't think she knows herself."

"It's obvious to anyone used to the signs. Chloe's bound to blurt it out sooner rather than later, which means we'd better get this mess taken care of fast or your wife might possibly kill you. What's Madame Lambert working on that's got her in trouble?"

"Josef Serafin. He's trading intel for immunity. Right now he should be filling her in on the inner workings of some of the worst fascist governments of the last twenty years."

Bastien froze. "Hell and damnation," he said. "He's trading nothing but lies."

"I imagine he'll try, but Isobel's too smart to fall for anything like that. Why don't you think he'll tell the truth?"

Bastien grimaced. "Because he's not a professional mercenary, working for the highest bidder. He's CIA, and always has been."

Peter's bad day suddenly got a great deal worse.

19

Suzanne Brockmann. But don't take my word for it. She is a highly decorated veteran. Got hit, took fire in Mauritzia. Been CIA and always has been...

Isabel had only a few seconds to ponder that, then without...

19

"You're lying to me," Isobel said.

"Now why would I do that? I haven't anything to gain—I expect the Committee's generosity is going to be contingent on the quality of intel I bring. I have no reason to hold back." Killian turned his head to look at her. He was stretched out on the sofa, his long, lean body taking up the entire space. Not that she would have wanted to sit next to him. She was happy to keep her distance, and the uncomfortable chair was perfectly adequate. She'd fed him, simply because she was famished herself, and in a battle of wills he probably would have won. And she'd spent the last three hours grilling him. And getting nowhere.

He told her absolutely nothing she didn't already know. It wasn't common knowledge, but the Committee wasn't a common organization, and their intel was first-rate. Killian wasn't bringing anything new to the table.

"What happened in Mauritzia?"

He shrugged, perfectly at ease. "One of my more spectacular fuckups, I have to admit. I was in charge of removing the ethnic population of three small cities to a holding area where they were to be exterminated under my supervision. Which is where I got the charming name Serafin the Butcher. Unfortunately, someone let word slip, and the neighborhoods were emptied before I even got there. Personally, I didn't see the problem—the local governments wanted these people gone, and they were, having slipped over the border into refugee camps. Unfortunately, Busanovich didn't see it that way. I got out at the last minute."

"It didn't seem to hurt your future employment prospects any," she said.

His smile was cool and deadly. "There's always employment for a man with my skills and moral...flexibility. I'd be more than happy to give you names, positions of President Busanovich's advisors, but like the president himself, they're all dead, and Mauritzia is discovering the wonders of democracy. I like to think in my own modest way I contributed to that." His tone was mocking.

"Next you'll be telling me that you were saving the world with your incompetence."

He shrugged. "You could look at it that way. I'm afraid Fouad Assawi was a bit more determined than some of my previous employers. Which is why I decided to throw myself on the mercy of the Committee."

She said nothing, closing the lid to her laptop.

"If you're done with that do you mind if I check my

e-mail?" he said, sitting up. "I was bidding on a couple of things on eBay and I wanted to see if I won—"

"Oh, shut up. You've probably never been on eBay."

"Now that's where you're wrong. There's quite an interesting bit of black market trade going on—you just have to know how to find it."

"And what's the e-mail for—online dating services?" Her voice was caustic.

"No, princess. I've already got you."

She stood abruptly, needing to get away from him. "As a matter of fact, we don't have Internet service in here. No cell phone service, either—we're completely cut off. The walls are lined so that nothing, not even a telecommunications signal, can get in or out."

"Then how are you going to know what to do with me?" he said lazily.

"The door still works, if you know where to find it and how to open it. If you don't know the codes you'll die, but Peter doesn't make mistakes like that."

"Which is why he walks with a limp nowadays." Killian swung his legs over the side of the sofa, stretching, and she moved back, skittish.

It was too much to hope he hadn't noticed her retreat. And responded. He came toward her, and she told herself she wouldn't back up, but her feet moved, anyway, until she ended up against one of the blanketed walls, and there was nowhere else to go. He was standing too close to her, and she couldn't remember ever being so intensely aware of another human being.

"That means no one would hear you scream," he said softly. "No one would come to your rescue. You're just as trapped as I am."

"Yes." Her voice didn't waver, her gaze was clear and steady, and even if her heart was racing there was no way he could know that.

He put his hand against her neck, cradling her throat with his long fingers. "Your pulse is too fast, Isobel. Are you afraid of me?"

"No. I don't feel anything at all."

He moved his face closer, his mouth hovering just over hers, and it took everything to keep her lips from trembling. "Are you lying, princess?" He was stroking her throat, the roughened pads of his fingertips brushing against her soft, vulnerable skin. "I think you're lying to me."

He could tighten his hand, crush her larynx and she'd drown in her own blood. He could move his mouth a fraction of an inch closer and kiss her.

Or he could step back, away from her, releasing her from the prison of his cool gaze. "If we're finished for now I think I'll take a shower," he said, dropping his hand.

"There should be new clothes in the bedroom. Our people are good about such things." Her voice was only slightly husky—most people wouldn't notice. She didn't make the mistake of thinking Killian was most people, but her control was good enough, considering the circumstances.

"I'd suggest you join me, but I can imagine your reaction."

"I've already had a shower."

She waited until the door to the small bathroom closed behind him before she sank down on the couch. Then jumped up a moment later because it was still warm from his body heat.

"Snap out of it," she muttered under her breath. She was out of control, reacting to stupid things, and Killian was playing her like a master.

In the last eighteen years she'd come up against some of the most monstrously manipulative people in the world. People who made a fictional character like Hannibal Lecter seem merely eccentric, and never had she faltered. This had to stop, right now. She needed a break, but it wasn't coming. With the organization compromised, everyone had gone to ground, and there was no way she was drawing Peter into a tricky situation like this one. She had nothing to lose. Peter had Genevieve, who'd somehow managed to be his salvation.

Isobel was still reeling from the discovery that Hiromasa Shinoda was Reno. The Committee's operatives could blend in in almost any situation—Reno stood out like a brightly colored parrot, flame hair and all, and any other time she would have sent him packing. But right now he was watching over Mahmoud, keeping him safe, and she couldn't think of anyone better suited for the job. Peter would have probably strangled the boy.

She sat back down in one corner of the sofa, curling

her legs up beneath her and leaning her head back. She was so tired. She hadn't dared sleep last night; Killian was so unpredictable that there was no telling when the drug she'd given him would wear off, and when that happened she'd expected him to be royally pissed off. So she'd dozed, off and on, telling herself that eventually she could rest. For now she had to stay on full alert, drinking cup after cup of coffee. It was no wonder her hands shook and her heart raced. It had nothing to do with him.

He was taking his time in the bathroom, probably trying to find a way to escape, but that was one area she could feel completely secure about. Unless he was going to dig through plaster with a toothbrush, he wouldn't find any way out. This safe house was a prison as well as a haven.

The wind had picked up outside; despite the sound-proofing there was no way they could totally obliterate the noise of the wind whistling through the old house. It was probably raining again. November in England was cold and wet. She'd lived here so long she'd almost for-gotten how bleak it was. The desert sun would have been a reprieve, if she hadn't been on this particular mission.

She could smell water and soap and shampoo when he opened the door—pleasant, normal scents in a crazy world. And then he walked into the small living room, wearing nothing but a towel around his hips.

She was speechless. Not because of his near nudity—she wasn't that innocent. And not because of the undeni-able beauty of his long, wiry body. She already knew she liked the way he looked. She'd accepted that almost two decades ago.

It was the scars. A knife wound above his right hip, crescent-shaped and deep. The tear bisecting his chest, his skin still faintly pink where the incision had been. The abrasion marks on the right side of his throat, as if someone had tried to strangle him. Or used a rope.

He must have known what she was looking at in silent, hidden horror. "Like what you see?" He mocked her, turning slowly so she could get the full picture. Whip scars across his back. His elbow must have been smashed at one point—it had healed badly, though it didn't seem to give him any trouble.

His knee had been destroyed as well, and replaced at some point—she recognized the long scar. And along the back of his right shoulder were scars that could only come from bullets. It was a wonder he was alive.

"I do make a pretty picture," he drawled. "But unless you're taking off your clothes as well, I think I'd better get dressed. Where are the new clothes?"

"In the closet." She'd seen people who'd been tortured. Seen people who'd died from it. What she couldn't understand was how Killian had managed to survive such a brutal life.

He dropped the towel, tossing it at her, and headed back into the bedroom. Somewhere she found her voice. "Don't be so damned predictable," she said. "I'm surprised you bothered with the towel in the first place."

He appeared back in the open doorway, but by now

had a pair of black jeans on and was zipping them up. "I wanted to make it more interesting for you." He'd brought a shirt with him, pulling it from the plastic sleeve and shaking it free. As he unfastened the buttons, she watched, trying to keep the question from forming.

But it came out, anyway. "Where's the scar?"

He glanced at her, still holding the shirt in his hand. "What scar? My body is a veritable road map of pain, princess. Was there a particular one you were interested in, or just a global tour?"

"Where I shot you. I thought it was center body mass."

"You didn't even know those terms back then, Isobel," he chided gently. "And you were so nervous, you were lucky you even managed to wing me."

"Your arm?" She could see a long, thin scar above his elbow, but it didn't look right.

"Shoulder." He came up to her, and this time she didn't retreat. "Look closer."

She couldn't see anything. Just smooth, golden flesh crisscrossed by a faint network of lines. He took her hand and placed her fingertips against his shoulder, pushing, and she could feel the scar tissue, a small knot beneath the warm skin.

She pulled her hand away. "You had a good doctor," she said, uneasy.

"One of the best."

"Who?"

"If you don't want to hear the answer, then you shouldn't ask the question."

He still hadn't put the shirt on, but she was past caring. "My husband," she said in a dead voice. "That's Stephan's work."

"Indeed it is. But he wasn't your husband at the time. Granted, he was a lot more interested in stabilizing you than digging the bullet out of my shoulder, but then, I was in no particular danger of dying. You, however, had lost a hell of a lot of blood, and Stephan much preferred a challenge. Besides, even all cut up you were still pretty, and he knew I wasn't particularly interested."

"In me?"

"In him. Your husband was gay, remember? He gave me a shot of morphine to tide me over, and let me watch as he put you back together again. It was very impressive."

"Why didn't you kill me?"

"Why should I kill you? I was the one who brought you there."

She turned away, because she couldn't look at him a moment longer. "No," she whispered. Knowing it was true.

"Don't take it so hard, Isobel," he said. "You can still hate me. I killed five men that night, three with my bare hands. Hardly the kind of heroic behavior you would have expected."

"What five men?"

"General Matanga. I was paid to take him out and I did. His aide got in the way as I was escaping. And then there were my three confederates, the ones with the knives. After all this time I'm afraid I've forgotten their names."

"Why did you kill them?"

There was no humor in his smile, no warmth in his blue-gray eyes. "They'd dragged you back to the warehouse and they were having fun with you. You weren't conscious anymore, but you could still feel pain—each time they cut you your body twitched. This annoyed me, so I killed them." His words were casual, his eyes watching her.

"And then you took me to Stephan?"

"Well, since I was heading there myself it seemed the gentlemanly thing to do. I have to say it was a bitch and a half carrying you with a bullet in my shoulder. On top of that I had to sit and let him save your life while I almost passed out. And then the son of a bitch decided I could spare a pint of blood, despite all the stuff that had poured out of me thanks to your bloodthirsty actions."

"A pint of blood?"

"You needed a transfusion, and he was fresh out. We both happen to be AB negative, princess. Just one more sign we're destined to be together."

She wanted to throw up. His blood was running in her veins. She'd shot him, and he'd saved her life. And he was standing there, looking at her out of enigmatic eyes, and she wanted to scream.

She cleared her throat. "Interesting," she said. "You really are full of surprises."

"And you don't fool me for a minute, princess. You're ready to fall apart, but you aren't going to let yourself do it. Part of you is wishing to God you'd killed me when you had the chance, another part knows you'd be dead as well. I'm a nightmare, a monster who saved your life when I should have left you to bleed to death. Now, how are you going to make peace with that unpleasant truth?"

"Quite easily. You've been trying your absolute best to manipulate me, but I'm not the puddle of emotions you seem to think I am. I know what you're doing, and I know what's behind it. What's wrong with you."

"Please share," he said amiably. "I've always been interested in other people's opinions about my sociopathic behavior."

"You're afraid of me."

This time she'd managed to shock him, and she could feel her fear ebbing, the icy strength taking over. She was far from defenseless, and she'd finally realized the weakness in his armor.

"Afraid of you?" He laughed lightly. "I hate to tell you, but I'm not afraid of anyone or anything. It's both my strength and my weakness. I don't care if I live or die, I don't care who I hurt. I'm not afraid."

"You're afraid of me," she said again. "And I think you always have been. You kept me drugged and pliant in that hotel room in Marseille—I remember it better than you think. And you never let me touch you. It was as if you were experimenting on me, to see just what you could make me feel, and you never were there at all."

"You were drugged, Isobel, and it was eighteen years ago—"

"And two nights ago," she continued ruthlessly. "On board the ship. You just wanted to prove you could make me feel. But *you* didn't feel anything at all. You didn't let yourself."

He was looking no more than remotely interested in her theory, but she wasn't fooled. She knew the truth this time, and she wasn't going to be distracted.

"You didn't climax. You couldn't. You could manipulate me enough to make me feel powerless, and then you pulled away. Is it women you're afraid of, Killian, or just me?"

He looked at her for a long moment, his eyes hooded, unreadable. "What are you trying to do, Isobel?"

"Call your bluff. Get you to leave me the hell alone. You don't want me, you just want to fuck with me. So here I am, you son of a bitch. Take me."

She could feel the power coursing through her, a strangely mournful power. It was a triumph to realize he'd only been playing with her, a triumph to know that she really didn't matter.

His smile was almost wistful. "You're right about two things, Mary Isobel Curwen Lambert," he said. "I absolutely want to fuck with you. I'm calling your bluff. So why don't you go down on me and prove yourself right?"

The silence in the room was muffled, absolute, and the caffeine must have finally hit overload, because her heart was slamming so hard against her chest that surely he must have heard it. And if she turned her back, gave in, he would win, and she could never let him do that, never again.

Her knees hit the floor as she sank down in front of him. Her hands were shaking as they worked on the snap of the new jeans. He didn't move, just stood there and let her fumble with the zipper, his hands at his sides.

He wasn't wearing underwear. She grasped the denim and yanked it down, and in the murky light his cock was hard, bigger than she'd expected.

She looked up at him, her eyes cold and hostile. "So you can get an erection," she said. "Too bad you can't come."

And she put her mouth on him, a deliberate taunt, an insult, a sly, erotic challenge that she knew she would win. She closed her mouth around him, sucking at him, pulling with her lips, letting her tongue swirl around the rigid, unfeeling length of him, as she proved to him...

She felt his hands on her head, oddly gentle, his fingers threading through her hair, pulling it loose from its tight bun so that it spilled over her shoulders. He was stroking her scalp, kneading her, letting her taste and suck and then swallow, as he froze, his body rigid, his cock pumping into her mouth as he held her there.

She fell back, shocked, wiping her hand across her mouth, and she could barely see the expression on his face in the murky light. "You're right about something else," he said, his voice ragged. "I'm scared to death of you. Because I want you, when common sense and a lifetime of experience tells me I should kill you. I want you, and if I give up then you'll own me, and I'll have nothing left to fight with."

She said nothing. She could taste him in her mouth, feel him between her legs where he hadn't touched her—and she was ready to climax from thinking about what she'd just done.

"But then, it's too late, isn't it? You win, princess. Now let's take this to the bed and get it done right."

20

He reached down to pull her to her feet, but she fought him. His jeans were halfway down his legs, trapping him, and when she struggled, he fell, taking her with him onto the cold, hard floor of the apartment.

He kicked the jeans off, rolling on top of her, and he had her clothes off her, those plain, expensive clothes, in less than a minute. She fought him, hitting him, not knowing what she wanted. He was hard again, that fast, and he shoved her down on the thin carpet, kneeling between her legs, waiting for her to tell him to stop. Whether he would listen was another matter entirely.

But she didn't. She lay in a welter of discarded clothes, her hair loose and tousled, and he looked down at her body. A body he remembered, even after all Stephan's handiwork.

She still had pale freckles, spots of gold, dancing across her stomach. She still had red hair, and he stopped thinking about his cock and put his mouth there, kissing her, so damn grateful that something was still the same.

She put her hands in his hair and yanked his head up, hard, and her eyes were a storm of pain and confusion. "What the hell are you doing?" Her voice was no more than a raw whisper.

"You know what I'm doing. Returning the favor." He half expected her to keep fighting, hitting at him. But she didn't. She dropped her hands to the floor, trying to will her body into that ice-fogged state she'd lived in for so long, and he wanted to laugh. That was one battle she'd never win. He was an expert when it came to using his mouth, and he'd never done it with someone he...cared about. He was enmeshed with her, body and soul, and he knew just how to touch her, with his mouth, his tongue, to make her shatter in a matter of seconds.

And before she had a chance to come down, he was inside her, pushing into the tight wet sleekness, feeling her tighten around him, first trying to keep him out, then pulling him in deeper, and he put his hands under her butt and yanked up, hard, so that he was in so deep she could probably taste him.

She *was* tasting him, and the knowledge almost made him lose it again. He loved her mouth, the cold things it could say, the hot things it could do. He arched back, looking down at her, deep inside her.

He'd forgotten her breasts. Small, perfect, the nipples hard in the warm room. He'd forgotten the soft, muffled sounds she made when she was ready to come. Like she was right now.

And he'd forgotten the dark, bleak pain in her eyes

when she had no defenses left, and he'd trapped her, used her, and there was no love at all.

He'd pull out. Away from her, before he could destroy her completely. That's what he had to do—he couldn't, he shouldn't...

Her hands came up from the floor and touched his face, gently. Her fingers brushed his mouth, slowly slid down his tense, sweat-dampened body, light and caressing. She was crying.... A woman like Isobel Lambert shouldn't cry. And then her hands gripped his hips and she arched, bringing him in deeper still, and she said yes to his unasked question. Yes, and yes, and yes.

He kissed her, because he couldn't stop himself. He tried to go slowly, to make it good for her, to make it the best she'd ever had, but she was already past that point, making those strangled little cries that sent him over the edge, and there was nothing but heat and damp and the smell and the touch and the taste, and he could have no more stopped himself than he could have stopped the storm outside.

He was a man who fucked in silence. And when he climaxed, long, hard, endlessly, inside her tight body, he heard his voice in the darkness. Calling her name.

Reno stretched out on the floor, a beer cradled in his hands, his eyes drifting closed as he listened to the sound of the storm outside. Tiny pellets of icy rain were beating against the windows, mixed with the noise of the video game Mahmoud was playing.

It had been a strange day.

He opened one eye, glancing at the kid. He was sitting cross-legged on the mattress Reno had dragged out for him. The second bedroom was crowded with discarded furniture, but he could at least get out the mattress. Mahmoud would have been happy enough sleeping on the hard floor—clearly he'd slept in far worse places—but Reno had a soft spot for the kid.

Besides, he probably wasn't going to sleep at all— he was going to stay up all night playing video games. It had been love at first sight; one taste of Mortal Kombat and the boy was hooked. Reno had battled him for hours, opponent after opponent. Sometimes he let Mahmoud win, at other times he'd simply slap his character to the ground and rip out his spinal cord. Reno didn't let himself dwell on the eerie thought that Mahmoud would have lived in a world like that. Well, the ripping out of spinal cords was not usually seen outside of a video game, but the blood had been real for him.

He looked relaxed, happy, with his newly spiked purple hair, rude T-shirt and ripped jeans that had cost more than a child soldier would make in a lifetime. And they'd figured out how to communicate, a crazy mix of French, English, Arabic, Japanese and video game terms. After two hours of silence Mahmoud had started talking, and he hadn't stopped, as characters battled on the HD television screen and fake blood spattered.

Reno understood only part of it, but it hadn't mattered. Mahmoud had needed to talk, and he listened. They moved from fight games to first person shooters, and Reno found himself hopelessly outclassed by a kid fifteen years younger than he was, something he wasn't about to put up with. Older brother kindness could only go so far, and he moved him on to RPGs, fantasy role-playing games where Mahmoud could wander through enchanted forests, kill trolls, turn into a wizard and collect potions. The kid was in heaven, and Reno could retire to his bedroom in peace.

They'd already had a solemn exchange of presents, Japanese style. He'd given Mahmoud his most prized possession, his handheld game system that was still in beta mode, unavailable on the open market and so advanced it made PS3 look like an Atari. And Mahmoud had given him a string of beads, cracked, ancient, worthless. The beads had belonged to his foster sister. He'd taken them from her dead body, and had sworn on them to kill the man who'd murdered her.

He'd given them to Reno, along with his blood oath of revenge, finally letting go. And Reno, cold, unsentimental punk that he considered himself to be, had wrapped them around his wrist, knowing he would carry them with him until the day he died.

He could hear nothing from the floor below. He'd never even realized there was a closed-off living space down there—he was just glad Peter Madsen hadn't decided to put him in it during his training period. England was bad enough; being in a prison wouldn't help.

Madame Lambert had looked like a different woman than the cold, efficient robot she'd appeared to be the only other time he'd been in England. But then, that had been miles away from the plain, middle-aged cult follower that had been the first disguise he'd seen her in. Maybe the robot was a disguise as well, and the bloody, torn and troubled woman who'd been waiting for them with an unconscious man and a furious Mahmoud was the real Madame Lambert.

Normally Reno wouldn't care. It was none of his business. But it didn't look as if he'd be getting back to Tokyo anytime soon, and he held the firm belief that if he was going to do something, even if coerced into it, then he should do it completely. And in order to accomplish that, he needed to understand the people he worked with.

What had she been doing all day with the man she'd drugged? He was more than just a hostile—Reno could figure that out by the expression in her eyes when she'd thought no one was looking. They'd dumped his unconscious body on the small bed in the closed-off apartment, and she'd stood there, looking down at him with an unreadable expression on her face.

Maybe she'd killed him at some point during this long day. But then, he would have been called to help Madsen move the body. The Committee's operatives had gone undercover, and right now there seemed to be only the three of them.

Reno hoped Taka was looking out for himself, that son of a bitch. He was the one who'd arranged to have him shipped out of the country, and while there was no doubt Reno had made the mistake of losing his temper with some very unforgiving people, it also had something to do with the fact that Taka's sister-in-law was coming for a visit. He and his wife kept Reno as far away from Jilly Hawthorne as they could, even if it meant exiling him halfway across the world.

He pushed himself up off the floor, considering his annoyance with his entire family, women, the Committee, England and life in general. "I'm going to bed," he told Mahmoud.

The boy simply nodded, staring fixedly as his video game character rode a dragon through a flame-colored sky.

"Don't stay up all night," Reno said, and then could have kicked himself. He'd turned into an old man. The kid could stay up for days if he wanted to, playing games, and be none the worse for it. Reno had done it often enough.

Empty Red Bull cans were piled high in the trash bin; boxes of cereal, Chinese take-out containers, bags of chips were littered all over the place. The boy hadn't stopped eating. Reno had taught him how to use chopsticks rather than his hands, but it had been harder convincing him not to leave them stuck in the rice. Mahmoud had argued with perfect logic that it should only be bad luck to leave them stuck in Japanese rice, not Chinese. But then he'd carefully removed them.

No, the kid was okay. Tomorrow, maybe he'd take him to a video game arcade and let him try Guitar Hero and DDR. Or steal a fast car and drive out into the countryside, and maybe they could find a castle or two.

At least Reno was no longer so damn bored.

Mahmoud made no sound when they came for him. The struggle was silent, muffled, and Reno wouldn't have woken up if they hadn't knocked over the bin of soda cans. He came flying through the darkness toward the shadowed men, and he took out two of them with the sheer element of surprise. But then he heard the crack of his arm breaking, as if from a distance, and felt a flash of blinding pain. Then nothing at all.

Bastien Toussaint glanced around the pristine offices of Spence-Pierce, wondering what the hell was happening behind the double-thick walls. It was three in the morning, and he wasn't any more eager to face Chloe than Madsen was to deal with his very annoyed amazon wife. They weren't much further than they'd been when they'd started out that morning, and there was no way either of them was going to stop until they figured out what the hell was going on. So far they'd come up with bugger all.

Bastien sank back in the chair, taking the mug of coffee Madsen offered him, liberally laced with Scotch. He had no fears the Scotch would slow him down——he was riding on pure adrenaline, as if the last three years of peace had never happened. Old habits died hard, he thought, looking at the high-tech arsenal Peter had laid out on the teak desk.

"You want to tell me why you never thought it important to share the fact that Josef Serafin was CIA?" Peter said, absently rubbing his bad leg.

Bastien shrugged. "We had an arrangement. Thomason sent me to Central America to kill both Serafin and his boss, Ideo Llosa, the head of the Red Terror. Once I made Serafin, he agreed to take care of the other half of my mission. It was why he was there in the first place. I left him to it. The question is, why did the CIA want him to make contact with the Committee? Why stay under deep cover?"

"I can think of one good reason. They've never liked the fact that we don't have the same political agenda they do. Most of the powers-that-be in the American government think they know what's best for the world, and the Committee doesn't always agree."

"Don't we feel the same way?" Bastien said. "We don't willingly share intel with the CIA any more than they share it with us. You'd think we'd learn to work together."

"Not in this lifetime," Peter said.

Bastien took a sip of his coffee. "Probably not. I expect they sent Serafin in to try to take us down." He didn't like the way he'd automatically slipped into "us" mode. He was no longer part of the Committee, and never would be again. "His real name is Killian, by the way."

"Thomason said he and Isobel had a history."

"Is that old fart still around? I thought he was put out

to pasture long ago." Toussaint picked up one of the smaller guns, weighing it in his hand. He was more used to a hammer than a gun nowadays, and he preferred it that way. But someone had come after him, and he had no choice. And he was going to blow the son of a bitch's head off, when he'd promised Chloe he would never kill again.

Shit, he'd broken that promise a few days ago when those men had invaded his house and threatened his family. And she hadn't said a word of reproach. At this point she was probably ready to kill someone herself, but the least he could do was take care of it for her. She didn't need the darkness on her soul that would never leave his.

"He's still around, still a pain in the butt. He said Isobel and Serafin have a past, but he didn't say anything about Serafin being CIA."

Bastien set his coffee down, very slowly. "You know, I wonder why good men and women are being killed, and a piece of shit like Thomason gets to retire and live out his life in peace and luxury. Why don't they go after the people who deserve to die?"

"Are you asking me a philosophical question?" Peter drawled. "Because I don't think fate or God have much to do with it. I don't believe in fate or God, or anything at all, and neither do you."

"You spend a lot of time trying to convince yourself of that?" Bastien asked. "Give it up. We both know otherwise." Before Peter could protest, he moved on. "And I'm not talking fate. I'm talking practicalities. Thomason's made a hell of a lot of enemies over the years, including just about everyone who ever worked for him. Operatives are being picked off, one at a time, and no one's going anywhere near Thomason. Why not?"

Peter slowly turned his head. "You think Thomason could be behind this? For God's sake, why?"

"He's not the kind of man who'd give up power easily. I was surprised he'd let Isobel take over."

"He wasn't given a choice in the matter."

Bastien closed his eyes for a moment. "I think we need to pay Mr. Thomason a visit."

"Sir Harry. He's been knighted for his service to the crown."

"Christ," Bastien muttered. "You're sure he doesn't know about the secret room?"

"Only Isobel and I know about it. And now Reno and you."

"And no one's realized that these offices only fill up half the floor?"

"Not even Harry."

"Then we're going to need to inform him. And find out exactly what he's been doing and who he's been talking to during the last few years."

"It's not Thomason," Peter said, not sounding convinced. "It can't be."

"We'll find out soon enough. In the meantime, do we need to check on Isobel? Make sure she and Killian haven't killed each other?"

"Why would they?"

"You tell me. I haven't seen her in three years."

Peter grimaced. "I admit she's been having a hard time recently. You know what this job does to people. I've been worried about her."

A brief grin flashed across Bastien's face. "I never thought you'd be worried about anything but your own ass."

"And my wife's ass," Peter reminded him.

"And a very nice ass it is."

"Watch it," Peter said.

"Not as nice as Chloe's," Toussaint added. "Sorry, I couldn't resist. We'll leave Madame Lambert and Killian in the room while we—" He stopped abruptly. "What was that?"

"That thumping noise? It couldn't have come from the apartment—things are sealed so tightly you could have a jackhammer going in there and we wouldn't hear. It can't be the stairwell, because it's rigged. It probably came from overhead. Reno's a noisy little bugger. Maybe he's teaching Killian's little buddy some karate moves."

Another thump, heavier, and Bastien was out of his chair, Peter right behind him.

The door to Reno's flat was open, though the room was lit only by the eerie glow of the wide-screen television. Video game characters were paused, pulsing, waiting for someone to move them, but there was no sign of Mahmoud or Reno.

Bastien switched on the light and swore. There was blood, too much blood, and Reno's body was sprawled out on the carpet, his arm at an odd angle, his head in an ever-spreading pool of blood.

And Mahmoud was gone.

Sir Harry Thomason lit his cigar, puffing slowly, majestically. He'd taken his grandfather's gold pocket watch from the family safe, the one given to him by Winston Churchill himself. Harry was wearing it in his waistcoat pocket, and it felt good, snug against his belly. It was four o'clock in the morning, an ungodly time to be awake, but things were coming to a head, and he was too excited to sleep. Vindication was thick in the air, along with the sleet and rain.

Stolya and his men were back already, the child with them. One of them was dead—they'd dumped his body in a ditch on their way back—and another was unconscious and unlikely to revive. That Jap punk must have put up more of a fight than they'd expected. But Stolya said he was dead as well, so there'd be no more complications.

The boy was locked in one of the bunker rooms, still clinging to his stupid video game. Stolya had wanted to take it from him, but Thomason told him to leave him alone. It would keep the brat occupied, less of a nuisance. If Stolya wanted it he could wait until he killed the boy. That would be happening before long, as soon as they got their quarry in place.

Once Serafin knew the child had been taken he'd come after him, though Thomason was damned if he knew why. Someone like Josef Serafin shouldn't care about one less child. But he'd kept the kid with him like an albatross around his neck, and Thomason was banking on him following.

And Isobel would come after Serafin. She was a perfectionist, never left a job unfinished. Her job had been to bring Serafin in, debrief him, and nothing but death would stop her.

Astonishing that she'd managed to avoid it so many times in the last few days. His traps had been well set, and Stolya was one of the best, from a long line of Russian military who made an automaton like Isobel Lambert seem made of sentimental mush.

There'd be no more mistakes. Madsen was a thorough man, and once he found the child had been taken and his new recruit murdered, he'd go straight to his boss. Thomason didn't need Peter to lead them to Serafin and Isobel—his enemies would come to him. Making the thing so much neater.

He looked out the leaded-glass windows in the library of his country house. It had been in his family for generations, and though he'd had to sell off some of the farms, he still maintained a goodly portion of land. Including the network of tunnels that had served as bunkers during World War II, when his father had been one of Churchill's staunchest supporters. They'd run all sorts of covert operations from the tightly sealed rooms, and unlike the empty halls in the bunkers at Dover Castle, these were still secret. Stolya and his men had been living there for the past three months, planning, training. The brat was locked in one of the whitewashed cement rooms.

That was where Isobel and Serafin would die, as well. Harry hoped Stolya would make it hurt like hell, but in the end, he really didn't care. The Russian was smart and experienced, but he had no idea that those tunnels and bunkers had been booby-trapped. The police would think the explosion was a gas leak in an abandoned section of Sir Harry's estate, and no one would have any reason to comb the rubble for bodies.

No, it was all coming to fruition. He would have liked to be in at the kill, but he'd waited a long, long time for this kind of satisfaction. It would be worthless if his presence did something to endanger its success.

Tomorrow afternoon there'd be a huge, collapsed section of earth in the west field. Both Isobel and Serafin would have disappeared, leaving Madsen behind to help clean up the mess. Harry was rethinking his decision to get rid of Madsen—he could find work for a man like him. Peter was an unsentimental individual, cold as ice, and he could be relied upon to do what needed to be done, with no squeamishness.

It was a shame Bastien Toussaint had disappeared, but he was a bit of unfinished business that could always be dealt with later.

For the time being, the Committee was almost back in hand. And some night, very soon, Harry would take his King Charles spaniels and stroll out to the sunken field and spit.

He was too old and dignified to dance on their grave. But he could count on the dogs to do their business, and that would have to suffice.

He'd step in and save the Committee. And with any luck, in a few years the Queen's Honours List would include his life peerage. "Lord Harry" was so much nicer than a paltry "Sir Harry."

In the meantime, he needed to exercise all the patience he had at his command. The trap was baited and set.

He just had to wait.

21

The bed was very small. Killian was very large. Long legs and arms wrapped around her as he slept, and she should feel suffocated, trapped.

She didn't.

Her body hurt. He hadn't meant to hurt her—in fact, she was probably to blame for it. She'd pushed him. He'd pushed her. They'd done everything she could think of and then things she'd never imagined, as the long, endless hours stretched into the night and beyond, and she'd taken him every way she could.

And now she was lying in his arms, entwined with him, her body aching, her soul hurting, her heart ready to explode. They'd had rough sex, kinky sex, silly sex, deliciously nasty sex. And then, God help her, they'd made love.

He'd moved deep inside her body, his eyes looking into hers, his hands cradling her face with devastating gentleness, and he'd been motionless as he came inside her. And then he'd said, "I love you."

The monster, the butcher, the man who'd put a bullet in the head of a pregnant fifteen-year-old, who worked for terrorists and sadists and genocidal maniacs, had told her he loved her.

And even more horrifying was the undeniable fact that she loved him, and always had. Even when she'd thought she'd killed him. Even if she had to kill him again, she loved him.

And there was no way she could live with that sick, awful knowledge.

She could run. She, who never ran, never faltered, never shirked her duty. She could slip out of his sleeping arms, pull on her clothes and leave this place. Just vanish, into the night air.

She could do it—she had the skills. Peter wouldn't find her. He'd certainly be able to, but he wouldn't do so. He'd let her go, because he'd know that she wouldn't run unless she absolutely had to.

And he could take over the Committee in her place. He was better at keeping Harry Thomason's delusions at bay, and he knew everything she knew. She still had to fight her emotions, the feelings breaking through her icy calm. Peter had made peace with that long ago. He had no emotions, except when it came to Genevieve. He could take care of business with icy composure, find out who and what was behind this latest string of disasters, and make sure whoever they were were stopped. He could see that Killian was set up in the style he was demanding. And meanwhile

Isobel would be gone. Where no one, not even Killian, could find her.

It was almost as if he were hearing her thoughts in his deep, exhausted sleep, because he stirred, his grip tightening, and muttered a soft grunt of protest under his breath. As if he knew she was going to run.

He'd try to stop her, of course. He was good enough to get away with it. Almost.

But in the end he'd let her go. Because he didn't want to love her any more than she wanted him to.

Their lives were ones to be lived alone. Solitary, empty. No room for other people.

The room smelled of sex, creating a thick, drugging atmosphere, and her body hurt. She slid out of his arms, carefully enough that he didn't waken, and made her way to the small, rusty shower, closing the door and turning on the water full blast. They hadn't been able to upgrade the plumbing, not without involving outsiders, and as she'd told Peter with macabre humor, they'd then have to kill them. But the water was hot and plentiful, and she let it stream down over her as she cried.

And then Killian was there with her, crammed into the metal cubicle, holding her, pressing her head against his shoulder as she wept, her face against the place where she'd shot him.

She thought they'd have sex again, and she wouldn't have argued, though her legs were so weak she could barely stand. But he only held her, taking the cloth and washing her body with a slow, exquisite tenderness that had nothing to do with sex.

He kissed her gently, brushing the water and tears from her face. "It'll be all right," he whispered, meaningless words of comfort.

She didn't believe him. It didn't matter. Taking comfort from him was even worse than loving him, and after a moment she made herself push away from him, step out of the shower and grab a towel.

She expected him to follow. She expected him to take her back to that bed, and she would have gone.

But he didn't. He stayed in the shower, and through the glass door she could see him leaning against the wall, the water beating down on him, his eyes closed. He looked…defeated. Just as she felt.

There was fresh underwear in the closet. Her clothes were still on the living room floor, and she didn't want to put them on. Not the tailored trousers, not the cashmere sweater, not the leather heels. She didn't have any choice. She dressed quickly, twisting her wet hair up into a tight bun at the back of her head. There was a mirror, and she didn't want to look. But pride made her.

No one would think she was ageless. She looked exactly like what she was: young and stupid again. In love with a monster.

She heard the signal from the hidden doorway, and she snapped to attention, pulling the mask of Isobel Lambert back over Mary Curwen's lost face.

By the time Peter made it into the room, there was no sign that poor girl had ever existed.

"Sorry," he said. "Were you awake?"

He had blood on his clothing. "What happened?"

"They took Mahmoud."

"Who did?" Her last moment of weakness vanished, replaced by an icy rage. "Did they kill him? Whose blood is that on your clothes?"

"As far as I know, Mahmoud's still in one piece. They're holding him for ransom. In exchange for Serafin, in fact. And it's Reno's blood."

She could feel the ice spreading through her veins, stinging, numbing. "Did they kill *him?*"

"No. He's got a gash on his forehead and a broken arm. Maybe a concussion, but there was no way we could keep him in hospital. We figured it would be easier to keep an eye on him if we had him with us—otherwise he could be nothing but trouble."

"'We?'"

"Bastien's here. He brought Chloe and the children—they're staying in the Golders Green safe house with Genevieve. Someone tried to take them out, back in the States."

"No one could get through the kind of security he had set up there," she said, her voice flat. "No one even knew where he was, outside the Committee."

"Exactly." Peter pulled a small piece of equipment out of his pocket and set it on the table. "The kidnappers left a GPS with instructions. Killian's supposed to follow it, alone, and they'll let Mahmoud go."

"Why would they think he'd do that?"

"Why would he insist on bringing the kid halfway across the world with him? It doesn't matter why, only that he hasn't let go of him and isn't about to."

"Were you able to download the information from the GPS?"

"Not yet. But Bastien figured out the coordinates. It's someplace in Wilders."

"Shit," Isobel said, as things fell together in her mind. "Have we been complete idiots all this time? That's where Harry Thomason's country house is. But why? He'd kill all these people because of his hurt pride?"

"Oh, it's more than that," Peter said. "I expect he wants to take over the Committee again, and the best way to do that is to prove how incompetent you are. Operatives dying under your watch is a perfect example."

"Hell, he put out termination orders on half the people working under him!" Isobel snapped.

"I don't think he's planning to give you a chance to argue. These attacks on Serafin—Killian—have been just as dangerous for you. I think you were the real target."

"I already told her that." She hadn't even heard Killian come into the room. He was dressed, his hair still wet from the shower, his eyes hooded. She could see the mark her mouth had made on the side of his neck, and she turned her face away, shivering. "Isobel didn't want to believe it."

Peter looked at Killian for a long moment, sizing him

up. "You haven't given us much reason to believe you in the past. I'm Peter Madsen, by the way. I'm one of the people who carried you up here. If you've got a few bruises you can thank me for them."

"Oh, I think Isobel contributed her share," he said, casting an oblique glance in her direction. She ignored him, keeping her expression stony.

"How long have you been listening?" Peter said, his voice cold.

"Since you got here. They have Mahmoud and they want me in exchange. Simple enough."

"Not so simple. They really want Isobel."

His smile was slow and cool. "It's still simple. He's the bad guy. We don't give him what he wants. I go get Mahmoud and you keep her here."

"You think you can just waltz in there and pluck Mahmoud out?" she asked, her calm cracking. "I wouldn't have thought you'd be fool enough to underestimate an enemy."

"Sounds like he's more your enemy than mine," Killian said. "And I never underestimate anyone. Except you, perhaps." The enigmatic words hung in the air. "I'm quite good at ingratiating myself with bad people, Isobel. Like to like. I'll tell him that I'll set you up if he gives me Mahmoud."

"Would you? Give up Isobel for Mahmoud? Why?" Peter didn't bother to disguise his hostility.

"I didn't say I would. I'm not very trustworthy," he said with a wry smile. "Once Mahmoud is safe, you and whatever operatives you have left can go in and clean up the mess."

"I've got an old friend of yours downstairs," Peter said. "Bastien Toussaint."

Killian didn't even blink. "It's been a long time."

"But Bastien has a long memory."

"As do I."

"What the hell is going on here?" Isobel demanded. "There's something you're not telling me."

Peter glanced at Killian. "You want to enlighten her? Or shall I?"

"I think this isn't a very good moment to complicate things. We need to get Mahmoud out of there, though if the boy is still armed I'd back him against whatever thugs Thomason has managed to hire."

Isobel felt Killian's eyes on her, but she wouldn't look at him, wouldn't meet his quizzical gaze. She'd betrayed everything she'd believed in, by falling into bed with him, and now the worst kind of disaster had happened. There were a hundred different ways she could have handled this, each of them an improvement over what had happened. She had to become who she was, make the hard decisions, do what needed to be done.

"You're staying here," she said. "No arguments. You're much too valuable a commodity to risk for one small child. I've told you he's too much of a liability— you should have gotten rid of him long ago."

"Is that why your back got shredded when you protected him from the car bomb?" he said, his voice silky.

"Mistaken impulse. We'll get him out if we can. But this is internal business—they're just using you, and I'm not going to let that happen. You're staying put."

"And if I choose not to?"

"No choice. This place is as hard to get out of as it is to get into."

She was prepared for anger, for arguments, but he simply shrugged. "All right. If I'm out, then I'm out. I'm going to make myself something to eat. For some reason I've worked up quite an appetite."

No color flooded her face, no expression flitted through her eyes. She was back in control, and the crazy, endless hours might never have happened. "Just give me a minute, Peter," she said.

She'd left her elegant leather purse in the bedroom, next to the rumpled bed. It was custom made; the inner pockets held two handguns, a syringe, a Tazer that could be set to kill levels, and an emergency tracking device. She moved into the bedroom and switched on the overhead light.

And froze for the briefest of moments. It still smelled of sex. The mattress had slid halfway off the bed, the sheets were a tangled mess, the pillows gone. She could see her purse under one corner of the bed, and made herself kneel down on the floor to get it. When she felt the presence of someone in the doorway, watching her, she froze.

It was only Peter. Peter, who took in the room with his cold blue eyes and didn't miss a thing. "Are you okay?" he asked.

She started to put her hand on the bed to push herself up again, but didn't want to touch it. With anyone else she could have held up, but this was Peter, the only family she had, so she smiled crookedly. "I screwed up. I guess everyone gets fucked by a monster at least once in their lives."

"There's something I should tell you...."

"What's Killian doing?" She sat back on her heels. "How did you know his name is Killian, by the way? Is that even his name?"

"It's his name. Bastien told me."

"What else did he tell you?"

There was a faint, creaking noise deep within the walls, inexplicable. "What's that?"

"Rats?"

"I don't think so. There's no way out of here, is there? He can't open the windows?"

"You know as well as I do how secure it is. They're nailed shut." The squeaking noise got fainter, and a look of horror crossed Isobel's face. She surged off the floor, running past Peter into the empty living room. The deserted kitchen. There was no sign of Killian anywhere.

"How the hell did he get out?" Peter demanded, coming up behind her.

"The dumbwaiter," she said. She yanked open the aging kitchen cabinet to expose the empty shaft. "How did he even know it was there? We left it in place in case someone needed it for an emergency escape, remember?"

"I guess it came in useful, after all," Peter said.

Isobel whirled around. "Don't you care? He's going to screw everything up. And I know damn well he's going to disappear, getting away with appalling crimes against humanity, and we'll get nothing in return, though I always thought the deal was revolting—"

"Calm down, Isobel. Forget Killian. We need to concentrate on bringing Thomason down, and Reno's in a pretty violent mood. He said he killed at least one of their people before they took him down, and I believe it. It wasn't just his blood all over the floor upstairs."

"Killian hasn't simply taken off, Peter," she said. "He's gone for Mahmoud."

"Shit." Peter limped into the living room. "He took the GPS."

"Of course he did. He's going after him."

"Bastien will stop him."

"He'll get past Bastien. Maybe he couldn't have three years ago, but Bastien's been out of the game. We need to go. Maybe we can get to Thomason's place before he does. He's going to need to steal a car, and he's not familiar with this area, so we're bound to have a head start on him. If we're lucky. Unless he's even more of a monster than I think he is, and he puts a bullet in Bastien's head on his way out."

"He'd have Reno to contend with. And as far as I know he doesn't have a gun."

Isobel opened the purse she'd collected. Both firearms were gone. "Yes, he does. Two."

"All right. But he's still not going to kill Bastien."

"Why not?"

Peter hesitated for only a moment. "Because Killian's CIA. This is just one more undercover sting, trying to take down the Committee, but this time Harry Thomason is getting to it first."

"What?" Isobel felt as if she were falling, twisting and turning, and she grabbed on to the kitchen counter, her knuckles white. "He's what?"

"One of the good guys. Or let's say one of the not so bad guys. We should have figured it out, since each time he fucked up, disasters were averted and lives were saved. He's good at what he does, he's very good. But he and Bastien came to an understanding years ago. He's not after us."

"I'm going to kill him," she said in a tight, determined voice.

"I would have thought he'd told you," Peter said. "Considering…"

She knew he was referring to the wrecked state of the bedroom. "I would have thought so, too," she said grimly. "Let's get out of here. We need to get to Thomason before he does."

"Why? Thomason will keep him alive until he gets his hands on you."

"Because I want to be waiting there to kill him myself," Isobel said.

"Thomason or Killian?"

"Both," she snapped. "Both."

22

Killian had a solid head start. By now Bastien or Peter would have told Isobel what he couldn't tell her. She'd know just how deep his lies had been. In a dream world she'd be relieved that he wasn't the international war criminal he'd pretended to be.

But it wasn't a dream world, and even when he could have, should have, he hadn't told her the truth.

It wasn't his truth to tell. He couldn't compromise his mission, couldn't walk away without telling his superiors first. He'd spent too many years doing what had to be done, and that was a part of him he couldn't change. His moral code would never be recognized as such by most people, but it existed.

The Committee was imploding, eating itself alive from within. It didn't need his help to bring itself down. He wasn't even sure the Committee needed to be brought down. He tried to keep things simple, follow orders, never question the how or why. Though in truth he always had. Blind obedience had never been his thing; if he'd always followed orders he'd be dead.

He couldn't afford to be thinking about her right now. She'd put a bullet in his brain if she had the chance—and right now she'd be sorely tempted. Fortunately, Harry Thomason was higher up on her shit list.

Killian actually didn't give a damn what happened to himself. Happy endings weren't made for the kind of man he was, the kind of life he'd lived. But he was damned if Mahmoud was going down, too. He'd saved the murderous little brat's life time and time again. Right now the kid had one thing to live for—Killian's eventual, torturous death. It didn't matter that Mahmoud would have died along with his foster sister—he didn't see it that way. Killian was responsible; Killian must pay.

And Killian didn't have much of an argument with that.

If he didn't get out of this alive, and there was a very good chance he wouldn't, then Mahmoud would be cheated of his eventual revenge. But maybe Isobel would see he had something else to live for.

Killian could count on her for that. He could see through the lies she told him, the lies she told herself. She'd protect the child with her life, instinctively, without question. He'd be leaving Mahmoud in good hands.

If he made it through…well, he wasn't going to think about that. One thing at a time.

He could feel the ice-laden fog in his bones as he slipped down the quiet streets of Kensington. He'd already figured out they were somewhere near the Committee's phony office front, which made orientation easier. In an expensive part of town it wasn't that hard to find a late model SUV with killer tires, and no alarm system known to man could slow him down. He had to get the hell out of town, following the instructions on the tiny little GPS to the letter.

But he had one important stop to make first.

"Good to see you, too, Isobel," Bastien murmured as she pushed past him, climbing into the backseat of the car and slamming the door behind her. Reno was sitting in one corner, looking like hell. He had a bandage across his forehead, his arm wrapped, his clothes bloodstained, and there was death in his eyes. No cat's-eye contact lenses. Just black, implacable rage.

She said nothing, settling into the opposite corner, frozen with fury and disbelief. Her whole world had been turned upside down, and worst of all was how damn stupid she'd been. Why hadn't she seen the signs? Now that she knew the truth it was painfully obvious. The botched missions that had saved so many lives. The unprecedented access to intel he would have had over the years.

She knew what deep cover was like, but that was nothing compared to what Killian must have lived through. Two decades of lies and betrayal, of dealing death while he was ostensibly on the side of the bad guys.

Of killing people who didn't deserve to be killed, just to keep up his cover. Yes, she knew what that was like.

In their life there was no such thing as good guys and bad guys. He was still a monster. He was simply the same kind of monster she was.

"There was no sign of him," Peter said from the front seat as Bastien pulled out into the rainy street. "It's going to take him some time to get there—first he has to steal a car, then he was to figure out the roads, and there's been some bad weather out there. Freezing fog. It'll coat everything with ice, and he's not likely to steal a car that can handle it."

"Don't underestimate him," Bastien said. "He hasn't stayed alive this long without paying attention to details. He'll find an SUV, maybe with studded tires."

"Studded tires are illegal over here," Peter said.

"He'll find one anyway."

"I'm not talking to you," Isobel told Bastien in a sharp voice.

"Don't be petty. Killian and I had an arrangement. He was out of the picture at the time I retired."

"And you didn't think I needed to know a piece of information that crucial?"

Bastien shrugged. "I wasn't particularly interested in anything the Committee needed."

"I think Peter should drive. You've been driving on the wrong side of the road for the last three years."

"Don't worry, Isobel. I've lived on top of a mountain—I know how to deal with ice and snow."

She sank back, resisting the impulse to snarl. There was no place for emotions right now, no time for anger. There was simply the job ahead of them and no room for anything else.

She glanced over at the silent Reno. He had something in his hand, a string of beads he was running through his bloodstained fingers. They looked familiar.

"Are those Mahmoud's?"

He jerked his head, startled. "Yes," he said finally. "He gave them to me. They belonged to his foster sister."

"The one Killian shot?"

"Yes."

Isobel had been hoping that was a lie. "Why did he give you the beads? They were his most valued possession."

"We exchanged gifts. He was ready to give these up, he said. Along with his oath to kill the man responsible."

"Why did he kill her?" She ignored the men in the front seat.

"He didn't tell you?"

"Killian told me nothing but lies."

"Mahmoud's foster sister was a suicide bomber. She was in the middle of a crowded marketplace, holding on to Mahmoud with one hand, the detonator with the other. Killian shot her before she could detonate it."

Isobel closed her eyes for a moment. In the darkness no one could see her reaction. She swallowed. "He took a big chance," she said. "The girl could have hit the button in reflex even as she died."

"She could. Either way there would have been scores, maybe hundreds of people dead. He took Mahmoud and got out of there."

"And the girl? She was pregnant. The baby...?"

"From what Mahmoud said it sounded as if the people in the marketplace pulled her body apart. Too many suicide bombings, too many deaths."

There was nothing Isobel could say. At another time she'd wonder about the kind of life she lived, that someone could tell her something so horrific and she couldn't even respond. But not now.

She concentrated on the present. "You should be in a hospital," she said.

Reno's dark eyes met hers. "No," he said simply.

She didn't bother to argue. She leaned back, trying to will her body to relax, to get ready for the upcoming battle. She could still feel Killian inside her, still feel his hands on her. Like a tape, playing over and over again in her head.

"How long will it take us to get there?"

"We're not even sure where we're going," Peter said. "The coordinates we lifted off the GPS get us within a mile or so of where we want to be, but it's not exact."

"So we head straight for Thomason's country house and kill him," Bastien suggested in the calmest of voices.

"I doubt Sir Harry is doing this on his own," she murmured. "His skills were always organizational, not field-ready. If we kill him, we leave Mahmoud at risk."

Reno made a protesting noise, but Peter overrode him. "I thought you didn't care about the boy? Isn't he just collateral damage?"

"I really hate you all," she said irritably. "You know as well as I do that I draw the line at children. Sometimes innocent people have to die. Mahmoud isn't innocent, but he's still a child, and we're not having his death on our hands. That's the difference between us and Thomason."

"I know," Peter said gently. "I just wanted to make sure you did."

Isobel counted to ten. It was a very good thing that she was, temporarily, without a gun. "Does anyone in this goddamn car have a cigarette?"

"You gave them up."

"I need one." She turned to Reno. "You must have cigarettes on you."

Reno shook his head. "And no weed, either. I gave that up, too."

Isobel leaned back against the seat, muttering. She could still feel the dozens of tiny cuts from the shards of glass that Killian had carefully, even lovingly picked from her skin. She hadn't even noticed them during the endless night.

"What was that?" Peter asked.

"What was what?" she snapped.

"Did you moan?"

"Just fucking drive. And if we pass an open store we're getting me some cigarettes."

"Here," Bastien said, passing a gun over the seat back. "Play with this instead."

It was a nasty piece of weaponry, heavy, solid. It would blow a good-size hole into anyone she aimed it at. Right now she was thinking Killian would make a good target. They could explain it to their so-called allies later.

"Just keep driving," she muttered. Stroking the gun.

Mahmoud sat cross-legged on the cot, leaning back against the rough stone walls, the violent waltz of the video game reflected in his blank eyes. Reno was dead. He'd seen him go down, seen the blood before they'd hauled him out of there. His friend, his brother. He'd lost too many.

The man who'd brought him here, the one with the blond hair. Russian, Mahmoud thought. He'd seen Russians before. They drank too much, but they bled as much as any man. The one who took him, who'd ordered Reno's death, would die.

He knew what they were waiting for. He was unimportant—Mahmoud had learned that long ago. They were using him to get to the man who'd killed his sister, and a month ago he would have helped them.

Not now.

Reza would have killed him, and a hundred others. He hadn't known until the last minute, but he wouldn't have stopped her. She had loved him, looked after him. He wouldn't have minded dying with her—it would have all been over in a flash.

But the man had stopped her. Killed her. Saved him. And in the end, maybe it was all even.

They would come for him. He had fought in the wars long enough—he knew how these things worked. They would promise the man that they would let Mahmoud go, and the man would come, because he hated what he had done. Weakness, Mahmoud thought. Killian had had no choice but to kill Reza. It was a waste of time to feel guilt.

But the man would come, and they would kill Mahmoud, anyway. Unless he did something to stop them.

Right now he wasn't sure what that was. Mahmoud didn't care whether he died or not—the way he saw it, death was an old friend, one who took everyone he cared about, from Reza, the sister he'd known for years, to Reno, the brother he'd known for a day. It could take him as well.

But it would take the Russians, too. In the meantime he stared at the video screen, the only light in the dark, cold room, and set the blood-splatter level on high in the game he was playing.

And he killed.

Killian knew they would be waiting for him. For the last ten miles the road had been a skating rink. As the sun began to rise the freezing fog had coated everything, and the first glints of sun sent prisms of color through the heavy mist. They'd routed him along back roads, and there'd been no other traffic out in such dismal weather. He nearly missed the turn to Wilders—one touch of the brakes and he went skidding past it. Cursing, he let the car drift to a stop, put it in Reverse and carefully backed up, taking the right-hand turn toward Harry Thomason's estate.

Not that he was supposed to know that. He'd had just enough time to pick up a few things, including some basic intel. There were a few deserted cottages on the far end of the estate, scheduled to be torn down and turned into high-priced country housing. And there was an old bunker that had been used during World War II for some sort of covert activity. He was guessing that was where he was heading.

He had little doubt Isobel would be close behind him, but with only the coordinates, she wouldn't be able to pin down his location exactly. Chances were they'd head for the main house first, giving him even more time to put his hasty plan into action.

Killian pulled the stolen car up in front of one of the old cottages. The roof had caved in long ago, and birds flew up into the dawn-lit air when he slammed the door of the vehicle. The ground was slick and icy underfoot. It would be damn funny if he were to fall and—

He knew where they were moments before they appeared out of the mist, reaching for him. He already had one of Isobel's small guns in his hand, and he shot the thug on the right, sweeping his long leg so that his companion fell on the ice. The man rolled as he slid, coming up on his knees with a gun pointed straight at

Killian, but he just had time to pull the trigger before Killian finished him.

The bullet hit Killian, knocking him back against the stolen car, and after a breathless moment he laughed. It had hit the fleshy part of his shoulder, in almost the exact same spot Mary Isobel had shot him eighteen years ago. That hadn't killed him; this wouldn't, either. He needed to stop the bleeding, and then find Mahmoud before they sent reinforcements.

He could see a heavy door in the side of a hillock. So it was going to be the bunkers. Even better. An enclosed area had a great deal to recommend it.

He was freezing cold, the icy mist clinging to his body, and blood was oozing from his shoulder at an enthusiastic rate. He'd learned to deal with pain a long time ago, and he knew just how long he could go without getting a wound treated. The cold would slow down the bleeding. All he needed to do was pack it with something for the time being.

It was a good thing the dead man's aim hadn't been a little lower, or everyone in the surrounding area would be very unhappy, he thought as he stripped the leather jacket and T-shirt off the first man he'd killed, leaving him lying on the frozen mud. The T-shirt was bloody already, but he pressed it against his wound, beneath his own shirt, then pulled the jacket around him. It was big enough—the man had been a little shorter than he was, but burly—and it still held the dead man's warmth.

Killian started for the bunker as the morning mist began to rise, the birds began to sing and the stink of death filled the air.

23

Harry Thomason pulled out his father's gold pocket watch for the hundredth time and wound it very carefully. It was half past five in the morning. You had to have a delicate touch with fine clockwork—too rough a turn and it broke, too light and the watch stopped prematurely. His father had worn it every day of his life since the day Winston Churchill had presented it to him, and Harry had hidden it when his father died and his older brother inherited everything. Maurice was long dead by now, childless, thank heavens, and Harry had stepped up to the task at hand.

He wouldn't have children, either, unless he adopted someone. Perhaps a pretty young boy, innocent enough to be molded. It would be a shame not to leave all this to someone, and life did get lonely.

He snapped the watch shut. Stolya should have called him by now. The sun had risen on an ice-coated world—maybe the roads had slowed his quarry down. Stolya was supposed to notify him when it was done, and Harry had been patient for three years, ever since that bitch had taken his job and his power. He could be patient a few more minutes.

The day staff would be coming in soon. He had a housekeeper and an executive assistant, but both of them knew to keep their distance unless their presence was specifically requested.

There was just so long a man could sit and stare at the frozen landscape. He was truly going to enjoy setting that charge once Stolya called him. If there was one thing Harry couldn't abide, it was incompetence in underlings.

The mobile phone made a quiet little chirping sound. He hated the things, but it was the only way to ensure absolute privacy, and he punched the button, growling into the receiver.

"There's been a hitch." Stolya's thickly accented voice came over the line. "Your presence is requested."

"Out of the question. You know your job. Do it!"

"Not possible. Not this moment. Your presence—" The voice ended abruptly, and a new one came on the line. An American voice, drawling, annoying.

"This is Killian, Sir Harry. If you want any chance to get to Isobel Lambert, then I suggest you come down here. Immediately, or I'll kill the three men who are still alive, take Mahmoud and leave you holding the bag."

"I'm afraid you're mistaken, Mr. Killian. I don't care what happens to those men—they knew the risks when they entered my employment."

"But you do want Isobel Lambert, don't you? And all I have to do is walk out of here and warn her."

"Dear me, now why do I have trouble believing you?" Harry said softly. "You and Isobel were once involved, a long, long time ago. Surely the gentlemanly thing would be to protect her."

"The bitch tried to kill me. More than once. You've got ten minutes, Thomason. And then I'm gone, and Isobel is never letting you get near her again."

The connection was broken. Harry set the phone down gently on the table. And then he picked it up and smashed it against the stone fireplace.

It took him less than a minute to get the gun. He would have liked to take one of the matched set of dueling pistols, also a present to his father, this time from Lord Mountbatten himself. Pretty things, antique. But he needed something more functional and totally deadly. He was going to put a bullet in that woman's brain himself, and he wanted to make sure he had plenty of them. By the time he got his hands on her he'd deserve it.

He wasn't fool enough to think he wasn't walking into a trap. Somehow Killian must have gotten away from his keepers, but they'd be close behind him. And once Isobel realized they were heading to Wilders, they'd know who was behind everything. Chances were they'd come straight for the house, but he was better off waiting for them in the bunkers. He needed them there because the only way he could wipe them all out was to blow the place.

He regretted having to kill Madsen. Peter could have still been useful, and he was pragmatic. Even if he knew Thomason had been behind the deaths of his compatriots, Madsen would take it in stride. He had no weaknesses, except for that wife of his, and Thomason could get to her easily enough.

He left the house silently, walking across the ice encrusted field in his old pair of Wellingtons, his Barbour coat, his walking stick—the epitome of a landed English gentleman. The kind who didn't exist anymore. He would outlast them all.

He wouldn't do that by walking into a trap, or by letting anyone warn Isobel. There were tunnels crisscrossing the lands, including one that ran from the old stables down to the back of the bunker. Last time he'd checked, it hadn't caved in—he could get there quite easily, with no one suspecting him. They didn't realize what an old fox they were dealing with. They were fools to think they could best him.

He could see the headlights in the distance, pulling into the long, winding driveway that led up to the main house. It must be Isobel. She wouldn't stop until she confronted him, wouldn't stop until she found Killian. She'd walk into the trap her pride had set for her.

He made his way into the stables, down the deserted brick alley to the far stall. To the hidden entrance to the tunnels, where he and his brother had once played pirates. And now he was a real pirate, about to claim his prize.

* * *

"Killian hasn't been here," Bastien said, pausing at the end of the driveway. "There are no tracks in the ice. With this kind of crust there'd be no missing him."

"Then find him," Isobel snapped.

He backed into the empty road, the car slipping. "I'll follow the tracks. He can't be far—the coordinates were close enough, and this is the only place that makes sense."

"There's a lot of land connected with the estate. He could be anywhere," Peter said. "Maybe he hasn't gotten this far yet. The roads are hell."

"He's here," Isobel said. "Find him."

It was taking too long, she thought, leaning back in the seat and deliberately letting the pain from her cuts move through her body. Strengthening her will. They'd taken main highways for as long as they could, but eventually had to travel icy back roads. The sun had risen, and sooner or later the ice would begin to melt, but right now it was a wonderland of crystal death.

An endless ten minutes later, Bastien pulled to a stop. "Found him," he said in a grim voice.

She could see the abandoned car—and the two bodies lying on the frozen mud, blood pooling and freezing around them. Isobel let out an anguished cry, fumbling with the car door. "No," she said, scrambling out and almost falling on the ice.

Reno was already beside her, surprisingly steady as he caught her. "He's not one of them," he said.

She pushed her hair away from her face, pulling the

mask back on. "Of course he isn't," she said. "Though I imagine he's responsible for them. The head shot is his specialty."

"Fast and clean," Bastien said in an approving voice. "Do you think he left anyone alive in there?" He nodded toward the door to what looked like an old storage cellar.

"Not if he could help it," Isobel said, moving forward. Her leather shoes were crap on the ice, but she didn't care. Nothing would stop her, not Mother Nature herself. "He'd better hope he's taken Mahmoud and gotten the hell out of there before I kill him."

Peter was moving ahead of her, Reno behind her, and she was getting the unpleasant feeling they were trying to guard her. "I don't need protecting," she said in her iciest tone.

"You're the target, Isobel," Peter said. "We're not being gentlemanly, we're being practical. Reno, I need you to keep out of the way and wait here. Make sure no one follows us in. We'll send Mahmoud out."

She half expected him to argue, but he simply nodded, vanishing into the morning mist, moving as quickly and as silently as the fog itself. She followed behind Bastien and Peter, hating the necessity, as they made their way into a whitewashed tunnel. The murky light of dawn made it only partway into the cavernous mouth, and she could see that a bare lightbulb overhead had been smashed. They moved silently, the three of them, passing another body lying in the shadows. None of them Thomason.

"What the hell is this place?" Bastien whispered.

"An old bunker of some sort," Peter said. "They used them during World War II as hospitals or covert training areas. Thomason's old man was a general. Rolling over in his grave, I expect."

"I expect not." The voice came from behind them, and Bastien moved swiftly, slipping in front of Isobel.

"Sir Harry," he said in his deep, cool voice. "What a surprise."

The old man stepped into the light, switching on the torch he was carrying. It illuminated his squat figure, dressed in tweeds and carrying a semiautomatic handgun. "The surprise is all mine, dear boy," he said. "I thought you left the business."

"I had, until you sent someone to mess with my family," he said.

"I am sorry about that. It's from a lifetime of tying up loose ends. I'm sure you understood the necessity. If one of our enemies found you they could torture you, make you tell them all the things you've learned over the years. And even if you could withstand the torture, you wouldn't if your wife and children were threatened. You were a liability—surely you see that?"

"Surely I see that," Bastien echoed ironically.

"Why don't the three of you put down your weapons?" Thomason said in the amiable voice of a kindly uncle offering tea and biscuits. "My people are waiting in the room beyond, along with your recent failed mission, my dear. We should join them."

Out of the corner of his eye, he must have seen Peter move and the blinding beam of torchlight fastened on him. "Another bullet in that leg would be both debilitating and painful, Peter," Harry said. "I don't think you want that. Put the gun down."

Peter set his gun down on the littered stone flooring, and Bastien did the same. Isobel wasn't ready to panic—she expected they carried other weapons, and both of them were capable of killing with their bare hands. They still stood more than a fighting chance.

"And you, my dear," he said. "Put it down now, or I'll put a bullet in your head this very minute."

She set it down, because she had no choice. "You're planning on doing it anyway, Harry," she said. Her voice sounded nothing more than bored. She'd learned her craft well.

"Yes, we both know that, but as long as there's life, there's hope, and you're not going to willingly take a bullet until you have no other choice."

"You're very wise," she said sweetly. She still had her Swiss Army knife, although it wouldn't do much good against a semiautomatic.

"After you, my friends." Thomason gestured toward the circle of light farther down the tunnel. "And do be careful. I believe your friend Serafin—or should I call him Killian?—has cut a bloody swath on his way down here. I wouldn't want you to trip over any more bodies. Hands on your heads, please."

Isobel's back screamed as she put her hands on the

back of her head. "Why are you doing this, Harry? Have
you been behind everything? The car bomb in Plymouth,
the pilot in Algeria, MacGowan's disappearance?"

"Of course. But don't expect me to make some long
confession full of braggadocio. I do what needs to be
done. And what needed to be done was to take you
down, Madame Lambert. You're weak. You put the
safety of the world in jeopardy because you won't do
what needs to be done."

"That's why you're doing this, Harry? To save the
world?" Peter murmured.

"Sir Harry, my boy," he snapped. "Remember, I was
your mentor."

"I haven't forgotten."

"This place is wired, isn't it?" Bastien spoke
suddenly. "You're going to blow it."

"You always were quick, Toussaint. Practically
psychic, except that I know you've been around explosives long enough that you can probably smell them.
That's exactly what I plan to do. But I'm not leaving a
thing to chance—you'll all be dead before I hit the
switch. I'm a thorough man."

"So you've said." Isobel kept walking. She could
feel his eyes, his gun, trained on the middle of her back,
and suddenly the tiny cuts from the glass seemed like
the least of her worries. "Then I presume Killian's
already dead?"

Harry sighed. "I fear my employees have not been
as efficient as I might have liked. But you'll find out

soon enough. There'll be time for a touching lovers' farewell, and maybe I'll even let you die in each other's arms."

"Don't make me ill, Sir Harry," she said coldly. "Have you ever known me to be sentimental?"

"Not particularly. But you have a weak spot as far as this man is concerned, I know that much. Who would have thought the head of the Committee would be fucking a *terrorist?*" The word sounded strange in his elegant voice, clearly an obscenity.

"But he's not a terrorist, Harry," Peter said. "You missed that one completely. He's CIA."

"Preposterous!" the old man exclaimed.

"And are you sure we're all present and accounted for?" Bastien asked slyly.

As a judgment call it was questionable. Harry didn't need to know Reno was skulking around, but then, anything that dented Thomason's self-assurance was an asset. "There's no one else," he said.

"What about our new recruit?" Isobel murmured.

The old man laughed. "He's dead. My men saw to it. The nasty little punk killed one of them, and another one's not going to make it, but *he's* dead."

"If you say so," she said. The light was getting brighter, but there was no noise coming from the open doors ahead. Were Killian and Mahmoud already dead? Harry wouldn't be nearly so sure of himself if he didn't have the upper hand.

Peter was holding back, and she knew he was going

to try to get between her and Harry. To take a bullet for her, if he had to, and that was one thing she couldn't let happen. Not and live with herself.

She halted, turning to look at Sir Harry. He had always seemed a somewhat comical little man, until you gazed into his pale, blank eyes. She'd been a fool to underestimate him. A man who'd ordered as many deaths as he had over the years wouldn't take to being marginalized with any grace.

"Keep moving, Madame Lambert," he said, waving the gun toward her. "And tell your friends to keep their distance. I see Peter looking for his chance, and I have time to blow his head off and still kill you."

"But that would leave me," Bastien said in a silky tone.

"I'm not alone down here. Move ahead."

She followed them through the doorway, into a large room. There were two low-wattage lightbulbs overhead, and standing in the middle was Killian, wrapped in someone else's coat. Slightly pale, but alive.

He had no gun, and yet he seemed to be in charge. There were two more bodies on the ground, and three armed men watching him warily, like tourists watch a polar bear in a zoo devouring its meal. There was no sign of Mahmoud.

Killian didn't look at her when they stopped, focusing instead on Thomason.

"What's all this about?" Harry demanded, sounding querulous. He turned to one of his men. "Why are you just standing there? He's not armed. Shoot him!"

"Not exactly true, I'm afraid," Killian said in his laziest drawl. She looked at his hands, and saw the blood running down his left hand, dripping onto the ground. He opened the coat, gingerly, and she could see the belt he was wearing. Packed with the latest fashion in lightweight explosives.

"How did you get that?" The words came out before she realized she'd spoken.

"Shut up!" Thomason snapped, his temper fraying. "Or I'll shut you up!"

"I don't think you'd like the consequences," Killian said. "You touch her, and we're all going up."

"I think you'd best believe him," one man said in a heavy Russian accent. "He'd do it."

Thomason fired, and the man collapsed on the ground, half his skull missing. "Does anyone else have something to say?" he inquired in a dulcet tone.

"Your aim has gotten better, Harry," Isobel said, her voice cold. "You didn't used to be able to hit the broad side of a barn."

He swung in her direction, his face purple with rage, but Bastien had already tackled her, throwing her to the ground, covering her body, her head, as the gun rang out, over and over again. She could feel chips flying from the stone wall, stinging, and she wanted to shove Bastien away, but he was much too strong and determined, and too damn big, and then, shockingly, the gun was silenced, and he rolled off her.

She kicked him, scrambling to her feet, to see Peter

standing over Thomason's huddled figure. Killian hadn't moved—he was leaning against a table, seeming perfectly at ease, if it weren't for the bomb strapped around his middle and the blood dripping from his hand. "She never was grateful," he said to Bastien.

Isobel wouldn't look at Killian. She stalked over to Thomason's figure. "Is he dead?"

The old man looked up at her, hatred in his milky eyes. "Only slightly damaged, thank you," he said in a voice thick with loathing.

She kicked him, too, just for good measure. "Where's Mahmoud?"

"He's locked in one of the rooms, but he's fine," Killian said. "Reno can take care of him."

"I wasn't talking to you," she said in her iciest voice. Peter was holding the handgun that she'd handed over to Thomason, the one that would stop an elephant in its tracks. "Too bad you're wearing that belt or I'd shoot you where you stand."

"Be my guest," Killian said gently, unfastening the belt and setting it down on the table behind him, very carefully. More blood on his hand; he'd obviously been shot. She didn't care, she absolutely didn't care. He could die for all it mattered to her, and she'd dance on his grave.

"I'll get him," Peter said, limping past Thomason's unmoving figure. A moment later Mahmoud came flying out of the room, his video game clutched in one hand. To Isobel's amazement, he flung himself at Killian.

Killian grunted, falling back for a moment at the

child's onslaught. A child who weighed very little, and Killian was very strong. How badly was he hurt?

He put his hand on the boy's hair, ruffling it with affection, speaking to him in Arabic. "Is Reno here?" he asked Isobel. "He wants Reno."

"He's here. Come along, kid," Peter said. "I'll take you to him."

Mahmoud was already racing ahead of him, but he paused for a moment to look at Isobel. He said something to her, something long and incomprehensible, and then took off, Peter trailing behind him.

Bastien made a choking sound, and she remembered he knew Arabic. She wasn't about to ask Killian, who was looking strangely amused beneath his pallor. "What did he say?"

"Just good wishes for your future health and happiness," Toussaint said.

"Vermin," Harry said, struggling to his feet.

"Bastien," she said, "do something about these two, would you?" She gestured toward the remaining men Harry had hired.

"What about Thomason?"

"I'll take care of him."

"You sure?"

She arched an eyebrow. "You think I can't handle a pathetic old man, Bastien?"

"Of course you can, *chérie*. You're the Ice Queen." He glanced toward Killian. "What about him?"

She had no choice but to look at him. He still had that

vaguely ironic expression on his face. "Get out," she said in a low voice. "Go back to Langley and tell them that if I ever see you again you won't be left standing."

"Not the forgiving sort, are you?"

"Get...out," she said.

He started after Bastien, moving slowly but with no particular limp. Maybe it was someone else's blood on him. Maybe it was a flesh wound. Maybe he was dying.

She didn't give a flying fuck.

She ignored him, turning back to Harry. "So what am I supposed to do with you?"

"There's nothing you can do. You can't prove anything, not without bringing our entire business to light, and you wouldn't want to risk the few operatives that are still alive. Though I'm not sure quite how many there are.... I've got someone in Japan about to take out Takashi O'Brien and his new wife, and the operation in Somalia is in ruins. My men must have got to MacGowan, as well. They're going to take your toy away from you, Isobel, and there's nothing you can do. You were too weak to run an organization like the Committee. You couldn't do what needed to be done, so in the end I win. I may not have control back, but you can't touch me without getting yourself dirty. The Committee will replace you, and I wouldn't be surprised if they put me at the helm, after all. We're run by some very pragmatic people, and the end justifies the means. I'll be ready to accept your resignation, of course."

"They're not that stupid."

"Not stupid. Just not bothered by sentimental nonsense about human rights and fair play. We're fighting the forces of evil, Isobel, and you haven't got what it takes to wage that war. You haven't got the stones to do what needs to be done."

"Yes, Harry, I do," she said. And she pulled the trigger.

The expression on his face was shocked, almost comical, as he slid to the floor. A head shot, quick and silent, as Bastien had taught her. His body splayed out, and something slipped out of his pocket, a gold watch falling onto the stone floor, the engraved cover flying off as it dropped into the pool of blood, the glass face shattering on impact.

She didn't move. The gun was heavy in her hand, shaking, and someone came up behind her. She knew who it was. He took the gun away from her with his bloody hand. "I would have killed him for you, princess," he said softly.

She wouldn't look at him. And after a moment he walked away, slowly, down the empty corridor stained with blood, never looking back.

24

They got back to Golders Green by five. Cleanup had been no easy matter, but Isobel had simplified things by ordering Peter to blow the charges when everyone was at a safe distance. The ensuing explosion had been a bit of overkill, but Harry Thomason and the bodies of five Russian mercenaries disappeared in a collapsed field and tons of rock. By the time anyone got around to excavating, there would barely be enough left to trace their DNA. No one would look too hard—the Committee would see to it.

Peter was exhausted. He needed a shower, a meal and a good night's sleep. But most of all he needed his wife. Bastien had been silent since they dropped Isobel off at her flat; she'd refused to come with them, and he'd been wise enough not to push. Bastien would be taking his family back to the States as soon as they could get a flight, and Peter had every intention of dragging Genevieve back to Wiltshire as soon as she was willing to go.

And if she argued, he'd throw her over his shoulder and haul her there.

He'd had a few rough moments during the last twenty-four hours, one of the absolute worst being when he'd dragged Reno to the hospital and the admitting nurse had asked, "Your son?"

"Christ, no," Peter had replied in total horror, earning a smirk from Reno. But he'd done a good job, cool-headed in a crisis, deadly when he needed to be. He'd make an excellent operative. If they could get him to cut his ridiculous hair.

In the meantime, someone needed to warn Takashi O'Brien that all of Harry's stratagems hadn't died with him. Taka was more than capable of taking care of himself and his wife, but a heads-up wouldn't hurt.

Mahmoud had refused to leave Reno's side, and in the end Peter had dropped them off in Kensington. They were both kids, outlaws, brats, brothers. For the time being he didn't have to worry about them. They could play video games and drink Red Bull to their heart's content. With Reno's arm in a cast, Mahmoud might actually be able to beat him. No, Peter didn't have to worry about them.

Isobel was a different matter. She was cool, calm, the Ice Queen personified. She hadn't even asked where Killian had disappeared to. Which was a good thing, because Peter had no idea. He was simply gone by the time they'd left the bunker.

* * *

Genevieve was sitting in a chair by the fire, Bastien's daughter Sylvia in her lap. She only looked half-ready to kill Peter—maybe there was hope, after all. She looked up when he walked in, and then for a moment all was chaos as Bastien followed him, to be inundated by his wife, his baby son and his daughter.

Peter moved past them, to Genevieve's side, and knelt down beside her. Which hurt his bad leg like hell, but he figured she was going to demand some serious penance for disappearing on her.

"I love you," he said, hopeful.

She gave him a look. "Is it over?"

"Yes," he said.

"Is Isobel all right?"

"I don't think so. I don't think there's anything I can do about it, either."

"No," she said thoughtfully. "I expect not. By the way, I don't have the stomach flu."

He had to tread carefully. "You don't?" he asked, trying to look innocent.

She laughed at him. "Why is it you can lie to everyone on earth except me? You already know. You probably knew before I did." She took his hand and put it on her still-flat belly. "Are you going to stop trying to get yourself killed?"

"I'll do my best."

"Humph," she said. "Let's go home."

And it was that easy.

* * *

Isobel walked into her apartment, dropping her purse, kicking off her shoes. It was dark outside, but she didn't turn on the lights. She walked through her flat, straight into the bathroom, and climbed into the bathtub, still wearing her tailored slacks and her cashmere sweater. They were stained with blood. Her soul was stained with blood. She sat in the tub and turned on the shower.

The water was icy, but she didn't flinch. It quickly grew warmer, but she didn't move, letting the water soak into her hair, her clothing, her skin. She sat until the water grew cold again, then she rose, stripping off her clothes and moving through her darkened apartment to her bedroom. She pulled back the duvet and climbed into bed, her hair soaking wet, the room cold. Sooner or later the heat would come on by itself. If it didn't, she could always freeze to death.

They'd replace her, thank God. She'd have to face the Committee, and there was no way she'd flinch from what had happened. She'd done the right thing, the necessary thing, and she'd do it over and over again if she had the chance, with the memory of Charles Morrison, of Finn MacGowan, of all the other operatives keeping her company. Their hands had held the gun along with her.

She'd killed her last man. The first time she'd ever done it point-blank, with no hesitation, an unarmed man of pure evil. It was too steep a price, and she couldn't do it anymore. This was a world she could no longer live in.

She wasn't sure where she'd go. Somewhere far away, someplace warm and lush and green, where there were no ice storms and freezing fogs, where no one could ever find her. Not that anyone would look.

Maybe the South Pacific, maybe the Caribbean. Did it snow in New Zealand? She could get lost among the sheep.

He'd been bleeding, and he'd disappeared. The car he'd stolen was gone—she could only assume he'd taken it and left. She could at least be grateful for that much. She wouldn't have to face him again.

She rolled over on her stomach, hiding her face in the feather pillow. Saint Lucia? The Canary Islands? Hawaii? She wanted the ocean and soft breezes, she wanted hot sand, palm trees and flowers. She could almost smell them now, except they were roses, and roses weren't tropical, were they?

He was standing in the doorway, a silent silhouette. She kept a gun under the other pillow, complete with silencer. She could roll over and shoot Killian in the head, and it would be called an accident.

But she'd killed her last man, no matter how badly this one deserved it.

She sat up, turning on the light beside her bed, keeping the duvet pulled up in front of her. He looked like hell. He'd changed clothes, and she could see the bulk of a bandage on his left shoulder. The same place she'd shot him so many years ago.

"I couldn't tell you."

She just looked at him. He didn't come any closer—he probably knew just how dangerous she was. "I quit. I had to tell them before I told you the truth. They aren't going to like it, and we have our own Harry Thomasons who aren't going to want to let me just walk away. But I will. If you will."

"Why should I?" It wasn't her voice in the darkness, the cool voice with the clipped British accent. It was Mary Curwen's voice, young, vulnerable.

"If you don't know, I'm not sure I can convince you." He was edging closer. If she pulled the gun out she could get a clean shot. Fast and clean.

"Why?" she said again.

"Because you love me. For eighteen years you've haunted me, and I don't want to let you go again. So either shoot me with that gun you have or ask me to come to bed."

It was raining again, another cold, icy rain. But it was warm inside. The gas fire behind the grate finally had clicked on, and a soft glow filled the room. The cold had vanished, and she could feel the heat building inside her.

"Come to bed," she said in her coolest voice. "I can always shoot you in the morning."

"Of course you can, princess," he said. And he got into bed.

MIRA®

NEW YORK TIMES BESTSELLING AUTHOR

STELLA
CAMERON

'Tis the season to be wary....

Christmas is coming and all is far from calm in Pointe Judah,
Louisiana. Newcomer Christian DeAngelo—Angel to his
friends—is at his wit's end trying to manage Sonny, the
hotheaded nineteen-year-old everyone believes is his nephew.

Angel has been commiserating with Eileen Moggeridge,
whose lonely son Aaron has latched on to Sonny and gotten
into deeper trouble than ever. But nothing could prepare
Angel and Eileen for the boys' latest crisis: as they are horsing
around in the swamp one afternoon, a shot rings out....

A COLD DAY IN HELL

"If you're looking for chilling suspense and red-hot
romance, look no farther than Stella Cameron!"
—Tess Gerritsen

*Available the first week of November 2007
wherever paperbacks are sold!*

MIRA®

MSC2495

New York Times Bestselling Author

SHARON SALA

He killed her once...

Throat slashed and left for dead next to her murdered father, a thirteen-year-old girl vows to hunt down the man who did this to them—Solomon Tutuola. Now grown, bounty hunter Cat Dupree lets nothing—or no one—stand in the way of that deadly promise. Not even her lover, Wilson McKay.

Suspecting that Tutuola is still alive, despite witnessing the horrific explosion that should have killed him, Cat follows a dangerous money trail to Mexico, swearing not to return until she's certain Tutuola is dead—even if it means destroying her very soul....

CUT THROAT

"The perfect entertainment for those looking for a suspense novel with emotional intensity."
—*Publishers Weekly* on *Out of the Dark*

*Available the first week of November 2007
wherever paperbacks are sold!*

MIRA®

www.MIRABooks.com

MSS2507